T0328500

THE FLAME TREE

Kim H. Rasmussen

Safari Books Ltd
Ibadan

Published by
Safari Books Ltd
Ile Ori Detu
1, Shell Close
Onireke
Ibadan.
Email: safarinigeria@gmail.com
Website: http://safaribooks.com.ng

ISBN: 978-978-59508-7-8

When he switched on the light, he saw the long dark-green snake on the bed from which he had just sprung. It had its head turned directly towards him as if it had already known in the darkness exactly where to find him.

The snake raised its head and the front part of its body about three feet in the air and opened its mouth. Its mouth was black inside, which was a bad sign; the black mamba whose poison could kill a man in a very short time.

They stood facing each other like two gunslingers, but with the slight difference that only the snake was armed. Luckily, the snake was not aware of this.

His heart was hammering away and he was dripping sweat yet he had ice cold hands and felt like his feet had been glued to the cold tiled floor. There was no sound except for the cheerful humming of the air conditioner and his own short breaths.

The distance between him and the snake was small enough for it to reach him had it thrown itself towards him. However, it just stood there impressively high and seemingly evaluating how threatening the enemy was.

'I am no danger to you at all so please don't attack me,' he thought, and he would have prayed to God if he had been able to remember any suitable prayers at the time.

TWO WEEKS EARLIER

Chapter One

// NIGERIA," Frank shouted. "You can't be serious, Simon. Do you know what it's like in Nigeria? It's dirty, noisy, corrupt ... and ... and ... well, it's also bloody dangerous with all those armed robberies and suicide bombers. I won't make it out of there alive, man." Frank paused and looked out at the grey skies above central Copenhagen. 'Dreary,' he thought.

"And the women are a solid bunch who look like dock workers. Haven't you seen the former minister of finance on CNN. Extremely competent, but imagine waking up with her one morning," he said, shaking his head despairingly.

Frank had a couple of good friends who had also made their careers on the African continent. One of them now worked in Ghana, the other in Uganda. They had both unambiguously expressed that Nigeria was a place they would never set foot and they were both old and hardened Africa hands. Should Frank now be the first to throw himself into such a challenge? He had heard all the horror stories for many years but perhaps these stories were exaggerations and rather worse than the realities in the country ... perhaps not.

Simon Larsen was head of the Danish branch of the small specialised recruitment agency, Africa Executive Search, with special focus on recruitment of managers for companies in Africa. He and Frank Grabowski knew each other quite well as their paths had crossed several times before.

"Listen, Frank. You were negative last time when I positioned you for that job in Liberia, which went so well for you in the end. You are just an eternal grumbler, aren't you?"

The traffic light turned to red at the junction opposite the office. An elderly lady with bluish grey hair was standing in the middle of the pedestrian crossing, desperately struggling with an umbrella which had unfolded the wrong way, while a taxi was impatiently giving way to her. A few brown leaves were already whirling around in the wind. Frank was imagining 34-degree humid air in West Africa and missed the sweat running down his cheeks and the shirt sticking to his body after only a couple of minutes outside in the heat. The contrast between the often very cold air-conditioned offices and the thick, embracing and hot air outside was remarkable. He took a sip of his cappuccino and looked at Simon over the edge of his cup.

"It's exactly the right job for you, Frank," Simon tried enthusiastically. "A relatively large company assembling cars. They have a sharp market position and good cooperation from authorities as far as import and tax regulations are concerned. Profitable government contracts and, just as important, new and strong investors from Saudi Arabia, who want things to be successful. And those Arabs, I am telling you my friend; they have money."

Frank felt that Simon was very keen to convince him that he should accept this assignment.

"I know that it's a bit hot with those Boka Harem robberies and a lot of unpleasant crime and corruption but this company is really interesting and your profile is perfect." Simon clicked his pen a few times with a smile spreading across his face. "Besides, the women are not that bad. There was this lady, Iman, the model who was married to David Bowie."

"Boko Haram." Frank said.

"Hmm?" Simon lifted his eyebrows.

"They are called Boko Haram and they are islamist extremists with connections to Al Qaeda who blow themselves and many innocent people up because they are against western education and influence generally. They are deadly." Frank touched his temples with his thumb and forefinger while thinking of his receding hairline and Wayne Rooney's hair transplant but then ignored the thought of doing the same. "And Iman is absolutely beautiful but she is Somali, you moron."

"Oh well. She's black isn't she and I heard you like black ladies, right?" Simon looked at him with an annoying smile while turning his ergonomically correct office chair back and forth – very different from the large soft chairs Frank was used to in Africa.

Frank ignored the last remark about the black ladies.

"Is there a managing director for the time being, and why do they need a new man?" he asked. Simon's gaze flickered, and he made circles with his computer mouse on the desk.

"There was a guy but he had an accident. So, for the time being there is nobody. The company is temporarily run by a group of departmental managers under close supervision by a board committee." Simon made a few more circles with the mouse.

"What happened?" Frank wanted to know. "Hmm?"

"I said, what happened? To the managing director – don't you want me to know?"

"Car accident with a petrol tanker which exploded. He was grilled, the former managing director. Only 39. Wife, three kids, nice guy. Was driving a sparkling new Toyota Avensis Automatic and there sure wasn't much left of that."

"Shit. That sounds grim," Frank said, while looking at his hands thinking that the lack of physical exercise had made them slightly chubby. He tried to imagine the scene with the burning car, shivered and dropped the thought. "But why me?" he wondered.

"You're single. You've solved other difficult tasks on the continent. You're a youthful guy in his mid-forties with solid Africa experience. On top of that, you probably need the money and you have a reputation for being a bit of a tough cookie who's not afraid of the difficult places.

Where others are reluctant to go, you don't mind taking on a tough challenge." "I do my best."

"Yeah, exactly. So, my point was spot on wasn't it, old chap? You're perfect," Simon said eagerly. "The new owners offer an interesting package with a decent salary, company house, car, travelling business class, holiday twice a year, and not least a share scheme with a good bonus depending on the bottom line. It's exactly what you need." Simon had folded a piece of copy paper and now pretended to open it as if announcing the result of an award. "And the winner is … Frank GRABOWSKIII."

"Are there other candidates for the job?" Frank asked.

"I heard there was a local guy, presumably one of the departmental heads who was interested and ran a strong lobby campaign but the board of directors want an expatriate and your CV is almost perfect."

Frank was still sceptical but he was becoming curious and wanted to hear more.

"I'm still not crazy about the idea but why don't they employ a Nigerian or another expatriate who's already in the country?" Frank asked, but then remembered the old debt, the children's maintenance as well as the long, dark and cold winters in Denmark.

"The board agreed that a Scandinavian would be ideal. They've had bad experiences with old British guys who were hard on the liquor. They don't even want to hear about French people." Simon confidently leaned back in his chair. "Well, and we, that is our company, have solved another assignment for the new investor to their utmost satisfaction."

"Yes, you are world champions, no doubt," Frank said, and asked: "What is the timing of all this?"

Simon held up a finger in the air. "Aha, now we're talking." He turned his chair around and picked up three large envelopes from the book shelf behind his desk. "Here's a list of the employment conditions. The contract needs to be signed by the chairman but, in principle, the board has already approved these conditions." He took the other and thicker envelope and showed it to Frank. "This is the latest annual report, a couple of months' management accounts, the organisation chart and some other stuff which I don't quite understand. Anyway, it should give you an idea of what it's all about."

The last envelope had a Carlson Wagonlit logo on it and Frank now had a feeling in which direction they were going.

"Yes, Mr Grabowski. You've won a trip to Nigeria. This is the first prize – a business class ticket to Lagos, Centre of Excellence, as I believe they call it from what I saw on Wikipedia.

Doesn't it sound like an exotic paradise?" Simon leaned forward with a smile and placed his elbows on the desk. "You're going to London on Wednesday to meet with the chairman of the board. Then he'll get a Nigerian visa for you because he is a big shot. Then you go home for the weekend before you travel to Nigeria on Monday. Isn't that a world class arrangement?"

Frank pointed his finger at Simon as if to threaten him, picked up the envelopes and emptied his coffee cup.

"I haven't decided yet but you'll hear from me first thing tomorrow morning."

"Good luck with it all and have a nice trip to Lagos," Simon said cheerfully. "Idiot," Frank answered while on his way out of Simon's office.

"And say hello to Iman," he heard Simon shouting when he passed the reception on his way to the lift. He had only just walked out of the lift on the ground floor when a message beeped in on this smartphone. The heading was: "West African Motors' chairman Chief Adeyemi – meeting in London". So, Simon had prepared the mail in advance, the bastard.

Frank zipped his jacket and pulled up the collar. Then he ventured into a windy Copenhagen and suddenly felt convinced that he would take the job in Nigeria. He had had a good long summer which had brought his bank account balance down to a level too low for comfort and, apart from that, the quarterly mortgage on his house was due soon. So, his financial reserves had been depleted considerably. Furthermore, there was the long and dark Danish winter lurking just around the corner. He walked briskly towards the Admiral Hotel where he had parked his car and paid an outrageous amount for the pleasure. It was just after midday, so he decided to grab a quick lunch in restaurant SALT. He checked the parking receipt which gave him just about an hour to have lunch, and he wanted to avoid having a parking ticket in addition to the already exorbitant fee.

Frank found a small table in a corner, sat down and ordered roasted mackerel and a soda water while he began skimming through the documentation Simon had given him. It all looked confusing, although it quickly became clear that the development in the company had been unstable. Some years with remarkable results and other years in between where it all looked rather critical – this was especially true for the last couple of years. The top line by and large looked impressive but was eaten up by some dramatically increasing costs. In any case, it did not at all seem transparent to him. He removed the documentation from the table as the food was served and smiled at the waitress trainee who was serving him. Her name was Marlene, the young rather long-limbed girl with long blonde hair, a tattoo of a small blue butterfly on her left wrist and a strong Funen-accent. He sent her an extra smile.

Time was getting tight so he did without a coffee, paid the bill and gave a good tip to Marlene who reciprocated with a charming smile and a polite; "Have a nice day, sir." He closed his jacket again and walked out to the Volvo. Traffic was still light at this time of day and Frank quickly reached the highway out of town and was well on his way to his summerhouse in Kulhuse where he set up base during his stays in Denmark. It was a well-insulated wooden house where he could easily spend longer periods of time when required. He had been lucky to buy it a few years earlier when the market prices were rock bottom.

He lit the wood-burning stove in a hurry and realised that he could not postpone the call to Kirsten any longer. They had been divorced for a little over four years now but still had a distinctly tense relationship. However, they had two children and were therefore stuck with each other in a somewhat scarily definitive way. Nikolaj was now 10 and Caroline 16. So they were not really kids anymore and sometimes they hardly had time to see him when he was home. Since the divorce he had always maintained close contact with the children. They knew each other well and usually had a good time together.

Frank's thoughts wandered back to the days when it went wrong between him and Kirsten, but he found it difficult to remember exactly when they had reached the critical point and realised that it was over. He had always been ambitious and aimed at building a career in international management and had already had some interesting but challenging assignments which pushed him in that direction. Primarily with jobs related to Africa.

Kirsten, on the other hand, was much more dependent on her network in Denmark and was not prepared to move abroad at all. It was important to her to use her education as a dentist and work towards opening her own clinic once the children had grown up. 'Perhaps it was just inevitable that it had to go haywire,' Frank thought. Perhaps their individual goals and ambitions were simply not compatible because there had been nobody else involved who could have caused their separation. Oh well, he had had a Christmas party fling with a younger colleague from the accounts department but that had stopped after a short while and he had never taken it seriously himself. And, as far as he knew, nobody had ever found out, except perhaps the cleaning lady who had surprised them one evening when his hands were on an exploratory mission inside her unbuttoned shirt rather than on the computer key board. 'In any case, it was an unrealistic project with Karina from accounts,' he thought, and now he was quite relieved that it had ended so quickly. Since then, he had not had any long-term relationships but he took it easy and tried to consider this as a time for career development where women were second priority. Later on, he could always join a dating website for single elderly people he thought and smiled to himself.

He pulled himself together, grabbed his mobile phone and pressed Kirsten's number.

She answered it immediately.

"Hello, Kirsten speaking." She sounded annoyed. "Hi. It's Frank."

"Oh, yeah. I was just thinking that it had been quite a while since I heard from you. I thought that maybe you were travelling again." She was indeed annoyed as Frank had guessed right away.

"No, but I am actually in negotiations about a job in Nigeria which could be confirmed very soon."

"Nigeria, well that's up to you but you haven't seen much of the children lately. But then you can earn some money, of course, because the ridiculous children's maintenance you are paying now is nowhere near sufficient." Now he remembered why he did not call her unless it was absolutely necessary.

She continued undaunted: "I also have to get a new car, Frank. I hope you can help me with the financing."

"We'll have to discuss that but what about the Astra? I thought it was still running OK."

"That old piece of shit. It costs me a fortune every time I have to send it for servicing or repairs. You know that damn well."

"Hmm. Maybe I could be a guarantor so you can get a loan from the bank," he suggested but apparently that was not the type of financing Kirsten had meant. They kicked the issue back and forth a few times without reaching any conclusion about replacing the Opel Astra or how a possible replacement would be financed.

"Now, listen," Frank tried to move on. "I'm going to London for two days but will be back over the weekend before I probably leave for Nigeria to take on the new job. I'll know for sure when I've met with the chairman of the board in London."

"Is it that soon, you're leaving? That sounds crazy. You can't just disappear like that as it pleases you," she sulked.

"No, but I have to make money, don't I?" To which silence followed and he tried again. "As I said, I'll be home over the weekend and I'd like to take the kids out for dinner and perhaps go to the movies."

"You can pick them up on Saturday afternoon around two. I don't think they have anything planned but you better call first." She was always able to make it sound like she was doing him a big favour but Frank was just relieved when he could finally hang up and avoid any more grumbling.

He stood there for a while, looking out into his garden where a hare ran past the terrace window. He shrugged, then found a pepperoni pizza in the freezer and threw it into the microwave. To accompany this delicious dish, he chose a glass of milk – something he really appreciated in Denmark; fresh milk.

Chapter Two

Frank switched on his mobile phone immediately after landing in Copenhagen airport on his return from the meeting in London with the chairman of the board. As soon as it had connected to the network a text message beeped in with a surprising wording.

"Congrats on your meeting with the chairman but watch out in Nigeria. It can be a dangerous place if you're not careful".

The message was sent from a private number. Frank put his phone in his breast pocket and thought about the message, then took out the phone and read the message once again.

'Surprising, but difficult to understand the exact meaning of it,' he thought. No doubt a warning, perhaps even a threat.

Frank was quickly through the arrival formalities as he was only travelling with hand luggage. He sent a text message to Nikolaj and Caroline suggesting that they have a steak at Hereford Beefstouw and perhaps watch the latest James Bond movie. They both confirmed that they were fine with that proposal.

During dinner, Nikolaj was mostly focused on consuming his large ribeye steak while Caroline was worried about her waistline and had ordered a small veal fillet accompanied by a selection from the salad bar. Frank had explained that the taste was more pronounced in a ribeye precisely because of the fat marbling giving taste to the meat but Caroline just shrugged her shoulders and he gave up his culinary lessons.

The children asked a few questions about his new job in Nigeria and he answered in as much detail as he was able to. After all, his own knowledge of the place and the job was still relatively limited.

"Where are you going to live there, in a house or an apartment?" Caroline asked.

"It's a furnished house where the former managing director lived. So I can probably move straight in. Otherwise, I will have to stay in a hotel for a couple of days." "Oh, that sounds fine but isn't it safer to stay in an apartment?"

"Hey, then you just need a big watchdog. What about a Great Dane," mumbled Nikolaj with food in his mouth and Caroline frowned at him.

"Will you send some pictures when you've moved in?" she asked. "Yes, of course."

"But in Nigeria they also have these terrorist attacks with suicide bombers, don't they?"

Caroline worried, but Frank tried to play down the seriousness of the problem in order not to leave his children too concerned.

"Yes, but that's mostly in the north of the country and I'll be working in the southern part near Lagos where it is not nearly as bad," he explained, but she was surprisingly well informed about the situation.

"Yes, Dad, but there's also something going on in that Niger Delta where armed people are sailing around in speed boats. I also read that some of the oil companies, wasn't it Shell amongst others, had several employees kidnapped?"

"My God, Caroline. You almost know more about Nigeria than I do." She pointed at her iPhone and lifted her eyebrows. "Internet, Dad."

Nikolaj also had some relevant input to the conversation: "Then you just have to get an AK-47 so you can shoot all of them." He showed with great enthusiasm on how to handle the weapon in question and added a brief burst of, "ratatatatatatata ratatatatatata". Frank calmed Nikolaj down and an elderly couple at the next table smiled at him.

"Oh, you idiot, Nikolaj – it's not a damn movie," Caroline snapped and continued updating her Facebook on the mobile. Nevertheless, Frank had felt her sincere concern about the dangers he might expose himself to.

Was it the right thing to do, to leave for Africa again? Shouldn't he stay in Denmark to continue building on the relationship with the children which he had established over the summer? He now knew that he would really miss them but it was also clear to him that he had financial obligations and it was not easy to find a decent job in Denmark these days. Furthermore, his key competence was management in Africa; something not everybody could do or even were prepared to do for that matter. He also had to admit to himself that he was ambitious and perhaps that was the most important factor when he had taken the decision. Yes, he needed a reasonable salary but he could perhaps have found an export-oriented job based in Denmark and with regular but shorter business trips. So, after all it was probably the ambitions playing the major part when he had decided to take this job. The interaction between him and Simon had almost been play-acting because he had quickly decided to take up the challenge in Nigeria.

Frank felt a little sting of conscience but tried to ignore it, ordered a double espresso and tried to change the subject to the movie they were going to watch later.

After dinner, which Nikolaj rounded off with an ice cream with hot chocolate sauce, they drove over to the underground parking near the cinema and walked back to the Palads Cinemas where the movie started at 9:20 p.m. They bought the traditional package of popcorn, coke, some chocolate and various other sweet stuff needed for a cinema visit. Frank was tired after his trip to London and the meeting with the eminent chairman so about half an hour into the movie not even Daniel Craig in full action could keep him awake. He closed his eyes for, what he believed to be, only a couple of minutes until Caroline pushed his arm and whispered: "Dad, you're sleeping," and he woke with a start.

"Hmm, hmm, no I'm not sleeping." From there he tried to get back into the plot. The movie ended and 007 had once more taken care of the bad guys and survived.

Frank drove the children home to Gentofte and stopped the car in the parking lot in front of the apartment. They sat in silence for a moment while he was thinking about how best to handle the farewell in the most decent way.

"Take care of yourselves until we see each other again," he said, and hoped that they had not noticed the slight trembling of his voice.

"Remember to send us some pictures when you've settled down," Caroline said.

"Yes, of course, and maybe you can come and visit me some time – perhaps the winter holiday," he said, well knowing that it was probably not a realistic possibility but he felt a heavy weight on his shoulders and did as much as he could to sound positive.

They got out of the car and he gave them both a big hug. "Remember that we can Skype from time to time. I'll keep an eye on when you're connected," he said, and he waved as they entered the apartment building; Caroline on her mobile, Nikolaj firing a round from an imaginary gun with added sound effects. He stood there for a moment and watched the door close behind them. He felt a lump in his throat, jumped into the car where he quickly found a radio station with music to distract himself from the farewell and went off towards his house in Kulhuse.

Chapter Three

George Akinrogbe was finance director at West African Motors and had worked for the company for 23 years during which time he had been promoted several times. There had been good periods, especially the first 10-12 years, and he was generally quite happy with the job and his respectable career. He had now turned 57 and knew that he might be asked to retire before long as the official retirement age of the company was 60.

Actually, it was not quite the same any more. Not after the latest changes in the management group where his own influence had been reduced and where the extravagant habits shown by some of the new people had led to a severe reduction in profitability. George considered himself a serious and modest man and did not like expensive habits. Well, he liked driving a proper car or eating a decent meal in a restaurant but a life in exaggerated luxury was not something he had ever dreamt about.

He looked out the office window without really noticing the activity out in the yard where car parts from a trailer were being offloaded and driven into the main warehouse. He thought about his cooperation with the former managing director which had been good, albeit not perfect. It had been a real shock when he died in a horrific car accident which George still had questions about. That a relatively young man with a family should die in such a violent way had shaken the company's organisation thoroughly, especially the management group. However, George had reached the point where he was looking forward and hoped the new managing director would prove to be a person who could properly address the serious issues they had been struggling with for a while.

He pulled himself back to the present, grabbed the internal phone and pressed 102.

"Yes, Mrs Adebayo, could you come in here for a moment please?" Any further explanation was unnecessary since everybody in the office knew his voice. In his position, he did not need to spend energy on presenting himself or to use too many expressions of courtesy to employees on lower levels of the organisation.

He was, after all, a member of the management group and had been so for a long time so his position meant that he could speak to people the way he wanted to. He treated the employees decently but the fundamental principle was that it was the duty of the younger staff to be polite to him and show the necessary respect, not the other way around. That was the way things worked and he certainly had no intention of changing that.

A moment later someone knocked on his door, Mrs Adebayo opened it and peeped in. George waved her in and she sat down in the guest chair in front of his desk. He noticed that she looked slightly uncomfortable.

"Well, now your new boss is on his way to Lagos. I have just received confirmation that he is on board the KLM flight arriving this evening. He will then spend the night in Lagos and be here in the morning. Therefore, you will have to make sure that everything is ready for him on arrival.

Has his office been prepared for him?"

"I have agreed with the cleaner that we go through the entire office this afternoon. Then we are sure that it is neat and clean when the new managing director arrives tomorrow," she said, and now seemed a bit more relaxed.

"That's fine, Mrs Adebayo but have you also made sure that his house is ready. It has been vacant for a couple of months now?" He wanted to make sure that there was nothing to criticize when the new managing director arrived as they were going to work closely together in the future.

"Yes, I went out there last Friday and went through the entire house with the steward so he's in full swing cleaning it. I also gave him a cash advance to buy some food and drinks just to make sure the managing director can get through the first day."

"That's perfect," George said, and thought that, as always, she was dependable and responsible.

"I have also ensured that there is a mobile phone ready for him and the IT manager has created him in the system so he can access the internal system and e-mail right away."

"Very good, but if there are any problems please let me know," George said, and she understood that their brief meeting had ended. "Oh, and another thing, don't tell him too much about how things went for his

predecessor in the end. There is no point in making him
too worried. Understood?"

"Yes, of course," she said, and left his office.

He had a good look at her large bottom as she was
leaving his office. She was a lady in the heavyweight
division, probably late 30s with four kids. Not the most
dynamic secretary he had known but she was loyal to
her boss and knew the company very well. George had
arranged for her employment about 11-12 years earlier
when his uncle, who was also president of the golf
club, had recommended her. Since George owed him
a favour and had an interest in becoming cashier of the
golf club, he had found a discreet way of positioning
Mrs Adebayo for a job interview. There had only been
a few candidates and she had been employed quickly,
without too much of a fuss. She had never really shown
her appreciation to him for his assistance in that respect
but that was all right because she was not his type at all.
Also, he usually preferred to sit with a few friends over
some cold Guinness instead of having all the hassle
with young girlfriends. They always ended up being
too demanding with high maintenance costs. Finally,
he had his own arrangements in place as far as female
company was concerned and that suited him just fine.

George leaned back in his large heavy office chair. If
only the new man could pull through and avoid being
exposed to situations like the former boss encountered
and that he would not give up until they had things
under control again. George sighed, opened the Punch
newspaper on his desk and started reading the news.

Chapter Four

II Good evening ladies and gentlemen, your captain,"

Frank heard over the public-address system onboard the KLM plane. He had been sitting squeezed into seat 41A for about six hours, cursing that it had not been possible to find space on business class as he had been promised.

"We have now started our approach into Lagos. We will be flying through some rather heavy clouds during our descent and should expect some turbulence but nothing to be worried about. We thank you for choosing KLM and wish you a pleasant stay in Nigeria." The passenger in seat 40A had reclined the back of his seat fully since the "fasten seat belt" sign had been switched off above Rotterdam southbound. So, Frank was firmly fixed between the two seats with sore knees as a result and could not properly see the TV screen in the seat back in front of him. He was about to empty the small bottle of drinkable red wine from Chile – the third of the trip – and reminded himself that he needed to reduce his alcohol intake and get started with some serious exercising as soon as possible. He emptied the glass and started mentally preparing for arrival. It was his first visit to Nigeria but he had heard the horror stories for many years and had to admit to himself that he was quite anxious.

After having been thrown around in the cabin for almost ten minutes they broke through the clouds over Lagos where dusk had set in. A confusion of rusty roofs, half-finished buildings and yellow busses in hopeless traffic jams revealed itself to the passengers. Frank had never seen anything like it but tried to convince himself that this had to be one of the more chaotic areas of Lagos. The city could hardly be as disorganised as this throughout. They flew over what looked like a green swampy area before the plane made a turn, flaps came out and the wheels were locked in place with a little clunk. Then they, once again, passed over the confused mixture of rusty roofs and yellow busses in dense traffic, only this time at lower altitude. The word chaos sprang to mind.

As soon as the plane landed and started taxiing towards the terminal building a veritable cacophony of mobile telephone sounds erupted. The cabin crew had sincerely requested that mobile phones remain switched off until the plane had come to a complete standstill and the "fasten seat belt" sign had been switched off. However, this request was completely ignored by a large majority of the passengers. Moments later many happy conversations with family members, colleagues, loved ones and drivers to discuss personal matters, homecoming to the Nigerian fatherland and not least agree on meeting time and place were heard. The plane stopped in front of the terminal and the captain rounded off with the mandatory; "cabin crew, doors may be opened".

'Arrived in Nigeria. What kind of experience will this be?' Frank asked himself but there was no time for philosophical thoughts when many passengers were already standing. They were struggling for their massive hand luggage and one passenger, a skinny lady of about 40, was even standing on an armrest. It was apparently important around here to be ready immediately. A couple of rows behind Frank, a young man pulled out his bag from the overhead compartment so quickly that another heavy and hard object fell on the head of an old man who complained bitterly. The young man's mother gave the boy a resounding slap in the face and screamed that he was a bloody idiot, while the old man sat with his arms around his head whining, "Oh my God," several times.

Frank realised that he would not get out of his window seat until his fellow passengers had started moving forward in the aisle. He remembered an episode, years before, involving an Air France plane which had an accident and a fire broke out. The plane had, under competent supervision of the cabin crew, been evacuated in just 90 seconds and nobody died. Frank thanked the higher powers that it had not proven necessary to empty this aircraft in 90 seconds. He sat there studying the scenery and hoping that other things in Nigerian daily life went by more smoothly than emptying of a Boeing 777 in Murtala Muhammed International Airport. He did, however, have a hunch that this was a sign of how things generally worked and his worries increased slightly.

When Frank finally reached the plane's door after about 20 minutes waiting, he instantly felt the different climate. Inside the tunnel on the way to arrivals a first drop of sweat ran down his cheek. Warm and humid, just as he remembered from other places in the region. It seemed as if the air was a thick liquid that embraced him to wish him welcome back to West Africa. At the stairs down to the arrival hall the escalator was out of order and people had to walk down the stairs. Halfway down Frank could not get any further as everything was blocked by many passengers from KLM and a couple of other planes just arrived from Europe. People were complaining loudly and pushing each other but there simply was no more space further down. A little boy had his toes trodden, twisted his ankle and started crying. His father looked angrily at the culprit, a very heavy and slightly intoxicated African with the surplus fat deposits around his neck hanging over his shirt collar resembling a big blood sausage.

Frank tried to wriggle out of his jacket as he was now sweating profusely. However, there was very little space and the talents of Houdini would have been required. After a long wait and slow advancement, he finally reached the lower floor from where he could now see that he was in the queue to the immigration counters. It was obvious to everybody that a certain amount of patience would be required and at the same time he had to be alert in order not be left behind in the queue. He guessed that this combination of skills would be honed intensively during his stay in Nigeria.

When he got a bit closer to the immigration counters, with the stern-faced police officers behind them, it also became clear that the forms required in order to enter the country were missing. The so-called landing cards were not available in the numbers needed and the newly arrived passengers showed the first signs of stress. Frank wondered how the authorities would handle the issue if the mandatory landing cards did not arrive in time. Exactly at that time a sweaty young policeman came running with a bundle of papers and started distributing them to the impatiently waiting crowd. Frank noted that he was the second to last person who received a card which turned out to be a distorted and unclear photocopied arrival form. He immediately started filling it in with his passport as support. Further back in the queue people expressed their dissatisfaction with the missing forms, but with little effect on the authorities.

Frank got through the chaos and was lucky enough to receive his luggage after ten minutes waiting. He threw his luggage on a trolley where three wheels were working and the fourth performed pirouettes in the air. He rolled out into the hot West African evening air where he was met by many offers ranging from taxi driving, money changing and baggage carrying to shoe shining. He rejected all these offers and stood by the wall for a couple of minutes from where he scouted for something recognisable since he had been promised that somebody would pick him up at the airport. That someone turned out to be a young African holding a cardboard sheet on which was written Garbovsky with thick blue letters. Frank wondered whether there had been Russians on the flight but then sharpened up and realised that is should have read Grabowski. He made a signal to the young man whose view was, however, set on infinite and he had to walk over and poke his shoulder.

Then he lit up in a big smile. "Ah welcome, sir," he said, and took hold of Frank's baggage trolley and started pushing it along the terminal building. Frank assumed that it would be a good idea not to let his suitcases out of his sight. So, he followed as closely as possible while rejecting an offer to change naira at an alleged extraordinarily good rate of exchange.

Frank almost lost sight of the young man and thereby also his luggage as the driver rolled through the crowd fast and expertly. They entered the main parking lot where it was considerably darker than in front of the arrival hall. Frank became slightly worried and considered how certain he was that he had found the right person who was supposed to pick him up. A moment later they stopped in front of a slightly battered old Toyota Camry and without any further comments his suitcases were dumped into the boot. Frank was about to get into the front passenger seat next to the driver but then noticed that this place was occupied by a seriously looking man with bulletproof vest, helmet, face shield and automatic weapon. So, he chose to sit in the right hand back seat.

"You're most welcome, sir," said the young chap and revealed a flawed set of teeth. "I'm Godwin, your driver, and I will take you to the hotel."

Frank considered whether it would be appropriate to greet, what he assumed to be, the policeman in the front seat. There was no sign that it was expected so he dropped the idea and leaned back. No conversation took place in the car during the 10-12 minutes it took to get out from the parking lot because an even older Peugeot 505 had broken down and now blocked the exit. This led to some aggressive shouting but fortunately no punches were thrown. Finally, a few men managed to push the old car out through the gate and the traffic in and out of the parking lot slowly started moving again.

The tyres of the Camry shrieked as the driver put his foot on the pedal and accelerated around through the first curve. He generally drove faster and closer to the cars in front than Frank liked.

The road was rough, traffic dense. Oncoming cars had poorly adjusted headlights and the street lighting virtually non-existent. Frank tried to convince himself that the impressions were made stronger because of fatigue from the long journey and the red wine he had consumed on the plane. Or perhaps Nigeria just gave such a strong first impression – he was not quite sure.

Finally, they rolled up in front of the Sheraton and Frank gave a sigh of relief. Everything suddenly seemed in order.

"You are welcome, sir," said Godwin, who had not become more talkative during the drive from the airport.

'Nigeria certainly is hectic,' Frank thought and prayed that his room would be clean and neat with a comfortable bed because he was completely worn out.

A uniformed hotel employee greeted Frank politely, loaded his suitcases on a trolley and asked him to follow. Inside the lobby, things seemed only marginally less hectic than out in the Lagos traffic but it nevertheless felt more secure. There was some waiting to check in at the reception because an elderly couple had a heated debate with the receptionist about the consumption from the minibar. They insisted not having used it at all, while the hotel claimed that they had consumed three small bottles of alcohol, an orange juice and a pack of peanuts. The elderly couple ended up paying the bill for the minibar consumption while they were assuring everybody that they would never make use of this mediocre hotel's services again ... ever. Then it was Frank's turn and his checking in was fortunately quite unproblematic. A few minutes later he threw himself on the bed in his room and sighed deeply. However, a rumble from his stomach reminded him that he was hungry and he sat up again. He spotted the minibar and felt like having a beer but when he opened the small fridge it turned out to be completely empty apart from one small bottle of mineral water. What on earth had the argument with the old couple been all about then?

Back in the lobby Frank made a little reconnaissance tour to investigate the possibilities of having a cold beer and something like a club sandwich as well as update himself on the breakfast arrangements. Outside at the poolside there was an orchestra playing but it was dark and warm as hell for a newly arrived northerner. Inside it was, if not cool, at least a bearable temperature.

Goodies Pub was situated in one corner of the lobby area but that was packed mainly with airline crew members. He even recognised a couple of the KLM cabin crew who seemed considerably happier than they had up at 35,000 feet between Amsterdam and Lagos.

In the central part of the lobby several business people were working on their laptops and Frank assumed that there was a functioning wireless network in the area. However, what seemed more attractive to him at that point was the lobby bar in the corner which looked like a place where one could get a quick and light meal.

He sat down at a small table by the wall and tried to make a waiter aware of his presence but quickly got tired of waiting and walked to the bar. Two waiters were absorbed in a serious conversation, of which Frank did not understand one word, but judging from their attitude it seemed incredibly entertaining. One of them had seen him but did not let himself be interrupted and they let Frank wait for about a minute before attending to him.

As soon as he had placed his order and sat down at his small table again he was approached by a young and lightly dressed lady. "Hi honey, can you buy me a drink?" she said. Frank made a quick visual inspection of her and concluded that the Sheraton apparently accepted professional ladies in their bar.

"Just a second," he answered and started working on his mobile telephone which he had hoped would be roaming in Lagos but he saw no sign of a signal.

"Can I sit down?" asked the lady, or rather the girl, because she could not possibly be older than 18 or 19. In any case, she was already sitting down in front of him at that time. "Did you just arrive?" she asked him. Frank was not in the mood for female company after the long trip. He would rather just have his club sandwich and another beer but before he could end matters the girl had already made herself at home.

"My name is Joy and I can do something really nice for you tonight if you want me to."

'Oh no,' Frank thought and considered how he could get rid of her as quickly as possible and without too much trouble.

He thought about the best possible tactics and went straight to the point. "Listen here, Joy. You're a lovely lady and perhaps another day we would have done something but I've travelled all day and I'm exhausted. We'll order a drink for you and then you'll go back to the bar. All right?"

'Sorted,' he thought, but the lady was employed in a distinctly competitive profession and did not give up that easily.

"Ah come on, honey. I give a fantastic blow job and you'll scream yes, yes, yes, more, more, more," and she apparently impersonated a former customer who had been in exactly that situation. Frank smiled but made it clear to her that it would not happen so she finally got up, winked at him and said, "See you tomorrow then, OK?"

Frank studied her tight butt threatening to escape from under the short skirt or was it the skirt that threatened to jump up over the butt? He shook his head and concentrated on his club sandwich which had just been served. He got one more of the large Star beers before signing the bill and feeling the exhaustion sneaking up on him. On the way to the lift he got a discreet wave from Joy who was now sitting on a bar stool with her legs opened and in intimate conversation with an elderly white man in canvas trousers, blue-chequered shirt and long hair in the neck. 'Congratulations my friend, you are going to get a good blow job tonight,' Frank thought and left the bar to make sure he would be well rested the following day.

Frank had exchanged some emails with one of the departmental managers in the company by the name of colonel Chukwuemeka. They had agreed that he would meet Frank in the morning so they could drive together to Ibadan where the factory was situated. They had not agreed on a specific time but Frank preferred to be ready early to avoid making the colonel wait for him the first day, so he was quite happy having retired to his room relatively early.

Chapter Five

Frank had just sat down on the edge of the bed and yawned, while adjusting the alarm on his mobile phone, when the hotel telephone rang. 'Oh no,' he thought. Who on earth could that be?

Before he could introduce himself, he heard a loud and energetic voice.

"Mister Frank. Welcome to Nigeria, sir. I hope you had a good trip down from Holland, sir." "Yeah, OK … hmm," he answered.

"This is colonel Chukwuemeka, sir. Won't you come down and have a welcome drink? I'm sitting in the bar with a few friends, sir." He made special efforts to emphasize "sir" and Frank was not quite sure whether it was intended to be serious or if it was just slightly exaggerated for the fun of it.

Frank would really have liked to go to bed and had absolutely no wish to go back to the bar. So, he started an unconvincing excuse about being tired and all the things he had to do the following day but he was interrupted by the cheerful major or whatever his title was.

"Just jump into a pair of slippers and come down. Then I'll order some champagne to celebrate your arrival. After all, it's not every day we have a new managing director," and then Frank simply heard a high click when the receiver was slammed down. Frank trudged to the toilet and for a moment considered shaving as he looked rather untidy. Then he gave up on the idea, brushed his teeth and found a T-shirt and a pair of jeans in his suitcase. He sighed, threw some cold water in his face and was ready for second round in the Sheraton's bar … well, sort of ready.

On the way out of the lift on the ground floor he ran into the Emirates Airlines' crew wearing their beige uniforms and identical grey suitcases. He smiled at an Indian-looking stewardess with a pretty face, red hat, matching lipstick and dark shadows under her eyes. Apparently, she was too tired to reciprocate.

Then he steered towards the bar where he had previously eaten and from afar he noticed a tall slender man who nonchalantly leaned against the bar while talking to a couple of young ladies. To his annoyance Frank recognised Joy. The man saw him before he reached the bar, stood up, took two steps forward and saluted with a big smile. 'Handsome fellow,' Frank thought, while he scanned the scenery around, what he assumed would be, one of his key employees. That much he had understood from the documents Simon had given him.

"Hello Mr Frank, and welcome to Nigeria. I hope everything is in order. I sent a policeman with the driver to make sure you were safe. We can't take any risks with an important person like you." The colonel pressed Frank's hand, hard and long. "But now you are safe and we need to have something nice to drink in company of these two beautiful ladies, not so?" He winked at Frank and showed him to the bar. "This here is Joy and over here we have Happy and all that's left is to find out who you like best. I'm sure they both like you very much."

Both the young ladies nodded in agreement while looking at Frank who started wondering how soon he could get out of this predicament without actually having to end up in the situation Joy had so vividly described to him earlier in the evening. Happy's skirt was only marginally longer than Joy's. On the other hand, her shoes seemed slightly higher but the makeup was on the same exaggerated level and the perfume scent was powerful. 'Unbelievable,' Frank thought, but the colonel had obviously felt his concerns and got them all seated at a corner table where the waiter promptly arrived with a bottle of Moët & Chandon and four glasses.

"There you go, Colonel Chuks. Champagne, as you requested." He bowed and moved backwards towards the bar with a nervous look on his face.

On no less than three occasions other guests in the hotel came over to greet the colonel and he introduced them to Frank as director this, engineer that and architect something. They all showed the utmost respect towards the colonel which Frank found remarkable. It was interesting to see and he no longer regretted having come down from his room.

A new bottle of champagne was served without Frank having noticed that it had been ordered. He immediately thought that there would be expenses on the entertainment account that needed looking into. During the champagne drinking, the colonel's focus gradually changed toward the two young ladies and Frank started wondering why it was necessary for him to come to the bar when the colonel was more interested in the ladies. He also spent some energy getting Frank interested in them. At one point, Frank, under the influence of several glasses of bubbly wine, started to consider whether he somehow found Happy slightly attractive, he got a hold of himself, stood up and said thank you for a pleasant evening.

This way he excused himself from the "meeting" and the colonel confirmed that they could meet up the following morning at 9 a.m. and drive to the factory in Ibadan together. Before entering the lift, Frank turned around and saw two men get up from another table to talk to the colonel who took out a bundle of naira which he gave to Joy and Happy, if that was in fact their real names. They had apparently completed the evening's assignment and were being settled. Frank could not completely rule out that they had been recruited to check his interest in the opposite sex and how easy it was to tempt him. It had, no doubt, been a wise decision for Frank to leave the group and go to bed alone.

Back in his room he noticed a small bottle of red wine on the desk with a small card attached. "Once again welcome to Nigeria, Mr Frank. Good luck with the new challenges. From your friend, Colonel Chuks," the card said.

'What a welcome,' Frank thought.

Chapter Six

It was not quite the start to his stay in Nigeria Frank had planned. He woke up much too late and had an upset stomach as well as a severe headache but it was too late to regret. Now it was just a question of getting ready in a hurry. First task was to find the packet of aspirin in his briefcase and swallow a couple. Then he almost stumbled when he entered the bathtub and wondered why every damn hotel could not just have shower cubicles. The small plastic bottle of shampoo, put at his disposal by the hotel, was half empty and he poured the contents into his short hair and got some in his eyes.

After having checked out of the hotel, and been informed that the bill had already been paid, Frank saw that the colonel, apparently in high spirits, was standing outside the hotel entrance.

There he was entertaining a couple of policemen equipped with green berets, shining black boots and machine guns.

"Hello, Mr Frank. How was the night?" The colonel really seemed on top of the world and had to be less sensitive to alcohol than Frank was or perhaps he just had some more efficient painkillers. He continued without waiting for a reply: "I'll go and get the car so we can get moving," and then he ran towards the parking lot.

The policemen studied Frank and one of them with a name tag on his shirt – his name was Okafor – opened the conversation with a polite, "First time in Nigeria, sir?" while he swung the machine gun over his shoulder.

"Yes," Frank had to admit that it was, and he now felt slightly better after the effect of the two painkillers had set in.

"It's an AK-47," the policeman said.

"What?" Frank asked surprised.

"This one here." He took the weapon off his shoulder again and continued, "you were looking at it with interest." Oh yes, Frank had perhaps been worried whether it was properly secured so he would not be wounded by an accidental shot. It would not only be embarrassing but also extremely inconvenient to be shot in such a foolish manner.

'Well, being shot is always inconvenient regardless of the way it happens,' he thought.

"Well, it was just because it's been a while since I saw one at close range and I was wondering if they have changed much," he said. This immediately led to the policeman handing him the weapon.

"Try to hold it, sir." Which was not exactly what Frank had anticipated but he did not want to look like a sissy and carefully took the AK-47 with both hands.

"I hope it's not loaded?" he asked with concern and knew very well that with great certainty it would be.

"Now, let me show you this." The policeman was very anxious to teach Frank how to handle an automatic weapon. "This is the magazine which you release with this little tap. Here is the trigger and here you change between secure, automatic and semi-automatic; there are three settings, OK?" he continued eagerly. Frank clicked loose the magazine, took it off and tried holding the weapon, as if he was ready to use it. A seriously looking elderly gentleman in a dark suit came out of the main entrance from the lobby and looked rather uneasy before he made a wide detour around Frank and got into a black Mercedes 500. Frank clicked the security lever up and down a few times and started feeling quite comfortable holding this famous weapon in his hands.

"So, if I insert the magazine and put this in the middle position, I will be ready to fire a burst?" he asked Okafor.

"Exactly, and now I better take it back before you shoot us," Okafor said, and his colleague roared with laughter.

At the same time the colonel raced up in front of the entrance, opened the side window and laughed: "Na wa o, have you been recruited by the Mobile Police Force or are you coming with me to Ibadan to run a car assembly plant?" Frank said goodbye to his newly found police friends, got his luggage loaded into the boot of the colonel's dark blue Avensis before he got into the front seat and put on his seat belt.

"Oh, you've already heard how I'm driving?" the colonel asked and made a sign towards the seat belt. He put the car into gear and saluted the policemen. "See you in Ibadan," he shouted, as they raced out of the hotel's driveway and ventured into the Lagos traffic once again.

The scene looked a bit less scary in daylight, Frank noticed, but by this time in the morning there were even more cars in the street. People were driving bumper to bumper, galloping on in small aggressive leaps, the horn was used frequently and strange hand signs were made to express one's opinion about fellow drivers' incompetence. The intensity of Lagos started sucking the energy out of Frank after a few minutes. At the first junction outside the Sheraton, the traffic policeman noticed who was driving their car. He bent forward, saluted and shouted: "MORNING, SIR."

'Apparently, the colonel is a well-known character even outside the international hotel,' Frank thought.

They got through the worst morning traffic and onto the highway towards Ibadan surprisingly quickly. The notorious Lagos-Ibadan Expressway which Frank had read stories about on the internet. "Expressway to Hell", as it was popularly called, and he had seen pictures of horrific accidents where petrol tankers had hit minibuses filled with passengers resulting in several burnt-out vehicles. The scenery was truly scary. After having circled a couple of large interchanges and negotiated confusing entry and exit lanes they finally seemed to be on the main highway.

After a little while Frank noticed an unusual advertisement which apparently offered services within the cleaning and sanitation segment. "Otunba Gadaffi: Shit business is good business," it said on the sign under which were shown what Frank assumed to be a row of mobile toilet units. He turned to the colonel who already giggled and started to explain. "Everybody is surprised when they see that but it's actually a former lawyer turned businessman and he now leases out mobile toilets for big functions. He is making a fortune."

"Which kind of functions? Weddings and such?" Frank asked curiously.

"When we approach Ibadan, you'll see some enormous religious camps where they often gather hundreds of thousands of believers who, despite their clean souls and holy connections, still need to relieve themselves of their faeces, isn't it?"

'Unbelievable,' Frank thought and asked himself how many big surprises Nigeria had in store for him. He thought he knew West Africa quite well but based on his brief experience he had to admit that Nigeria was different – very different.

Shortly after Otunba Gadaffi's profitable shit business the traffic thinned out, the colonel stepped on the accelerator and set a cruising speed of about 140 kilometres per hour. A bit too fast for Frank's taste and he discreetly checked the functionality of the seat belt while noticing that the colonel had not even bothered with his own belt. He was wearing sunglasses, sat with his arm out the window, smoking a thin cigar and humming along to a local song.

"There is fire on the mountain, and nobody seems to be on the run. Oh, there is fire on the mountain top, and no one is'ah running."

"So, are you looking forward to this assignment with West African Motors?" the colonel opened the conversation. "And what are your plans to get started? I really hope you have some good ideas because we have a few problems."

"Well, Colonel Chukwuemeka …," Frank started.

"No, call me Chuks or just Colonel. Most people do. Whatever you prefer."

Colonel. It sounded strange to Frank but he had to get used to it.

"First of all, I want to get to know everybody in the management group and hear what their opinion is about the situation. Then I want to understand the business fully and meet customers, suppliers, auditors, lawyer and so on." But in fact, Frank would rather hear Chuks talking, hear his opinion about the situation and he did not need to wait for long.

"That sounds really good. What we are doing is simply to import CKD cars which means a package with all parts that we assemble to a complete car at the factory. It isn't more complicated than that. Oh, and then we buy some components locally, mainly the windows, batteries, some cables and a few other small parts, but it doesn't add up to more than 5-6 percent of the car's value." All this Frank had already read in the documents he had received prior to his departure and which he had spent a few hours reading in the plane.

"But what is your own area of responsibility and who are the other key people?" He tried to get the colonel to open up.

"I am responsible for procurement, stores, import and export."

"I suppose import is clearing of goods in the port and that kind of activity but you also said export. I didn't know we were exporting."

"No, we basically don't but it sometimes happens that there are problems with some of the items we have imported. Then we have to send it out of the country again, back to the supplier," the colonel explained.

"Hmm, but that probably doesn't happen very often, I hope," Frank said.

The colonel changed the subject. "Yeah, and then of course I am also responsible for contact with the authorities and all security matters. Security is important because we are a very well-known company in the region and that always attracts criminal elements."

"I can imagine that but the police are also there to handle that kind of problem, I assume." The colonel smiled but did not comment on it immediately. After a couple of minutes' silence, he said: "I believe you are aware of how bad crime is in this country. We can't always count on the police, not officially in any case, so we must give them some incentives to ensure they're available when we need them.

"So, we are paying for the assistance that we are entitled to," Frank wondered.

"Well yes, but remember that these are lowly paid policemen who have a dangerous job and put their lives at risk every day."

Frank pondered over the situation until the colonel continued. "You have to remember that the country is functioning so poorly that none of us count on any kind of assistance from the government. We take care of ourselves in every way. We try to be independent of the system because nobody looks after us if we don't look after ourselves."

It sounded like a tough situation to Frank who was still pondering in silence.

"Of course, that also means that everybody is desperate to secure himself economically and, consequently, you must expect that many will try to enrich themselves at the expense of the company. I guess that's part of the cost of being a well-established company which is doing well," the colonel said and turned to Frank as if to see his reaction.

"I can understand that people are eager to make themselves financially secure but stealing from the company is totally unacceptable to me. You can be poor and find it hard to make ends meet but if you steal from your employer, you're a criminal. It's as simple as that," Frank said, and thought right away that it had sounded slightly more heavy handed than it was intended. So, he quickly added, "I just believe that modesty is a virtue and that it's one of the important qualities in a leader to show a good example to his employees," which somehow sounded even worse so he left it hanging. The colonel nodded with a smile.

They did not have the opportunity to expand on the subject because they presently arrived at a major police check-point. The colonel had to slow down while they were approaching a couple of heavily armed policemen wearing helmets, face shields and bulletproof vests. They did not look particularly friendly when they suspiciously looked into the car.

"Good morning, gentlemen. How now?" the colonel said and quickly added: "How is the commissioner? I hope you'll greet him from Colonel Chuks of West African Motors," while handing them a bundle of naira notes.

The two policemen obviously recognised the name and their faces lit up. "Of course, sir and safe journey to Ibadan, sir." They waved him through with a smile and the colonel drove through the concrete barricades before passing two more armed policemen on the other side. Then they were quickly back to 140 kilometres per hour and another cigar was lit. The colonel offered Frank one but he refused and explained that he had stopped smoking a couple of years earlier.

After a little less than an hour's drive they passed a place where a large number of trucks were parked along the roadside. This almost completely blocked the road only leaving one narrow lane free. The colonel drove slowly through this zone while he was studying the area behind the trucks. Suddenly he stopped, pulled the handbrake and jumped out of the car. The colonel ran around one of the trucks and looked around on the other side. Then he came back, jumped into the car again, drove a bit forward and found some space between two trucks where he squeezed in the Avensis.

"Come on. I'll show you something," the colonel said and winked at Frank who followed him to the other side of the long row of trucks where several small stalls were set up serving food and drinks. In most places, the drinks seemed to be large beers. A bit further down the row of vehicles they saw a man kneeling next to the tank of a truck. He was obviously in the process of emptying diesel through a hose out of the tank and into a large jar. The colonel ran over and stood next to the man who jumped up with terror in his eyes.

He shook his head and whispered: "Colonel! No, no, no, it's not what you think it is. Please oh, I beg."

The colonel stood there with his hands on his hips and looked at him for a moment. "You chop money from the company, isn't it?" he said.

The man, who Frank assumed was a driver on one of the company's trucks, opened his mouth but only managed to stammer "no" a couple of times before a hard slap hit his mouth and cheek.

Chapter Seven

// That's a lie," the colonel shouted to the truck driver who had clearly been stealing diesel from the truck's tank.

The next slap was harder and hit his ear. The driver went down on his knees desperately whining: "Sorry, sorry, I didn't mean to do it, Oga, I beg." Then he was suddenly lying down flat on his stomach in front of the colonel.

"Get up you idiot and listen well well. Drive straight back to the factory and wait there for instructions, oya." The driver got up with fear written all over his face.

The entire scene had attracted some attention amongst the customers eating and drinking in the small open restaurants only a few metres away. People looked on with interest, but nobody interfered. The colonel ignored everybody around him, turned around and said to Frank: "Come on, let's move on."

They continued up the famous Lagos-Ibadan Expressway for a few minutes before the colonel explained the situation.

"They all do it, the drivers. They steal diesel and make all imaginable tricks with overtime, spare parts and everything else but sometimes we catch them and then we have to be harsh."

Frank pondered over what he had just observed and noted that he had to look further into this problem. It was important for him to have a meeting with the human resources manager to get a better understanding of these things.

'Crazy,' he thought, still a bit shocked at the brutality with which the colonel had handled the situation. It would not have gone down well in Denmark if you slapped an employee a couple of times, even if he had messed with the company's fuel purchases. Even if doing some personal shopping with the company's MasterCard in the local supermarket such a reaction would have brought outrage in Denmark. Despite several years' experience in the region this was still somewhat more dramatic than Frank was used to.

When they were getting closer to Ibadan, Frank saw the huge religious camps the colonel had told him about earlier. They were not at all architecturally remarkable buildings. In fact, they could not even be called churches but rather gigantic hangars with open sides, surrounded by fields the size of many football pitches for parking. Frank's immediate reaction was relief that there were no religious gatherings of these churches on that particular day.

"How long does it go on when they have their mass or whatever it's called?" he asked the colonel who shook his head.

"Oh, you know it can take 3-4 days and there are pastors coming from all parts of the country. A couple of times a year even some from Europe."

"Wow," Frank said, and whistled. His headache from the early morning had started returning.

'It has already been an exhausting day,' he thought, 'and we've not even reached the factory yet.'

"I suppose you would like to go to the house to relax a bit before you come to the factory," the colonel suggested. However, Frank would rather start by showing some initiative and not seem too complacent. He insisted they drive straight to the factory to meet some of the colleagues. His decision did not seem to impress the colonel. Perhaps it even annoyed him.

They left the highway and drove into what had to be some kind of suburb of Ibadan, Frank imagined. Brown rusty metal roofs, partly plastered and peeling concrete walls in buildings with 2-3 floors, balconies with a wealth of battered signboards in faded colours gave the first impressions. All of this was accompanied by an aggressive noise and petrol smell from a sea of old cars. Frank noticed what, in Europe, would be called pedestrians – people who were running in and out between the cars for lack of a pavement, seemingly an unknown phenomenon Nigeria, as far as Frank had seen. Frank convinced himself that this had to be one of the more disorganised parts of the metropolis of Ibadan. However, it did give him an early warning that this was a place it would take time to learn to appreciate.

The colonel had captured the essence of what Frank was struggling with in his head. "This part of town is called Challenge," he explained.

'You don't say,' Frank thought, but refrained from commenting. He simply could not find anything interesting to say or ask about but spent all his energy observing. They drove through a few other areas very similar to Challenge which made Frank depressed.

Finally, they pulled up in front of a large black lattice gate on which Frank recognised the company logo. The colonel honked the horn hard to stir up hectic, or perhaps even panicky, activity on the other side. The gate was opened, guards bowed and saluted them but the colonel sped past the security men completely ignoring their greetings.

The colonel led Frank into the administrative office building and they walked up the stairs to the management part of the office. Modern architecture and open-plan offices were not the norm here and Frank already realised that some modernisation would be required. Inside the managing director's section there was a front office with a slightly old-fashioned looking desktop computer and an empty office chair.

The door was open to the corner office where Frank assumed he would be spending much of this time in the future. He turned the corner and almost barged into a chair immediately inside the office. His eyes following a line from the chair, up over a pair of low-heeled shoes that could have belonged to Daisy Duck, then a massive butt in a less than elegant beige skirt and a slip about an inch too long. There his glance stopped for a few seconds before continuing up to the ceiling where he noticed that the lady had her head through a dismantled ceiling tile.

The solid woman had obviously heard him entering the office because she pulled her head out from the ceiling and looked down at him. "Ah, that must be Mr Frank," she said happily and started climbing down from the chair. "I'm Mrs Adebayo," she said and held out her hand with a big smile.

'Big woman,' Frank thought, but he immediately also saw that she had a pretty face and a charming smile. 'Huge butt, solid arms, pretty face, unstylish skirt and Daisy Duck shoes. Oh well, it could be much worse. If only she can work, I'll be fine,' he thought and looked up at the ceiling.

"Is there anything I can help with up there?" he asked. "Maybe that's where I will be sitting?" "Oh, sorry, no, no, we were just cleaning and found some strange things here and there in the office. Some juju black-magic stuff - charms and that kind of thing." She showed him a handful of peculiar items amongst which he noticed a dried bird's leg and something that looked like a crooked nut ... black-magic, really?

Chapter Eight

II What's the meaning of all this?" Frank said, and shook his head.

Mrs Adebayo dismissed it quickly and wanted to get on with the programme. "Oh well, let me remove this chair and, eh, yes now … welcome Mr Frank. As I said, I'm Mrs Adebayo and I'm your secretary. Do you drink coffee or tea?" Frank felt more like a glass of water and a Prozac but he said yes to a cup of coffee. He tried to sit down in the large, heavy and much too soft office chair which threatened to tip backwards.

Mrs Adebayo came back with a mug of very black coffee which she placed in front of him on the corner of his desk then sat down in one of the visitors' chairs. "Don't worry about these juju things," she said. "We were cleaning the office and discovered these strange things in your office chair." Frank felt a slight tickle in his backside and hoped all the things had been removed. His secretary continued undaunted. "And then we searched the entire office to have it properly cleaned."

'Which apparently included the loft,' Frank thought, but he did not comment on it. He took a sip of his coffee, which was thick with sugar, and grimaced.

"Does it need more sugar?" Mrs Adebayo asked, and Frank explained to her that he did not use sugar at all. Then that was settled – an important detail for a future good cooperation.

"Mrs Adebayo, or what is your ... eh, first name?"

"Yemisi is my first name but it's probably better if you call me Mrs Adebayo. That's a bit more formal and that's the way I was raised. Then nobody can say that we've become too close, if you understand what I mean."

"OK, Mrs Adebayo. I fully understand and that's fine with me." He said and thought that she was a confident lady whom he could surely work with although there was no danger of him getting too close to her whether they used first or last names.

"Then there are a few things I would like you to arrange for me." He got straight to the point. "I would like to meet with all the heads of department tomorrow afternoon. So, if you would be kind enough to inform them. At 2 p.m. in the meeting room tomorrow." He looked around. "Where's the meeting room, by the way?" She sat with a little note book and a blue promotional pen, the origin of which he could not see.

"Right here next to your office," she said, and pointed behind him.

"Excellent, and then I need a mobile phone and a number. Oh yes, and I assume we have an IT person who can hook up my laptop computer to the internal system."

She was well prepared and had already arranged for the phone and the sim card which she fetched in her own desk drawer right away.

"Regarding the connection of your laptop to the system the password is written here." She gave him a yellow post-it note. "So, when your computer has found the network you hook up with the password. Your username is FRG since there was already an FG in the system. Let me know if there is any problem. I'm not an IT expert but I do know how to handle the simple things." "Perfect. I can see that you're well organised, Mrs Adebayo." He put emphasis on her last name to see if she would react to it and decide to change to first names after all. There was no reaction so Frank thought that they would just stay with the last name. From his side, that was, because she had no problem using his first name but if he used hers it could be misunderstood. "But, Mr Frank, there is a gentleman who has asked for a meeting with you ever since he heard that you were coming. It's one of the company's suppliers, Mr Okonkwo from Nigerian Glass and he won't leave me alone. Could you possibly see him tomorrow?"

"Well, that's a bit too soon. I've hardly arrived but OK then. Let him come the day after tomorrow, early, if it is really necessary," Frank answered.

Frank was not superstitious, but he was a little unsettled by the fact that somebody had placed strange items in his chair and in the loft. So, somebody was not happy about his arrival or was it just a coincidence? Maybe it was in fact targeted at his predecessor whom Simon had told him about in Copenhagen. He could not really decide whether to be worried, annoyed or simply not take any of it seriously. After all, a few tiny ridiculous juju things in his chair and in the loft, could be overcome even though the intentions might have been evil enough. In any case, he was too tired to worry about such things right now. He was also angry with himself for having been so easy to tempt into getting drunk with the colonel the previous evening.

Somebody knocked on the open door and a mature grey-haired and slightly overweight man stood in the doorway. "Hello, I'm George Akinrogbe," he said. "The finance director." Frank rose from the soft office chair with his hand outstretched to greet George.

"Yes, of course, George. Come in and sit down." This was exactly the man Frank wanted to see before any of the other senior managers. Mrs Adebayo got up and closed the door behind her when leaving his office.

"I'm terribly sorry about all this fuss and that you've had such a confused welcome to Ibadan." George seemed sincerely worried while he looked around in the office. "But don't take it too seriously. I am sure it was nothing personal," which to Frank sounded slightly naïve.

They continued with some polite and informal small talk before Frank got to the point.

"George, sometime during the day tomorrow, I would like to have various information so I can have an idea of how things are going. Then we could go through my questions later in the week.

George was ready to take notes. "Certainly, Frank. What exactly is it you would like to have?

Then I'll make sure my people prepare the information for you."

"I'd like to have the latest management accounts up to the end of last month, a cash flow analysis, a list of creditors and debtors, details of bank accounts and statements of account to begin with. Then we'll take it from there." He leaned back in the big chair, in which he did not feel comfortable at all, and he intended replacing it as soon as possible. He was wondering what to make of George and had not quite made up his mind about him yet. 'A bit dull but probably reliable enough although he seems a little bit humourless,' Frank thought.

Then the colonel peeked in. "I just heard that a lot of strange stuff was found in your office, Frank. I'm sure it was meant for the former managing director. I'm also pretty sure I know who put it there. So, don't worry." He smiled and closed the door again but Frank thought that his dismissal of the seriousness of the matter had seemed just a bit too convenient. There was something mysterious about this both charming and polished colonel who could replace his charm with brutality in an instant. It made Frank slightly uncomfortable. Nothing alarming, he could put his finger on, but there was just something not right. When he visited the chairman in London, Frank had seen the fear in the eyes of the chairman's servant but he understood that as being a big shot's tough way of dealing with his employees. They were probably always treated the same cold and cynical way and got used to it over time. The colonel, on the other hand, seemed jovial and charming but when his mood changed he became distinctly unpleasant, and the effect of the quick change and the extreme contrasts between the two sides of the man seemed shocking.

At around 5:00p.m. Frank had to admit that he was completely exhausted. The long trip the day before and the evening's programme with the colonel had depleted him of all reserves. He closed his briefcase and grabbed it but out in the front office the driver sat waiting for him. It was the same Godwin who had collected him at the airport the day before and he was very anxious to pull the briefcase out of Frank's hand. Frank quickly gave up, let Godwin carry the bag and followed him down the stairs and out to the car. A brand-new Toyota Camry.

"Look boss, we've got a new car," Godwin said proudly, and in such a way that it gave the impression that it was him and Frank, jointly, who were the happy owners of a brand-new car.

Frank would somehow have liked to be able to choose his own car but he did not want to be difficult and he was quite happy with the Camry. Frank was about to enter the front passenger seat where this time there was no armed policeman. However, since Godwin had followed him around the car and opened the door to the backseat in the right-hand side of the car, he understood that this was the place he was expected to take. And so he did.

Speedily they went past the big local Aleshinloye market and a couple of major junctions without traffic lights but controlled by energetic traffic police officers directing the circulation of mostly old cars. They crossed an ungated railway crossing where a triangular sign advised that "when light is blinking and bell ringing, train is coming". However, the equipment did not look like it had either blinked or rung for a couple of decades.

Upon arrival at the house, of which he made a quick external inspection, his briefcase was carried from the car to the entrance by the driver and from there into the house by the cook.

The latter presented himself with a big smile. "I'm Temitope and I'm your cook and steward. I take care of everything inside the house and right now I'm making some nice food for you, master." A welcome speech Temitope had probably worked on most of the day.

Frank did a quick once-over of the single-storey house. He identified which rooms he would use as bedroom, office and guestroom. It was actually more or less self-evident as it was already furnished; sparingly and not quite to his taste but with a few modest adjustments it could be made habitable also according to European standards. He sat on the sofa for a moment and noted, to his great relief, that it was not nearly as soft as that of the chairman in London – the comfort was approved. He walked around the sitting room and over to the bar where he tried out the bar stools which were the perfect height for the bar counter. The bar also had the required width thus leaving enough space for the legs without sitting sideways or with the legs spread out. So far, so good. He then tested the dining room chairs and the dining table which were approved - nothing more, nothing less. The back rest of the chair was uneven and the upholstery fabric so flowered that it reminded him of a visit to the botanical gardens in Copenhagen in the mid-1970s. The upholstery could be replaced, of course.

Temitope had made the safe choice and prepared a dinner consisting of a mixed tomato and green salad followed by chicken in a curry sauce with rice. Frank ate with great appetite and then went through the fridge, store and bar with Temitope to check what was missing. The latter was the easiest as the bar was completely empty apart from the bottle of Gammel

Dansk, a Danish bitter, he had bought in Copenhagen airport. So, Frank basically needed to buy everything else he could possibly feel like drinking.

The cook had been attentive enough to buy a carton of mineral water and a couple of beers which he had put in the fridge. There was also some bread, cheese, and eggs for breakfast, so the situation was not too bad.

After dinner, Frank tried the TV which was a modest 32-inch flat screen without any fancy functions. When he switched it on, it started on a local news channel. 'Ah-ha, so the cook is watching TV,' Frank thought. He flicked between news and sports channels and hung around BBC World for about half an hour after which he was so tired that he had to hit the sack.

He found a relatively new exercise bike of pretty good quality in the bed room.

'So, my predecessor did not have time to wear out this one,' Frank thought, and tried to ignore it. He hoped to spend more time on the bike than the poor chap who had burned to death in a new Avensis with automatic gears.

He spent a little time emptying one of his suitcases, made a quick inspection of cupboards and drawers and, of course, the bed. He found everything sufficiently clean and, considering his level of exhaustion, he had reached the point where he could without a doubt sleep here in his new residence.

Chapter Nine

When George entered the meeting room at 1.55 p.m., Frank was already there. They had been called for the first management meeting on the second day after Frank's arrival, which George thought was a positive move by Frank who wanted to make himself familiar with the company's heads of department and their areas of responsibility right away. He had asked them to be ready by 2 p.m. but he would, unless George was seriously mistaken, now find out that their discipline in relation to punctuality left much to be desired.

At 2.02 p.m. the National Sales Manager, Funmi, entered the meeting room with a slightly awkward look on her face. She greeted Frank, shook his hand and nodded towards George. He had never been able to find out whether she was looking at him or something else in the room as she had a squint in one eye, or was it both eyes. Funmi sat down at the opposite side of the round table to Frank.

Then they started dropping in one after the other. The factory manager, Duncan, an older and overweight Brit.

He had been there forever which meant a combination of vast experience and many bad habits often seen in expatriates who had spent decades in Africa. He arrived out of breath and sat down between Funmi and Frank.

The internal auditor, the human resources manager and at last, around 2.20 p.m., Colonel Chuks came barging in through the door and closed it behind him. Apparently, he took it for granted that he would, as always, be the last to arrive.

Frank spent about ten minutes introducing himself and then gave a summary of his experience from the companies he had worked for in different African countries before coming to Nigeria. He had a rather impressive C.V. and George just hoped that it would suffice to make it in Nigeria.

Frank's presentation was rounded up with a few PowerPoint slides in which he explained the decision process he wanted to implement and work with, in the company. He drew their attention to the fact that according to this process, a problem had to be tabled and thereafter discussed by all involved parties – it could, for example, be the management group. Everybody in the group would then have the chance to express their opinion. However, in all situations you would inevitably reach a point where a decision had to be taken even though everybody may not be in agreement. He made it clear that he did not believe in reaching complete consensus in every situation. In the end a leader had to live up to the responsibility bestowed upon him and make a decision even when it was an unpleasant decision. Frank emphasized that the leader could be himself or anyone of them depending on the nature of the problem. He expected that they would all have to live up their responsibility … and earn their salary. It was straightforward, with no beating around the bush, which George thought was about time for some of the colleagues several of whom had put on a serious face.

The very last slide in Frank's presentation simply had one large text box in the middle in which was written: "We start meetings on time." So, he had been prepared for some of them to show up late and wanted to make sure that everyone was aware that he found that unacceptable.

'Brilliant,' George thought.

"Need I say more?" Frank said, and looked around at them one by one. There were no comments.

Then Frank asked each of them to present themselves in the same way he had just done which created some uncertainty about who was supposed to start. George caught Frank's eyes and gave him a discreet sign that he would like to start. Frank noticed. "We start with you, George and then we continue clock-wise around the table," he said.

They went through a veritable examination and it was clear to George that Frank knew what he was talking about. Some did better than others but when they reached the human resources manager, he immediately showed signs of weakness and the pressure was on.

"What kind of pension scheme do we have?" Frank asked the human resources manager. "We have a pension scheme," came the short but hesitant answer.

"And how does it work? How much does the employee and the company pay respectively? Is it a percentage of the basic salary from each party?"

"No, it doesn't work that way. The employee receives a lump sum when he retires or leaves the company for other reasons. It is calculated based on the number of years of service and the last monthly salary," the human resources manager explained.

"So, it's not actually a pension scheme but a kind of golden handshake. A gratuity scheme in other words."

"We call it a pension scheme," insisted the human resources manager.

"Even though it is in fact something else but let's leave it at that. It means that the company is accumulating a debt to the employees and the amount becomes higher and higher every year ... especially when we implement salary increases. Correct?" "Yes."

"Very well then. How much do we owe the employees as of today if we were to pay all of them off?" Frank asked.

"That depends, of course, how long people have been employed and how many leave at the same time," the human resources manager tried to evade the issue.

"How much if it is all the employees leaving today?" Frank had got the upper hand and did not let go.

"Many employees have been here for many years so it could very well end up being a very significant amount." The HR-manager looked more and more insecure and probably knew where this was going.

"How much?"

"It is very difficult to estimate off-hand since it changes all the time."

'He is completely on thin ice,' George thought. He could have answered the questions about the accumulated amounts for staff gratuity better than the human resources manager did because he knew approximately how much had been provided for in the accounts, but he did not feel that it was the right time to get involved. So, he let Frank continue his cross examination of the HR-manager.

"HOW MUCH?"

"I'm not able to give a specific estimate here and now but I could investigate it as soon as possible." Frank sighed, and looked directly at the HR-manager who had his handkerchief out to wipe sweat off his forehead.

"Now we've finally, after wandering around in the dark for a while, reached the answer we should have had from the very beginning. That answer is that you have no clue but that you would like to investigate the matter. Isn't that correctly understood?" Frank had made a point and, unfortunately for the HR manager, he had been in the line of fire.

The HR-manager nodded to confirm his agreement and then looked down at the table in front of him. At that point Frank apparently let him off the hook.

"Lady and gentlemen. There are certain things I expect a head of department to be on top of.

BUT, if he or she, in a moment of mental blackout, should have forgotten, I would ask you to spare me all kinds of long rambling stories and thereby wasting my time as well as yours," Frank said, and looked around the group. Nobody gave even the slightest indication of disagreeing with Frank. However, George could not help but feel delighted that their new boss had shown how to create respect from day one.

Then Frank continued with a few questions to the internal auditor about existing control systems, the latest management accounts and expected result for the year to George. Then he went on to procurement procedures, customs clearance and general import regulations from the colonel. Questions about possible technical problems and future investment plans from the factory manager. Finally, he wanted to know a bit more about payment terms and status on trade debtors from Funmi. She did not have any figures for number of debtors with overdue amounts off the top of her head nor the actual amounts. In fact, she apparently believed that it was more of an accounts issue.

"No," Frank said. "If you sell a car, it's also your responsibility to collect the money and if you don't receive the required lists of overdue amounts from accounts department you have to complain, initially to George and eventually to me, if you don't get what you need. I hope there is no doubt about that?"

"The problem is that it's sometimes difficult to maintain a good relationship with the customers when you have to put pressure on them for payments," Funmi stated.

"It's always a sales person's responsibility to collect payment. That's the way it is. Otherwise it is much too easy to sell if you just leave the responsibility for payments to others, isn't it?"

Funmi did not answer and did not look like she was completely convinced but she understood that the subject had been exhausted for the time being.

"George, would you kindly make sure that we have an updated list of overdue payments divided into periods for instance from 30 to 60 days, from 60 to 90 days, 90 to 120 and more than 120 days?" Frank looked at George who took notes and confirmed that he would have everything ready the following day.

When the meeting was over, Frank asked George to come into his office.

"Well, George. That was a lot of pathetic nonsense and evasion by more than one of your colleagues," Frank said. "Fortunately, I can see that you are on top of the issues within your own area of responsibility and I'm pleased about that."

"Thank you for the kind remarks. I have been here for many years and I'm doing my best," George said.

"I appreciate people who put in professional effort and try to make a difference," Frank said. "You saw that I was a bit tough on a couple of your colleagues but they were sitting there fumbling with the issues not making any commitments. Things like that make me really annoyed. It's not because I like harassing people but I thought it was important to make it clear to everybody how I want things to run."

"That's absolutely crucial and I thought the meeting went well. It's unfortunate that we are not used to a boss who has a hands-on approach. That's probably why some of them were a bit shaken."

"Well, they'll just have to get used to that," Frank said to round up their meeting and George went back to his office.

George was quite content with the way the meeting had gone and the fact that Frank had had an opportunity to evaluate the management group.

Chapter Ten

II Good morning and welcome," Frank said to the man who had insisted on seeing him so urgently. "My name is Frank Grabowski and I'm the new managing director here at West African Motors. What can I do for you?"

"My name is Okonkwo and I'm the owner of the company, Nigerian Glass. We supply car windscreens and windows for most of your models, have done so for many years and we would very much like to continue doing so." He spoke rapidly while looking directly at Frank as if he were assessing what kind of man he was dealing with. "We have, however, experienced very significant cost increases and have announced planned price increases but your predecessor was very difficult to deal with indeed. He refused to hear any talk about higher prices and we understood that he was considering importing instead of buying from us." Okonkwo placed the palm of his hands against each other and studied his hands before continuing. "That would be extremely inconvenient for us and I simply want to make sure that we don't misunderstand each other, you and I, if you understand my point."

"I understand very well that there could be a need for price increases especially if the need for such had been clearly documented and justified. If we have not received such documentation, I would suggest that you prepare it most urgently and send it to us. I have just arrived, and I need to familiarise myself better with the details of our business. So quite frankly, I don't really understand exactly what I can do for you at this time," Frank replied politely.

"Of course, but you must understand that we could have common interests in many ways if only we identify how we can mutually benefit from various initiatives. If I may say so, we are known for remembering our friends and we would obviously also be prepared to remember you when things go well." The message was becoming clearer to Frank but he still did not find it particularly pleasant. However, he wanted to be absolutely sure that he had not misunderstood the situation.

"Does that mean that I would be, shall we say, rewarded if we can agree on certain issues?" Frank asked, and studied which effect it had.

Okonkwo gave a sigh of relief as he leaned forward and smiled. "Exactly Mr Graboski. I immediately saw that you are an intelligent man. It is always a pleasure dealing with people of your calibre."

'Now he is going too far,' Frank thought. I wonder where he's going with this bullshit.

"It is very important to us that we work together and I have actually brought you a small acknowledgement, a token of our friendship, just to wish you welcome to Nigeria and at the same time to show you that we are serious people," Okonkwo said, and pulled a narrow brown envelope out of his inside pocket, put it on the edge of the desk and pushed it over towards Frank with the slightest touch of his index finger as if the envelope was hot.

"Acknowledgement?" Frank asked and raised his eyebrows. "I certainly hope you haven't come to influence my decisions with money." He ended the sentence with a discreet, "hmm," and tried to raise his eyebrows even more while he waited for a reaction from Okonkwo.

"Please don't misunderstand me, Mr Graboski. We could all use an extra little contribution to cover the high cost of living. Don't you agree?" Okonkwo's tone had become slightly patronising and Frank was ready to wind himself up but he knew that he had to remain calm if at all possible.

"My name is Grabowski, not Graboski. I may be new in Nigeria and I may look like a boy scout but I'm not and I don't take bribes." Frank demonstratively placed his index finger on the corner of the brown envelope with all other fingers stretched out in the air. Then he slowly pushed the envelope across the desk back to Okonkwo while looking him directly in the eyes. "Thank you for a pleasant meeting, Mr Owonko," he said, and let go of the envelope with a little smile.

Okonkwo stood up quickly, took the envelope and put it back in his inside pocket from where it had come. "I had heard that you were a reasonable man but I must have been misinformed," he snorted. "Being as uncooperative as you are could be very unfortunate, Mr GRA … bowski. Remember! You're in Nigeria." He had exaggerated the pronunciation of Frank's family name, stood there for a second or two as if waiting for a reaction. Then he turned around and left the office without looking back.

Mrs Adebayo came rushing into Frank's office. "Oh my God, what happened? That man looked very angry when he left your office."

"An idiot came calling and tried to bribe me. I told him what I thought about that matter and asked him to get lost. That's the short version of the story," Frank smiled, and told Mrs Adebayo to ask George to come to his office. George did not let him wait for very long.

"What happened?" he already started out in the front office and continued when he had closed the door. "Was it that guy, Okonkwo, from Nigerian Glass who was here?" "Yes, exactly," Frank said. "I already don't like him at all."

"That's not someone you would want to have as your enemy. He's got a lot of influential friends in town," George explained. "I hope you didn't fall out with him."

"Ah, to hell with him," Frank said, and was more interested in the documents which George had given him the previous day and which he had gone through in the evening. "Tell me why we are not making more money when we practically have a monopoly on sales to the government and the public sector where we sell at incredibly attractive prices?"

George looked nervous. "All is not as it should be but I can't explain to you exactly what has gone wrong," he started. "We have a strong market position but we are spending too much money on purchasing diesel for the generators and trucks, spare parts, tyres and so on and so on." George shook his head and looked even more worried. "Hell, I really don't know – there are also substantial expenses to the police, security people and the authorities."

"We have to do something about this. Who is responsible for all these expenses, is it the colonel?" Frank interrupted him slightly annoyed. "And the expenses to the authorities, what does that cover?" he continued.

George was shaking his head and looked at the documents on the table in front of him. "I think it's important that you speak to the colonel and have him give you an overview of the situation," he said evasively, and almost looked as if it was all his fault.

Frank sat and pondered over what he had learned from George and became worried whether he could count on the man's full support. He did not strike Frank as being particularly energetic, probably even a bit weak. A man with that level of responsibility being head of the finance and accounts departments in such a large organisation gave him cause for concern.

"Listen, George, we are in October and we have the figures for September. So, I would like to have a statement showing all expenses specified by account – every single account – for the nine months of last year, nine months' budget figures and the actual figures for the first nine months of this year." George looked at him without speaking. "This is information which we have available at this time, isn't it?" Frank asked him.

"Oh yes, absolutely and this is certainly information you need." George sounded relieved that he had been given a clear assignment. "I'll get started immediately." He rose hesitantly but when Frank did not speak George just said: "Thank you, Frank, and have a nice evening," before leaving Frank's office.

'Competent enough but rather soft,' Frank thought. He was not sure where to get his support if he had to make changes to the company's way of operating. But he was aware that George – hopefully – was honest but under huge pressure and therefore careful what he said and did. He no doubt also wanted to size up Frank before he opened up completely to him. Frank thought that it was important for him to create a relationship of trust and confidence between him and George as soon as possible.

Frank was completely exhausted when he got home that evening. He had not seen the colonel all day and wondered what he was doing. George was apparently busy working on the cost overview which Frank had asked him for. The entire situation seemed quite overwhelming to Frank and on top of that he had a hard time with the Nigerian names which he often pronounced in the wrong way or put emphasis on the wrong syllable.

He was not in a very good mood and it certainly did not help that the cook had prepared a steak which was overcooked and rock hard. He asked for some bread and cheese and withdrew to his office which he had just furnished and once again started going through the documents George had given him the previous day.

The house that had been made available to him, and where his predecessor had also lived, was a one-storey building, but divided into two sections. Sitting room, bar, dining area and kitchen were placed in one section which also had the main entrance and a kitchen door. There were three rooms and two bathrooms in the other section, but no direct access from outside, so, one had to go through the sitting room or the kitchen to get in or out of the house. The two sections were separated by a steel door locked by an ordinary lock and an extra lock with a sliding latch. It was, after all, Nigeria and security was high on the agenda everywhere and rarely out of anybody's thoughts in daily life.

Since Frank lived alone, he had arranged an office in one of the three rooms in the secured section which had previously been a children's room. That was basically the only change in purpose as the utilisation of the house was almost given. It had been quick and easy to make the change because there had been some unused office furniture in the factory's main store which he had arranged to have transported to his house. From his office, as well as from the bedroom down the hall, he had a view over the front garden and down to the main gate and the driveway. The last room was situated on the other side of the corridor and had windows towards the back yard and a small hut with a bar which Frank's predecessor had apparently built because it looked relatively new. There were also a pair of children's swings in the garden. Frank shivered a bit when he saw it and was reminded about the predecessor's unfortunate passing and the young children left behind.

Frank sat in his office with a glass of red wine from the local grocery store which could not quite be described as a supermarket – that would have been an exaggeration. It was horrible – the wine that is. He guessed that it had never been particularly good but now it had simply gone off. He got up and went to the kitchen to pour it into the sink and replace it with a large Star beer. In Nigeria, beer in large 66 centilitre bottles was still very popular and that corresponded to two beers of the Danish standard size. Large country, large population, extreme richness amongst the few, extreme poverty amongst the many and large beer for everybody.

When Frank had acquired an overview of the contents of the documentation from George, he started on the unopened letters he had brought from the office. He took an old-fashioned paper knife with a meticulously carved wooden handle and attacked the envelopes. What a bizarre situation it was sitting in southern Nigeria cutting open envelopes with a special knife created for this purpose. This kind of tool had to have a short life span in these internet times, although in this part of the world a lot of memos were still printed out instead of being sent by email. Even internal documents were often printed and placed in envelopes before they were distributed by a messenger. Frank had seen a secretary typing a handwritten draft on her computer.

'Archaic,' Frank thought, and put the paper knife back in the holder with a logo apparently from a local clearing and forwarding company with which the company did business. The logo resembled that of Real Madrid. However, the company name was almost unreadable although the word "clearing" was clear enough on the over-decorated pen holder where he placed the paper knife.

He worked on the figures and calculated key indicators to evaluate the company's results and solidity, which only made him more worried. The figures somehow seemed unrealistic. It was especially the relatively good sales performance but surprisingly poor results which surprised him. The money was pouring in and pouring out again just as fast.

He took a short break, noticed that Caroline was online on Skype and sent her a short message. "Hi Caroline. Can you talk for five minutes?"

She quickly replied: "Hi, Dad. Yes, of course," and he called her.

"Hi Caroline, how is it going in high school, are you coping with it?" he started with the traditional question.

"Fine thanks, but what about you? How's Nigeria? Is it as bad as we hear in the news?" He quickly considered how much he should tell her and decided just to say that it was not nearly as bad as the reputation the country had in Europe. He did not want to make her unnecessarily concerned. After a couple of minutes, the internet connections weakened and they could only hear every second or third word until they finally gave up talking and continued writing. He had to admit to himself that it suited him quite well as he found the conversation difficult. It reminded him how much he missed his children and how far away from them he was.

"I really hope it's going well in school, Caroline," he wrote.

"Don't worry, Dad. I'm doing fine. Math is a bit difficult but otherwise I am doing very well. You don't have to be worried but take good care of yourself down there."

He suddenly felt how much he missed his children. Right there and then he would have wanted to be sitting with her and Nikolaj in the summerhouse in front of the fireplace having a good time watching a movie.

"I will and I'm sure it will be OK," he typed.

"When are you coming home on holiday next time?"

"Perhaps a short Christmas holiday but I'm not quite sure about that yet," he replied, although he knew well that it would be difficult to get away for Christmas when he had just started work in October. In a way he felt guilty being so far away and found the Skype chat testing. They continued with a few pleasantries before rounding up and saying goodnight.

Around 9.30 p.m. he was tired and watched a bit of sport on one of the satellite channels before going to bed.

Still he did not fall asleep immediately and lay in bed pondering all the challenges that were piling up in front of him. At one point he heard a slight noise, a sort of scratching sound, near the window which he assumed had to be an insect, perhaps a cockroach. The sound stopped but he suddenly felt something moving on the floor even though he was not completely sure whether he actually heard it or just felt the movement.

However, he was no longer in doubt when he felt something on top of his duvet above his feet – and it was definitely not an insect but something much heavier. His heart skipped a beat or two in total horror. There should not have been anything in his bedroom, yet something had moved from the window across the floor and up onto his bed. In one single movement he threw the duvet to one side, turned around to the other side, switched on the light and continued to roll out of bed. He had done so at the right time. In fact, it had probably been at the very last moment because on his bed lay a long green-grey snake which had now raised its head and the front part of its body into a vertical position. An impressively large part of its body was raised to a position where its head was almost level with his own.

Chapter Eleven

He stood there in the middle of the room completely frozen staring at the snake which stared back at him. They were standing in front of each other like two gunslingers each waiting for the other to draw first. Frank had no revolver to draw but fortunately the snake did not know that, and even though it was extremely well armed it was also frozen and hesitated attacking. Its mouth was opened slightly and Frank noticed that it was black inside – bad news. The most notorious snake in Africa – the black mamba – whose poison could kill a grown man in a very short time. Frank had forgotten just how long it took for its bite to be lethal. He did remember, however, that its poison affected the nervous system which basically meant that you were unable to breath and died from suffocation. He somehow already felt that he had difficulty breathing. It was scary, the black mamba, and Frank had never in his life been as terrified as he was now. He looked around in the room without moving anything but his eyes, while he desperately thought about what else he had read about one of Africa's most dangerous snakes. It could be aggressive when feeling threatened, he remembered. But how do you explain to a snake that you have no evil intentions and that it should not feel threatened?

'It's apparently also very quick,' he thought, and prayed that he would not have to race it.

The mamba took the initiative away from him when it lowered its head and slowly slid across the bed and down on the floor on the opposite side of where Frank was standing. He was standing barefoot in underpants and an XXL T-shirt with a company logo.

When he could no longer see the snake, Frank ran towards the door and out of the room. He slammed the door hard behind him and with shaking hands managed to open the security door. He ran to the sitting room where he switched on the lights and stood perplexed for a few seconds. Then he went back to the section of the house with the bedrooms and glanced towards his closed bedroom door. He then went into the guestroom where he found a pair of shorts and tennis shoes in the suitcase he had not yet unpacked. He shook the shorts and looked inside the shoes before he went into the sitting room and put on the light clothing. His mobile phone was still in the bedroom, and he had absolutely no intention of venturing in there again anytime soon. He decided first of all to wake up the security guards.

However, before doing anything else he went to the bar, took down the first bottle of alcohol he saw on the shelf and filled a glass generously. He emptied it in one swallow – it was whisky – then he poured another shot in the glass and took a sip. He then took a deep breath, put down the glass and moved out into the West African night.

The entrance door of the house faced the driveway and the small gatehouse at the main gate where an empty chair indicated that the watchmen had gone to sleep.

"Hello, security, hello," Frank shouted towards the gate but there was no reaction. He tried again a couple of times but received no response to his calls. So he had to go down there and wake them up. This made him more angry than afraid even though he did watch his step very carefully when walking down the paved pathway through the garden to the gatehouse. Through the window of the gatehouse he heard heavy snoring which was unaffected by a loud, "HELLO IN THERE". He pushed the door which met resistance from one of the watchmen lying on the floor from where he produced the snoring. In an old armchair, which looked like it had been scrapped sometime around independence, the other watchman lay sprawled as if he had been thrown there from a couple of metres away.

"Hello, you two, will you fucking wake up?" he roared into the little modestly equipped gatehouse. This caused veritable, or even hectic, activity in there. Both were on their feet in a split second and quickly started explaining that they had not been sleeping. Frank was in no mood to listen to long stories and interrupted them immediately.

"Listen now, you two shitkickers, you can explain all of that later. Right now, you're on an entirely different mission because you must go and kill a snake in my bedroom and it has to be in a bloody hurry before it disappears. Do you understand?"

The watchmen almost looked relieved that the scolding had blown over so fast and that they were now on a special mission. A VIP assignment where they might do enough good to ensure that any further disciplinary sanctions were forgotten. At least that is what Frank thought he read from their facial expressions and general behaviour. They grabbed their machetes and exchanged a few remarks in a local language after which, one of them took a long wooden pole standing in a corner of the little gatehouse.

"If you can get rid of this snake in a hurry you may avoid being sacked so you better get moving," Frank said, while he started trotting back up towards the house. The watchmen followed him with their weapons but inside the sitting room he showed them the general direction towards the bedroom and let them go in front. "It's the last room in this section and the snake was on the bed but it crawled down on the floor and under the bed I think, so maybe it is still there," he explained. The two, now completely alert and appropriately armed, watchmen moved into the warzone.

If the situation had not been as serious as it was, it would have been funny because the two men looked like a couple of characters from a Tintin cartoon in the way they sneaked in.

Suddenly, the amusing scene became dead serious though when the snake, fast as lightning, crawled across the floor and in behind a small chest of drawers along the wall under one of the windows. The watchmen showed no signs of fear and were in rather a combative mood. One of them quickly pulled the chest of drawers away from the wall and the mamba raised its body more than a metre high. There was no doubt what it thought about being disturbed this way. The battle was on and retreat was no longer an option. Frank kept his distance from the bedroom and observed the battle from outside in the hallway.

The watchmen did not leave the initiative to the mamba. One of them swung the long wooden stick with great expertise and hit it across the neck. Then things happened fast when the snake threw itself forward with open mouth and frightening teeth exposed. However, the distance was sufficient for the watchman to dodge the attack and he slammed the machete into the snake's body just behind its head as it passed him in its violent attack. The other watchman now made a second hit with the wooden stick and he definitely looked like he had done it before. The snake twisted and turned on the floor heavily wounded by the machete and the blows from the stick. One of the watchmen now solidly planted a black dusty military boot on the snake's head and then they kept hitting it with the machete and stick until it no longer moved. The watchman slowly removed his foot, but the snake had been neutralized and they both took a couple of steps away from it.

"Watch out, because it's still poisonous even though it's dead," one of them said, while they were admiring the result of their efforts as if they had produced a piece of art.

Over by the door to the sitting room section stood the cook, Temitope, who had been woken up in his small room in the boys' quarter and now looked distinctly worried.

"Eh, is that a poisonous snake?" he asked timidly.

"Hell, yes, it's a poisonous snake, a goddamned black mamba if I remember correctly from my biology classes back in school in Denmark," Frank shouted, and walked over to the cook and stared him in the eyes. "And do you have any idea how the hell it got into my bedroom?"

The cook looked uncertain and shook his head. "No, but there were some people here to service our air conditioners today," he answered hesitantly.

"Our air conditioners," Frank repeated. So now the cook felt some kind of ownership over the inventory in the company's house or was it just his clumsy English, Frank wondered. He opened his eyes wide and shook his head. "And they were in my bedroom while I wasn't around, were they?" The cook nodded. "What the hell is going on here? Are you completely mad?" Frank shouted and took a deep breath. "Did you know them?" he asked.

"No, I don't think they were the same people who used to come," was the unconvincing answer from Temitope.

Frank walked around in small circles a couple of times then over to the window where he looked through the curtain without seeing anything.

"You two watchmen, you're a couple of heroes – well done. Now, go out and find a sack or a cardboard box, then get this snake out of my bedroom." They looked proud and disappeared outside.

"You, Mr Cook, you go and check that all windows are properly shut and that there are no more snakes in the bedroom, or rats, or mice, or cockroaches or any other kind of visitor. Is that understood?" The cook confirmed that he fully understood and without any further explanations he immediately started the thorough checking of the bedroom.

Meanwhile, Frank went to the sitting room and found his drinks glass again. He took the glass and the whisky bottle to the dining table where he glanced under the table before sitting down. The two watchmen came thundering in with a couple of empty sacks from some Thai rice producer. They were in high spirits after their heroic act and babbled in their local dialect. The same could not be said about the cook who, after about half an hour, came sneaking out of the bedroom.

"OK, master, I done check it well well. No more snakes in that room," the cook said and tried to vanish into the kitchen.

At that point, Frank had enjoyed several large undiluted drinks and it had not softened his temper.

"Wo, wo, my friend, stop right there for a moment. Could you explain to me how that snake could have gotten into my room. Was there a window open?" But it did not look like the cook had any plausible theory or explanation about what might have happened.

"Well, I don't really know, those air condition people came and they brought a toolbox but I didn't know them." Frank put his head in his hands and shook his head but did not have the energy to insist on having a reasonable explanation.

"Go away," he shouted. Since the watchmen had also left the house with their trophy, Frank was alone again. He did not feel like going to bed at all but knew that he would have to do so sooner or later. Frank felt like smoking a cigarette but first of all he had stopped smoking a couple of years ago, secondly there were no cigarettes in the house and he had not seen any of his staff at the house smoking.

Did anybody place that snake in my bedroom to kill me or perhaps just to give me a serious scare? Could it really be a coincidence, pure bad luck? Frank went through the possible scenarios in his head, but he was too shocked to see it clearly and Johnny Walker was beginning to have an impact. Around 3 a.m. he was so tired that he thought he would be able to fall asleep without having nightmares about snakes. He was not especially relaxed though and lay stiff and tense for about an hour before falling into an uneasy sleep. Not surprisingly, he dreamed of plenty of snakes of different sizes and colours. When the alarm rang, he was sleeping very well and considered staying in bed for a couple of hours but did not want to show signs of weakness so soon after having arrived, so he forced himself out in the shower.

In the morning at the office, Frank was sitting with his first cup of coffee and the first cigarette for a long time which he thought tasted like shit. He went through the night's events but did not get any closer to a conclusion. He was at the same time exhausted and totally overwrought and had a hard time concentrating on the normal work. There was a knock on the door and Funmi opened it slightly and peeped in.

"Good morning, Frank. I heard that you had a problem with a snake last night and just wanted to say how shocked I am. Of course, we have plenty of snakes in Africa but it's very unusual that we find them in our houses," she said, and shook her head. "I am simply completely shocked."

"Thank you, Funmi," Frank said, and realized that this kind of dramatic news apparently circulated fast at West African Motors.

"I understand it was a black mamba and they are incredibly dangerous… deadly. Paralyse the respiratory system so you basically suffocate," she said.

"Yes, I am aware of that. It's shocking," Frank said, completely clear about the danger he had been facing.

"I can't imagine that anybody would want to hurt you, but we are in Nigeria and life is dangerous. You can't put anything past some people and they may pay young criminal area boys to attack someone." Funmi sighed and shook her head. "On the other hand, you have just arrived and couldn't have any enemies. It must be an unfortunate coincidence." She sighed again, wished him a nice day and left his office.

The thoughts from the night before about who could be behind the snake incident roared through Frank's mind again. He was, despite Funmi's attempt to convince him of the opposite, more and more convinced that it had been arranged and he shivered at the thought. He was far from reassured and lit another cigarette without any particular concern about whether he had started smoking again or if it was just the crisis situation demanding nicotine.

Chapter Twelve

Once a year, West African Motors gathered their biggest dealers for a grand event with live entertainment and presentation of awards for the best achievements during the past year. The first of its kind during Frank's time in charge had been scheduled for shortly after his arrival, and the planning had reached an advanced stage before he was made aware of it. The national sales manager, Funmi, was the head of department responsible for organising the event and she had been handling it for several years. However, when Frank was informed about the details he thought it sounded like too much of a routine job, if not even downright boring. So he asked Funmi to pep up the dinner a bit and spice up the entertainment. The guests were, after all, the dealers on which the company depended and for whom they wanted to show their appreciation.

Frank quite looked forward to the big day where he would not only participate but also give the keynote speech and hand over the awards to the most successful dealers. He considered it an important task to ensure that the dealers saw him as the new strong leader – someone they could have confidence in, someone to whom they would give their unconditional support. The chairman of the board was, of course, invited but had already committed himself to other more important engagements.

The sales people had rented a large hall in Lagos Airport Hotel, which Frank was not familiar with. It was not part of one of the major international hotel chains but Funmi had assured him that the standard was in order. It was a hotel where the invited dealers from out of town would appreciate spending the night.

Frank had agreed with Funmi that they would meet in Lagos so he did not depend on anybody else's time management. He had previously experienced this to be a big advantage in Africa if you wanted to avoid too much stress. Since the grand event was scheduled to start at 2:00p.m., he planned to leave home around 9:00a.m. Then he could check into the hotel and have some lunch before the event was to start.

Frank was ready shortly after nine and the cook carried his travel bag and his briefcase from the bedroom to the car where he gave it to Godwin who had been ready since 7:30a.m. The car had been thoroughly washed that morning. Then they were off on the notorious Ibadan-Lagos Expressway once again and Godwin seemed encouraged by the idea of doing some serious driving. In fact, it had to be slightly boring for an experienced driver to drive back and forth between the house and factory, but now they were going out on a real assignment where the driver played a significant part out there on the busy roads.

As soon as they were on the expressway and had passed the first police checkpoint, Godwin stepped on the gas and Frank had only read one page in The Economist's article about Donald Trump's woes in relation to his team's connections to Russia before he had to draw Godwin's attention to the fact that they were going slightly too fast.

"Oh Godwin, I don't remember if I have already said it, but you have to maintain a speed of maximum 120 kilometres per hour, OK?" Frank said, and it made Godwin's mood plummet. "You know, I'm not saying that you have to crawl along but stay on 120 kilometres per hour when the conditions allow it."

"The conditions?" Godwin asked, still with a serious expression on his face.

"Yes, I mean when it is not dangerous, when there are not too many cars and when you can see the road well ahead of you."

"OK, sir." Godwin smiled in the rear-view mirror which he had adjusted in such a way that he could see Frank in the back seat rather than the road behind the car. Frank took note that later he would have to make Godwin adjust the mirror. However, he preferred not to do so at a time when they were roaring down the expressway at 120 kilometres per hour.

Frank was looking at the landscape and remembered the first time he had been driven on the same road. It had been a couple of weeks since he arrived but it felt much longer. He sensed that he had got off to a good start with the first management meeting but he did not yet feel that he was completely on top of the situation. He was beginning to have a pretty clear picture of the competences of each of the individuals in the management group... and the weaknesses, although there were still many loose ends. A lot of issues remained to be dealt with, apart from the uncertainty in the back of his mind caused by the snake episode.

After about half an hour, traffic gradually became slower and slower until it came to a complete standstill. A bit further ahead they could see drivers and passengers getting out of their vehicles, glancing ahead and raising their arms in resignation. There was a general feeling of surprise and anxiety in the air. Since the traffic towards Ibadan had also come to a standstill there was absolutely no traffic in the opposite direction. Godwin quickly jumped out of the car to confer with fellow drivers while Frank put away The Economist and Donald Trump for later reading. Godwin came back to the car after a few minutes.

"They say that it's armed robbers operating ahead," he stated, apparently relatively undisturbed.

"What is it you're saying?" Frank asked.

"Well, it happens sometimes. They dress up as policemen and stop cars to rob them." Godwin, still rather relaxed about the issue did, however, add a matter-of-fact, "They can be very dangerous."

"But what the hell do we do now?" Frank was shocked by the statement of armed robbers in action. "And how do we know that's what's going on?"

"That's what the other drivers are saying," was Godwin's simple answer.

Frank got out of the car to see if there was any visible and significant activity further ahead. He had to relieve himself which he walked over to the side of the road to do. It was a completely surreal situation to stand there in the middle of a major highway speaking to other motorists about what might be going on a few kilometres ahead when in fact other people were perhaps being robbed and harassed, maybe even seriously harmed, by armed robbers.

After about 15 minutes a large truck passed in the opposite direction. The driver had his window open and with some gestures and a thumbs-up made it clear that it was now OK to proceed. The drama had, apparently, ended. Movements started slowly again and before long they were back on their way at full speed towards Lagos. Surprisingly, they did not see any sign at all, at any point, that something dramatic had been going on – nothing whatsoever. Frank wondered what had happened and how much the armed robbers had got away with, if indeed it had been a robbery that took place. He tried reading The Economist article again but suddenly thought that Trump's political troubles were relatively manageable compared to what he was up against in Nigeria.

Despite the delay on the expressway, Frank arrived at the hotel in good time and was able to check into his room before noon. He was not very impressed by the hotel's standard and would mention this to the national sales manager later in the day. He also observed a strong perfumed odour when he stepped into the room and when he sat on the bed it was obviously a solid foam mattress, rock hard in fact. The bed linen, upon closer inspection, proved to be slightly shabby.

On the plus side there was plenty of space in the room or rather the suite, because it contained a small sitting room with a sofa, a separate bedroom and a very spacious bathroom.

Of course, there were large flat screen TVs on the wall both in the sitting room and the bedroom.

Frank would have preferred a better smell, a softer mattress, cleaner bed linen and a smaller room but it was too late to change all that.

He walked down the stairs as the lift had made some rather plaintive sounds on the way up with the luggage. He had no intention of being trapped in a lift for hours after having driven this far to be one of the main players together with the biggest dealers. In the lobby he ran into Funmi who had just arrived.

"Oh, you're just arriving now?" He had somehow imagined that the responsible head of department would be on site much earlier in the day to oversee a proper preparation of the venue for the reception of the company's most important partners.

"But we have plenty of time," was her only argument. "They've been invited for 2 p.m. and most of them usually arrive late. They're all very busy and many are coming from other parts of the country."

"Why don't we just invite them for 3 or 4 p.m. then?" Frank asked, and thought it was a logic question.

"No, because then they'll only get here even later," she said, and that was the end of it. Frank realised that it was a discussion he had lost in advance. Nevertheless, he was incredibly annoyed when they entered the main hall where the event was to take place and which was situated in a separate building next to the hotel itself. Of course, there was hectic activity preparing for the grand event but he had expected that chairs and tables would have been put in place and the room decoration with coloured ribbons and balloons completed much earlier in the day.

At 2:40 p.m. Frank took off his jacket and walked around the room for his fourth inspection of the preparation team's slow progress. They were now almost ready and there were, just as Funmi had predicted, still very few dealers present. So basically, there was no reason to panic.

At 3:10 p.m. Frank went over to the hotel, found the bar and studied the well-equipped shelves behind the counter. He felt like having a beer and a cigarette but thought it would be inappropriate to smell of alcohol when later, wearing his best suit, he would be shaking hands with the major dealers and handing over awards for their excellent results during the previous year.

He ordered a club soda without cigarette. The floor in the bar was covered with a thick carpet and there was a distinct smell very similar to the one in his own room on the second floor. 'A smell of something like mouldy carpet mixed with strongly scented air fresheners – almost nauseating,' he thought. The bartender was wearing a formerly white shirt and a claret-coloured waistcoat with an almost matching bow tie placed in a position between horizontal and vertical. Frank imagined that it would suddenly start spinning and wondered whether it would do so clockwise or anticlockwise. The owner of the imperfect waiter's uniform was drying a glass with a tatty towel and smiled at Frank thus showing a hole where a tooth in the upper right side of his mouth should have been.

"Big day, eh?" the waiter opened the conversation.

"You can say that again." Frank tried not to get involved in a long and detailed discussion about the upcoming event. He had, however, regretted his previous decision. "And you know what, on second thoughts, let me have a quick brandy. That Remy Martin XO up there on the shelf looks good."

"OK, Oga. Should I put ice in it?"

Frank felt like educating the waiter on how to serve brandy but left it at shaking his head slightly. The brandy had only just been served and the first sip turned around in his mouth when Funmi entered the bar at full gallop.

"Frank, we are ready now. Please hurry up and come over so we can get started. The most important dealers have arrived and the master of ceremonies is also around ... and the orchestra."

'So now, almost two hours after we should have started, the whole thing suddenly becomes very urgent,' was Frank's initial thought but he said nothing. Downing the brandy in one gulp, a slight nod to the waiter and he was ready for action.

On the way from the hotel to the conference hall, Frank noticed that the colonel was arriving with his loyal bodyguard, Okafor, and two other men whom Frank had never seen before. The colonel saw Frank, waved happily to him and shouted: "We'll be there in a moment. I hope they haven't started yet." Frank shook his head and continued into the hall.

The hall was now ready and, to Frank's great surprise, looked quite presentable. At the entrance and at a couple of places between the tables, young ladies in identical dresses were waiting. These ushers would show the guests to their seats, carry out other miscellaneous assignments, such as looking good, and raise the level of the event in general. Most seats at the tables were now occupied by well-dressed guests in dark suits or various traditional attires for the men. Large colourful dresses and ditto head gear for the women. By far most of the participants were men of a mature age mainly African but also a few Middle Eastern and Indian looking men. However, there was also a few mature ladies, most likely wives of the major distributors and finally even a few pretty young ladies.

Frank was ready to proceed full speed up the stairs to the finely decorated high table, but he was stopped by a young lady whom he recognised from the sales department.

"Excuse me, sir. We have to introduce and invite everybody to the high table. Sorry, sir," she whispered with a mixture of cheap perfume, warm garlic breath and a big smile with white teeth.

"Yes, yes, of course." Frank felt her hand on his arm and was led to a vacant table where he sat down. It suited him fine because from there he was able to familiarise himself with the environment and get a feeling of the mood in the audience before he would be sitting at the high table where he would be distanced from the participants yet visible to everybody. The high table lived fully up to its name as it was placed on a theatre-scene about five feet above the floor. Frank's second, and slightly more thorough, scanning of the room revealed that one of the pretty young ladies was sitting at a table not far from his own. She had apparently come with an older man in the heavy-weight class wearing an expensive dark blue suit where the jacket was unfortunately a couple of sizes too small. He was in a concentrated discussion with a slightly younger light-heavy-weight sitting opposite him at the table. The young lady caught Frank's eye and he thought he noticed a discreet almost invisible smile. He continued scanning the room, taking his time, and returned to the lady who was again, or perhaps it was still, looking at him and she was definitely smiling now. It would be embarrassing if he just ignored her, but it would also be clumsy if he made too obvious signs, so he tried with a discreet smile and a little nod but managed to exaggerate both. She looked down for a brief moment before looking straight at him again with a couple of strongly made-up eyes which he could almost feel saying to him: "Oh, so you have seen me now, eh ... it was about time."

At the same time, the master of ceremonies was ready to start. First of all with a non- functioning microphone which he blew into and hit hard a couple of times. A technician had it replaced with another microphone. This also received a knock, a blow and a couple of, "check, check ... one, two, three, check," and then everything seemed to work. The MC started out with a little speech about how honoured he was, being present at this grand event with so many important people present. The audience got a longer story about how the MC had established contact with West African Motors through the former chairman with whom he had been to university, and he was in danger of getting lost in details from their student days. Finally, he tried with a joke which only lifted the spirits marginally and finally they were ready to begin inviting the biggest personalities to the high table.

They started, as it was the tradition, from the lower levels of the hierarchy and invited a couple of West African Motors' sales and marking people forward. They were then in doubt about which chairs to occupy, well aware that the seats in the middle were reserved for people of higher calibre, and one would have to be careful not to insult anybody. They were shown some appropriate seats while the MC flicked through his papers, had something whispered into his ear and then finally arrived at a union representative from Lagos State upon whom, for strategic reasons, had been bestowed this honour. Thereafter it was Funmi, who did not immediately hear that it was her turn and had to be poked by a junior staff. Then it was a representative of the important dealers, the reason for the entire festivities, and the choice had fallen on the dealer from Port Harcourt who had been one of the biggest for several decades. This was the big man sitting beside the young lady sending eyes and discreet smiles at Frank. The next important guest was a representative from the Ministry of Transport who had not yet shown up and his chair was left vacant until further notice. Frank guessed that perhaps he was reluctant to show himself publicly at such a big event organised by a private company and with massive press coverage.

Finally, and with big fanfare, Frank was introduced to the audience almost in a presidential manner and to such an extent that he felt it embarrassing and blushed slightly. After all, he had just arrived and could hardly take the honour for very much yet but perhaps some of them saw him as a kind of saviour. He had some ideas of necessary changes and had held internal meetings with his employees where this had been discussed. Apart from that, his biggest achievements had been to get drunk at the Sheraton, reject the company of a prostitute and, of course, supervise the killing of a black mamba in his house.

But he played the game and did his utmost to look important and determined, got up slowly, buttoned his jacked and walked confidently up to the central position at the high table. His importance was underlined by the fact that he was accompanied by two attractive ushers in nice dresses and that had its advantages as they had to team up to pull the large and very heavy chair out to allow Frank edge himself into his seat.

The MC had now begun a long speech about how far they had come in this grand event and how happy he was to be able to present such a group of so many important and distinguished people.

He spiced it up with a joke about the wife who suspected her husband of having an affair with the maid. Then one night, when she had sent the maid away, the wife went to her room and waited in the darkness. As expected, the husband came sneaking in and started making love to her. After the third time the wife thought it was enough, identified herself and complained that he was always tired after the first time with her, but then ... and then ... but eh ... the MC had forgotten the punchline and it took much too long for him to remember that it was the night watchman who said in pidgin English: "Ah ah sorry madam, I never know you are di one."

Frank thought that it was a pity that the MC had not known how to tell the joke properly and took note of it on a paper napkin. He could surely use it in another context at another future occasion.

Then it was time to activate the orchestra and they straight away got going on the local rhythms accompanied by, for Frank, completely incomprehensible lyrics. The musical interlude gave Frank the opportunity, from his elevated viewpoint at the high table, to get a clearer picture of the venue. First of all, he checked on the young lady whose partner now sat two places from Frank at the high table with his arms folded and resting on his voluminous stomach and eyes closed. Frank would have liked a short nap but it was not to be. The lady, who somehow did not fit into the crowd, was very well dressed for the occasion with a colourful dress and matching head gear.

'Traditional but extraordinarily stylish,' Frank thought. He once again met her eyes for a split second. Had she formed her full red lips slightly into something in between a smile and a kiss or was it Frank's imagination playing a trick on him? A very attractive lady with style but why was she sitting there making a pass at him. She had been doing so from the moment he entered the hall.

The music continued for what seemed as an eternity. It began feeling like torture and there was nothing but water to drink at the tables.

Finally, it was time to distribute prizes for remarkable results only interrupted by speeches with long openings, uninspired or messy contents and poor microphone technique. All of it connected by a very talkative master of ceremonies. At the end of the programme it was Frank's turn to give his speech and he felt a certain pressure as he walked up to the podium. First of all, it was the first time in Nigeria he stood in front of such a large and important audience. Secondly, he apparently had an especially interested listener and it did affect his confidence a bit.

Fortunately, he was well prepared and got through the speech without catastrophes and received a decent applause. Judging from the other speeches Frank had perhaps been too careful, his choice of words not sufficiently inflated, he felt. Now he knew how he would adjust his style towards the more highfalutin and bombastic next time.

Then Frank had the impression that they were finished but he had come to a country where formalities were important. There was one special speaker to thank all participants which he did with such eloquence that Frank had to admit that he was beaten by several lengths in the difficult art of public speaking. Then the enthusiastic and incredibly popular orchestra played a final number and the MC rounded up with a few anecdotes from his time in northern Nigeria during the 1970s.

Finally, it was time for the closing prayers and these were presented in professional fashion by one of the smaller dealers who was also a pastor in his spare time. The freelance pastor gave a practically-oriented but very animated prayer for all of them, actively supported by the audience shouting "Amen" whenever it was deemed appropriate. If all these prayers were heard in the highest places none of them would ever suffer any hardships, neither spiritually, economically, private or professionally.

The orchestra reduced the volume when the official event had been completed but then the noise from conversation increased significantly while drinks were placed on a long table and the buffet was prepared for dinner.

"Funmi, who is the young lady in the green and yellow dress and the big head gear? The one sitting down around the middle of the second table," Frank asked.

"I think she came with the dealer from Port Harcourt, the guy we had at the high table, but I've never seen her before." Funmi smiled at him. "Nice young lady but watch out," she warned with a lifted finger watching him alternately with the left and the right eye.

"Oh no, it wasn't that, but … eh, well, I don't know."

Frank circulated a bit on his own and found his way to the bar where a couple of the younger participants had started on some Guinness. He asked the waiter, who had served a brandy without ice cubes earlier in the day, for a gin and tonic.

"Hello boss, and welcome to Lagos." She stood behind him and when he turned around he was surprised how tall she was, perhaps because of her high heels. Not quite as tall as he was, though and her head gear made it difficult to judge. He felt her presence, physically certainly, but also her aura; calm and confident – in control of the situation.

"This is a good event you have organised here although a bit boring with all those speeches, don't you think? We Nigerians can talk forever when we get the smallest opportunity." She almost lost her balance, or pretended to, and put her hand on Frank's arm for a moment. "Apart from your speech, of course. It was … eh, short and sweet."

Slightly rough features and a bit too much lipstick, and then again maybe not, definitely well-equipped physically no doubt about that, was Frank's immediate evaluation.

"My name is Ifeoma," She said, and held out her hand. He hesitated just a little before taking it and feeling a soft and slightly moist hand, which held on to his for half a second longer than necessary.

"I'm Frank, but I assume you've heard that. Can I offer you something to drink?" was the smartest he could come up with and she showed him the wineglass she held in her left hand with a smile. "Oh, sorry, I didn't see that."

Her gaze wandered down over his body and up again for a brief eye contact.

"I hope you like it here in Nigeria and that you've been well received in the company," she said.

"Yes, thank you. I am actually quite positively surprised about everything so far, especially after all the stories I had heard before arriving."

"We are actually a positive and hospitable people. Incredibly enough, considering how tough life is for most people but the old negative stories about our country are much worse than the truth," she said.

Frank nodded but didn't say anything as he felt that she was going to add something.

"But there are many crooks and some of them are very smart. So, take good care of yourself and your money."

"Thanks, that's also what I had heard before coming."

She stepped a bit closer to him and showed that she wanted to whisper something in his ear. He bent forward slightly and caught her scent in his nose. He found it very pleasant.

"And watch out for the young girls. They hit like predators when they see an important person like you who's a handsome guy." She winked at him and stepped back a little. "Thanks a lot, but I usually don't have problems being attacked like that."

"I hope to see you later, boss, so you can tell me a bit more about your cars. I'm very interested in horsepower, acceleration, power steering and so on." She walked past him close enough for her shoulder just to graze his upper arm on the way. It was very difficult for him not to turn around and look at her while she worked her way forward through different groups of guests. He caught the eye of the waiter who sent him a quick wink and a smile, still with a tooth missing in the right upper side of his mouth.

Food was being wheeled in and the noise level from the conversations edged upwards while two longs queues at the buffet were created in a few seconds. Frank hated this way of organising the food. He did not want to queue up and grabbed a couple of small spring rolls and samosas from the starters buffet instead, had a glass of red wine and circulated around the room. He could no longer see the charming young lady and felt a slight disappointment as he would have liked to have a real conversation with her. He was annoyed with himself that he had not at least been able to give a more memorable impression, not that he knew why it mattered.

The young employee with the garlic breath reappeared and was clearly interested in more conversation. Apparently, she had just about enough seniority to allow herself to converse with the managing director without it being considered disrespectful. But Frank found it almost impossible to think about anything but the garlic smell, and had forgotten her name. She looked disappointed when he moved on.

Finally, the event was over. The food had been eaten, the trays were empty, and people left the room with quick goodbyes and thank yous. Participants from out of town, who were to spend the night at the hotel, retired to their rooms. Around 11:30 p.m. there was only the little group of Guinness-drinking youngsters left and they were getting a bit loud, but that took care of itself as the bar was beginning to close. He went upstairs in the clattering lift with Funmi while they agreed that it had all gone quite well and that everybody had looked pleased. He had a long list of details which he would like to improve for the following year but it was not the right time to take it up with Funmi. She yawned and got off at the first floor. Frank suppressed a yawn himself, said, "Good night," and continued up to the second floor.

The lift gave a little insecure beep when the doors opened and he strolled down the corridor to room 214. When he put the key in and opened the door, he noticed that there was light in the bedroom which he would not have expected but he was not quite sure whether he had switched it off earlier. On the desk stood a bottle of red wine with a little ribbon around the neck which was a pleasant surprise. Under the bottle there was a little envelope with the hotel logo which probably contained a welcome letter.

At the same time, he noticed the yellow and green scarf on the back of the office chair and he was absolutely sure that he had not brought any scarf of that colour, or any other colour for that matter. He stopped for a moment to think. The foul odour he had noticed when arriving had now been mixed with a scent of good perfume and he had to admit to himself that it improved the general odour in the room. Then he saw the dress thrown over the back of the armchair and that should definitely not have been there. He recognised it as belonging to the attractive young lady who had flirted so openly with him earlier in the evening, Ijeoma, Ifeoma – now he could not recall her name. The situation made him slightly nervous. Not as nervous as when the snake had crawled over his duvet but he certainly was a bit uneasy.

'How do I handle this particular situation?' he asked himself and took a few insecure steps towards the suite's bedroom.

Chapter Thirteen

II Hi boss, I thought you'd never come. Was it the little
    fat one from your company who delayed you?"
Ifeoma said, when she saw Frank appear in the door
to the bedroom. She had lain in the bed with a pile of
pillows under her head while waiting for him. "Why
don't you open the wine and give me a glass?" she
asked and sent him her best smile.

"Would you please tell me what's going on?" he
said seriously, but sounding a bit insecure. She felt that
it was going just as it was supposed to.

"I'm waiting for you. Aren't you happy to see me?"
She got out of bed and noticed that he studied her
body. She had found one of his company T-shirts in the
cupboard and that was the only thing she was wearing.
"Well, then I'll open it."

"But what are you doing here and how did you get
in?" He hesitated a bit and continued, "You have to
leave," but there was no conviction in his voice. So far,
so good.

Ifeoma decided that it was the right time to convince
him that she should stay with him. She quickly took
of the T-shirt and revealed her nakedness including
her newly shaved pussy. Frank's gaze focused on her

breasts which she put in a little extra effort of showing him by straightening her back. Then she walked over to him, put her arms around his waist and kissed him. There were no protests; on the contrary, he returned her kisses and accepted her tongue. She felt his hand slide down over her lower back to her butt which he grasped firmly.

She pulled back a little and teased him with a little, "Did you say that I should leave?" At the same time, she zipped down his pants, took a firm grip of him and felt that he was already getting hard.

"I have to think about that," he said, and sounded even less convinced than before.

"But it feels like part of you wants me to stay," she said, and gave his dick an extra squeeze. Then she started unbuttoning his shirt and helped him out of the rest of his clothes.

She took a hold of her breasts and lifted them a bit. "So, boss. Do you like these? You white men are crazy about big boobs, I've heard?" Then she threw herself on the bed and held her breasts again. "Come and kiss them."

Frank was quickly into the bed next to her and took his time kissing her breasts. She reached out and took one of the small green plastic sachets she had put under the pillow, tore it open and gave him the condom.

"Put this on," she said.

He quickly rolled it on and she showed him the way to her pussy. She played with him until she was wet enough then spread her legs a bit more and took him inside. Frank easily slid into her, found his rhythm and his breathing quickly became heavy until he came.

"Oh, Frank. Did you already finish?" she teased and kissed him again. "You won't get off that easily but let's get that wine opened now." She pushed him off to one side, stood up and moved her behind a little bit extra when she walked over to the desk to fetch the bottle.

"This must be your job. Isn't it normally the man doing that kind of thing?"

Frank looked like he wanted to say something but regretted it. Ifeoma knew that she was in control of the situation. He had been surprised to find her in his room, almost shocked, but he had never really wanted her to leave. She was pretty sure of that. Now, just after they had made love, was a critical moment where he may be annoyed with her or with himself and decide to throw her out. The fact that he had not been able to resist her when he saw her body and became horny did not necessary mean that he would not get angry afterwards. However, she expected to be able to handle that situation if necessary.

"Why?" he asked, while she was sitting on the bidet in bath room and washing herself. Then she put a large towel around her waist and went back to the bedroom.

"Because you're a handsome guy and then you're a big shot, so I wanted to get to know you. Well, and then quite frankly this event with the car dealers, long speeches and a ridiculous orchestra was rather boring." She put on his company T-shirt again and smiled. "But you must be used to the ladies being at your feet all the time. The short one from your company was drooling over you. She would have loved to score the boss tonight and then take advantage of it at the next salary negotiations."

"Oh, her. I never bother mixing with the employees privately. And she also smelled of garlic."

"Ha, ha, that's what you say now," she said, and thought that he would probably not quite be able to live up to that principle if only the employee was attractive enough ... and smart enough. "But how did you get into the room?"

She laughed and took one of the glasses he had filled with the South African red wine. "That wasn't very complicated. I ordered a bottle of wine in the bar and then I convinced the receptionist that I needed to borrow the key to your room because you had asked me to deliver the wine. I gave him a small token. That's the way things work in this country, everything is possible, but you didn't protest much either."

"No, that was difficult because you're a beautiful woman." He lay under the cover with a pile of pillows under his head and studied her. "You seemed very sure that I wouldn't throw you out," he said half matter-of-fact, half questioning.

"You said that I would have to leave but it didn't sound convincing at all and so I knew I could stay. If you really wanted me to leave you should have taken my dress, thrown it in my face, shouted OUT and looked really angry and determined." "Would you have left then?"

"Then I would probably have tried one more time with a smile and a quick remark but I would of course have left if you had insisted, I'm not a troublemaker," she said, and he looked like a big schoolboy who was being lectured on a difficult maths problem. "You have to understand that life is tough in this part of the world and people generally need a clear message. Otherwise they don't take it seriously but maybe you want to employ me as a consultant if you need more good advice."

She emptied her red wine glass in one gulp and put the glass on the side table, but she noticed that Frank was only sipping his wine and tasting it carefully. So, they drank wine in two completely different ways. She took his glass out of his hand and placed it on the side table. Then she slid under the cover next to him with a little satisfied sigh.

She was tired after the day's long program but lay philosophising over how it had gone. She had subtly hit on Frank from the first moment he looked at her and she had immediately concluded that it was working as his eyes kept returning to her. When she had a brief conversation with him during the reception, she became even more convinced that he was interested in getting to know her better. Therefore, she had felt confident taking the next step by gaining access to his room and simply seducing him there. She had fully succeeded and then it was only an added benefit that he was a handsome and pleasant guy who also knew how to treat a woman. Oh well, he probably had not been with a woman for a while because he had exploded inside her almost immediately. She smiled, cuddled up against him and fell asleep.

Ifeoma had no need for an alarm clock. She had always been able to wake up almost exactly at the time she needed to get up and this morning she better leave Frank's room early. She did not want anybody to notice that she had been there.

She sneaked out of bed and into the bathroom where she took a quick shower before finding her clean clothes in her backpack. Suddenly, she wanted Frank again and did not get dressed.

Instead, she lay down beside him and put her hand on his shoulder.

"Frank, Frank. I have to go now so my father doesn't find out that I've been here." "Your father?" he mumbled half asleep. "What time is it?"

"It's five, so there is just enough time for a quick one, OK?" she whispered in his ear, while she let her hand slide down over his stomach and into his underpants where it met a morning hard-on. He was ready almost immediately and she took out the second condom from her little stock under the pillow where she had placed it the evening before.

It was a quick one, as she had suggested, and she had the impression that Frank hardly woke up before it was over and he snuggled down under his cover again.

Ifeoma dressed in something a bit more casual than what she had been wearing the evening before. She kneeled next to the bed and did her morning prayer, then she got up and went over to Frank's side of the bed.

"See you soon, honey. I left my number on the table. Call me, OK?"

She was quite happy with the way the evening, night and morning had gone. Everything was entirely according to plan and on top of it Frank was a very sweet guy who she had nothing against being with. A guy she could easily have settled down with even if it had not been planned.

Chapter Fourteen

Frank was half asleep for a couple of hours after Ifeoma had left but could not really wind down completely after the evening and the morning's lovemaking. Just after seven he gave up and got out of bed, putting his heel down on the used condom from earlier in the morning. It spat out most of its contents on the floor with a farting sound.

"Ay, what the hell was that?" he snapped at himself and pulled off the condom glued to his heel and went to the bathroom to throw it into the toilet. Then he took a shower and packed his stuff.

Down in the restaurant he ran into the colonel who was in conversation with the heavy-weight gentleman from Port Harcourt. The guy who had been sitting next to Ifeoma last night and – he believed she had said early in the morning – her father? There was no sign of Ifeoma and she was not mentioned either so Frank felt that it would be inappropriate to ask about her.

"This is our dealer from Port Harcourt but you met yesterday and, as you know, he is one of the most important dealers we have," the colonel introduced him to Frank and they shook hands.

"Yes. I am aware of that. What did you think about the event?" Frank had a feeling that the two men knew each other better than just on a superficial professional basis. He also thought they looked at him as if they knew what he had been doing overnight. Hopefully, that was only his imagination.

"Next year you have to offer better prizes to those of us who have fought for the company all year but otherwise it was OK." Blunt answer from the fat gentleman who did not present any opportunity for a debate about the subject. "And then you offered unbelievably small discounts on the old models when we launched the new models towards the end of last year." It had nothing to do with the previous day's event but the dealer apparently found it appropriate to take this opportunity to complain a bit now that he was sitting in front of the new managing director.

"Yeah, the question of the prizes is something we will have to look at next year," Frank said, although he believed they had been quite generous but wanted to get going from the Airport Hotel and get out on the expressway again. He was served a greasy omelette with a couple of thick slices of dry toasted bread, a small pot of hot water and a tin of Nescafé. It was not exactly a big and impressive breakfast buffet but, in any case, Frank was not actually very hungry.

"Well, it was nice meeting you." Frank stood up and was ready to go. The bulky gentleman mumbled briefly and shook hands without looking at him.

"Just a moment, Frank." The colonel also got up. "I'm coming outside with you."

Out in front of the hotel, Godwin drove the car forward and showed that he was in fine form with a cheerful, "Morning sir, how was di night?"

Frank guessed that it was not a question that Godwin expected to be answered, so he abstained from getting involved in a detailed description of the nocturnal activities and left it at a short, "Morn' Godwin."

The colonel had followed him to the car and looked curiously at him. "I hope you were happy with the arrangements yesterday. I mean, that everything was to your satisfaction." A little smile followed the question.

"Yes, thank you. I think it went very well and the dealers generally seemed satisfied," Frank said.

"And the night? Did you sleep well?"

"Thank you, I slept like a baby," Frank said, a little annoyed.

"Well, it's just because I want to make sure everything is in order. After all, I'm responsible for security in the company and I don't want my boss to have any problems." Then he gave Frank a slap on the shoulder and walked towards his own car, then turned around. "Just let me know if there are any problems so we can help you." Frank let it hang there but felt a bit awkward.

The colonel apparently felt it and immediately continued, "And by the way, when we are back in Ibadan I'll come to your office and discuss our trip to Abuja tomorrow." "Abuja? Why are we going to Abuja?" Frank wondered.

"The import regulations are up for debate in the national assembly and we have to make sure that they don't decide something which goes against us as far as import of cars is concerned," the colonel laughed. "Drive carefully, Godwin." He pointed at the driver, waved to Frank over his shoulder and was escorted to his own car by Okafor with AK-47, green beret and newly polished boots.

Frank jumped into the car and soon they reached cruising speed on the way up the expressway towards Ibadan. Frank was too tired to insist that Godwin kept the agreed speed, so he checked the seat belt a second time, made sure the head rest was properly adjusted and took a nap which did him good.

"Would you please explain to me why we have to bring 20,000 dollars to Abuja for a meeting with the deputy finance minister?" They were sitting in Frank's office and he had a cash payment voucher in front of him, presented by the colonel for signature. Frank was of the clear opinion that the amount was extremely high, unless he could get a reasonable explanation what the purpose was.

"We have to make sure that the rules which apply for importation of cars, high import duties and other taxes that is, are maintained so we still have a pricing advantage. The responsibility for duty, import regulations and tariffs is handled by the ministry of finance and it is the deputy minister who is directly responsible for these matters. That's why we must have him on our side and that costs money. As simple as that," the colonel said.

"So, we have to bribe him in order to make him help us obtain a competitive advantage?" "No, I wouldn't call it bribing – that's much worse. It's a kind of motivation or incentive, as we call it here. Without that he wouldn't even bother talking to us." The colonel seemed unable to understand Frank's reaction.

"Hell, this must be damned illegal isn't it, even in Nigeria?" Frank started getting annoyed.

"We can't expect any kind of help if we are not open to, shall we call it, financial incentives," the colonel said and smiled. "That is the way life is here and we can't survive if we have to compete with all these importers who don't pay import duties when we have such high expenses to run a factory with everything that entails here in Nigeria." It somehow sounded plausible. A kind of assistance to the authorities to protect national interests of industry and work places – an employment package. Frank silenced his protests for the time being and parked them in a corner of his memory for later use.

"But can these 20,000 dollars really buy us a big enough advantage and, if so, for how long?" "Oh no, my goodness no. This is just to show him that we appreciate his assistance. The real money will come from our agent who is getting a commission on sales of cars."

"WHAT? That's completely insane," Frank said, and was shocked that the colonel seemed to find it amusing. "How does the agent handle it and how does he know who needs to get something and how much?" Frank had immdiately sprung his protests from the mental parking lot.

"Don't worry, there is a distribution formula which we have agreed with the agent and since he is meeting us in Abuja tomorrow he can tell you much more about it."

"Hmm," was all Frank could say while he ran his fingers over his temples and sighed. He wondered how differently things worked when you were dealing with the public sector compared to the type of business he had been involved in previously. When the customer was an individual and the product a fast-moving consumer item it was essential to use professional marketing to sell a good quality and correctly priced product. However, when the public sector was involved, it seemed like completely different methods had to be applied.

Chapter Fifteen

Next morning the colonel and Frank met at the Aero Contractors' check-in counter at the domestic terminal in Lagos and joined a long queue. Frank was still around 20 metres from the counter when the colonel arrived with his entourage and walked straight up to one counter where he immediately drew the attention of an employee to his presence. He looked around, spotted Frank and waved at him to come forward which Frank did not at all feel comfortable with.

"We don't want to be standing in this long queue," the colonel said to Frank. "When we know such a beautiful employee as Remi here." He sent the lady behind the counter, who was already in the process of checking them in, a broad smile. They heard some grumbling from people in the queue, who had been left behind, but the colonel ignored it completely. It did not seem to worry him the least and the system, or lack of same, seemed to work to their advantage. Furthermore, the young Aero employee, Remi, looked content and was probably looking forward to the small token which the colonel would no doubt give her when they had received their boarding passes.

After about 55 minutes unstable flight north, they landed in Abuja and were picked up by the agent whom the colonel introduced as: "Segun Ajibola, our important troubleshooter." They jumped into Ajibola's black Jeep Grand Cherokee and raced towards Abuja on the main road, which was under refurbishment by the big German construction company Julius Berger.

'I wonder whether they also have a troubleshooting agent,' Frank thought, but did not have the energy to imagine how a construction company secured their future business foundation in relation to the authorities.

On arrival at the Hilton, there turned out to be a very long queue in front of the hotel's main gate. This was apparently caused by a very thorough military checkpoint where they searched, or at least looked at, objects in the boot of every car as well as checked for bombs under the cars with a mirror on a long stick. It was something Frank had previously only seen in Colombia and it made him worried. There was no way of speeding up the process here as it had been the case at Aero Contractors' check-in counter in Lagos. The heavily armed soldiers, who carried out the control, looked extremely serious and in no mood for any smart remarks.

"You don't play with those guys," the colonel whispered to Segun who turned the corners of his mouth down and shook his head.

"At all, at all. Those are really tough guys."

After about 20 minutes of chaos in front of the Hilton they finally succeeded in getting through the control and Frank made a sigh of relief.

"It has become extremely cumbersome to get in here now. Maybe we should start using another hotel," Segun suggested.

The colonel shook his head. "No, no. The Hilton is the place to be. This is where it's happening, so we better accept the time it takes to stay in the best place," he said.

'Expensive habits,' Frank thought, and considered making a comment about cost control but decided that it was not the right time to bring up the issue.

Segun had already checked them into a VIP room on the 10th floor. It only took a few minutes to have the key card coded at the special counter for important people before they could go and drop their things in the rooms. Frank once again thought 'cost control' but had to admit that it was rather convenient to be checked in as a VIP. He specifically noticed the long queues at the normal counters where a Lufthansa crew had just arrived and was given priority over ordinary customers. Apart from that his room was in order, very much so in fact, and completely without comparison to the Airport Hotel in Lagos – several stars higher. Spacious room, top quality mattress, comfortable (and clean) bed linen, superb bathroom and view over the pool area – in fact it was impossible to find anything to complain about. He wondered whether it would include a young attractive lady in the bed later in the evening as happened at the Airport Hotel? 'Probably not,' he thought and smiled.

They had agreed to meet in the lobby bar 15 minutes later and had coffee while discussing the strategy for the meeting with the deputy finance minister. Segun had arranged the meeting at 12 noon but they considered it likely that the minister would not want to enter into the detailed discussions in the office. Both Segun and the colonel expected that he would ask them to meet somewhere outside the office, perhaps even at his house, at a later time. If that was the case, they only hoped that it would be the same evening as they had no wish to keep hanging around for several days at the Hilton, also known as "Nigeria's largest waiting room".

They drove off to the ministry which was a few minutes' drive from the Hilton and exiting the hotel was, not surprisingly, much easier than entering. Segun was familiar with the area and knew where he could park when going to the Ministry of Finance. He appointed a specific young man amongst the horde of self-established parking attendants to watch the car. They arrived shortly before 12 o'clock and waited for almost 45 minutes before the minister could see them. It was obvious from the conversation in the waiting room that this was not at all unusual. In fact, both Segun and the colonel were quite happy when they were called in "already" at 12:35.

The minister was relatively new and so did not know the colonel, but he had apparently met Segun before. They had a relaxed air between them so Segun made the introductions. Then the minister wanted his permanent secretary to be present at the meeting and they waited for a few minutes for him to join them after the minister had asked his secretary to get him as soon as possible. The permanent secretary came running into the office with a slightly panicky expression on his face and a large bundle of files under his arm, dropping a few on the floor when his jacket sleeve caught the door handle.

They opened with polite small talk about the general conditions in Nigeria but also touched upon the latest problems related to Sharia law in some northern states, the Boko Haram terrorist threat and, last but not least, had a brief exchange on the English Premier League. It became clear that the minister was a Manchester United fan and Frank abstained from mentioning his long-term and complete loyalty to Arsenal. 'After all, one must be careful not to disagree with influential people on subjects as important as football,' he thought.

After the general and relaxed talk, where they tried to tune into each other's wavelengths or at least switch onto the same frequency interval, they became slightly more specific from West African Motors' side. The difficult business environment they operated in, the high costs and the more than problematic energy supply situation were important factors for a big company. They made no secret of the fact that it was extremely difficult to make a profit under such circumstances. However, they did not reach the core discussion of import regulations for cars despite everybody being well aware that that was the purpose of the meeting.

"We fully understand, your excellency, if it is difficult for you to discuss all these details here and now as you have a busy schedule, but we will be in Abuja until tomorrow afternoon. So, if we could meet somewhere else, perhaps later tonight?" the colonel suggested diplomatically. Wise move to be specific about the alternative timing and lead the minister's thoughts towards a meeting the same evening. At least they would avoid him arbitrarily fixing the meeting for a couple of days later, after which it would become problematic to have it changed.

The minister looked inquiringly at his permanent secretary who quickly commented. "Yes, that could easily be arranged. Mr Ajibola, when we finish here, you'll give me your mobile number and then I'll arrange the meeting, if possible this evening, when and if it suits the minister."

'Excellent,' Frank thought, now we can hopefully avoid hanging around here for days without knowing when we can have a meeting. It crossed his mind that the whole game was following certain complicated, but generally and tacitly agreed rules – in a way a bit like chess where you had a chance if you knew the rules and played on a regular basis. Frank knew the chess rules but had mostly played ludo when his kids were smaller. He sincerely hoped that he was not a pawn about to be captured early in the game.

Frank had noticed that the envelope with the 20,000 dollars in crisp greenbacks had not seen the light of day or changed hands yet and now the meeting was over because the minister rose from his seat.

"So, gentlemen, that's the way we'll do it," he rounded up the meeting.

Suddenly, they were standing out in the front office where the agent went to the secretary and whispered many thanks to her while he gave her a little thin envelope. "We highly appreciate your invaluable assistance."

'Whatever it was that she had done,' Frank thought, and tried to guess how much money was in the envelope – it seemed that you had to pay for everything here.

The colonel indicated to Frank that they should go ahead while Segun continued his conversation with the permanent secretary.

"I think they have a mutual acquaintance or family relation so let them talk a bit. Segun is very good at this kind of thing," the colonel explained, and Frank began to have an idea of how to play this complicated game. It was not really a board game, castling did not exist and the pieces were not always moving according to established patterns but it was still some kind of chess game. At that point Frank felt like a pawn and only hoped that he would be upgraded to a knight before long. In principle he was not much in favour of this kind of game but had to admit to himself that he was beginning to understand a bit more about how the system was working. A kind of fascination was also getting a grip on him.

They waited for Segun at the lift, which took its time to reach them. He joined after a few minutes but still in good time for the lift.

"It's perfect. My uncle once recommended the permanent secretary's older brother for an important job so he is very helpful. He will call me later to explain how we find the minister's house and when we have to be there – it'll probably be late."

"Does that mean we are actually meeting the minister tonight at his house?" Frank asked naively.

"That's what it looks like. Isn't it great having such an efficient agent?" Segun laughed and they got into the lift which started moving towards the ground floor with a squeaking moan and with a brief stop at each floor. Frank exchanged worried glances with a young white lady in the lift but nobody spoke.

On the way back to the hotel in the car they only talked about insignificant subjects and agreed that they would not meet for dinner. If they did, they would risk being interrupted when the minister gave the heads up for the meeting. In other words, they had to be ready in the starting blocks from then on. Again, it took an eternity to enter the Hilton's compound. This time there was an additional explanation as one of the smaller telecommunications companies was celebrating having just exceeded ten million active mobile telephone contracts. The hotel's entrance looked like a car exhibition for Mercedes, BMW, large 4-wheel drives and surprisingly enough there was also a Ferrari and a Rolls-Royce. 'There is money here – it is quite incredible,' Frank thought.

"Yeah, as you can see, there is a lot of money in circulation here in Abuja. It is after all the capital and everybody is draining the system as much as possible," Segun said, and Frank asked himself if he was a mind reader.

They finally reached the main entrance where the colonel and Frank got out of the car, and Segun drove on to park the car. "I'll call you when I know where and when we are meeting the minister," he shouted out of the open window before proceeding to park his Jeep.

Frank walked around the hotel compound considering what he could possibly do. It was 4:30 p.m. and he had no clue when they would have the meeting with the minister confirmed, if in fact it would take place at all. He ordered a cappuccino in the piano bar which seemed to be dominated by various business meetings in the groups of large armchairs. Then he went upstairs to inspect the rather small but well-equipped gym. However, he did not want to be caught sweaty and out of breath if they were suddenly called for the meeting at the minister's house. After another tour of the hotel he went to his room, turned down the temperature on the air conditioning system, threw himself on the bed and quickly fell asleep. Frank did not fall into a deep sleep but just sufficient to dream a confused dream where chess pieces came alive and fought each other physically. A white pawn was hit in the head by a black knight's kicking hind leg but in the dream Frank had fortunately become a castle and stood down in his corner watching the ongoing battle.

He woke again when it had become dark and a rumble in his stomach told him that it was time to order some room service. He found the menu and ordered a Hilton burger and a large bottle of water which, to his great annoyance, took forever to reach his room. While waiting he flicked through the TV channels. CNN was informing their viewers what was on tomorrow, the day after tomorrow and on Sunday. NTA, the local nationwide station, had news about a crashed petrol tanker which had exploded and killed about 180 people who had all been involved in stealing petrol when disaster struck. The news programme showed some horrible pictures of bodies burned beyond recognition and they had also visited a primitive-looking hospital where survivors were, if not treated, then at least kept. It was nauseating. Another channel had one of the thousands of Nigerian movies which Nollywood produced every year – it advanced in slow motion and with lazy acting performances, Frank thought. He found a religious channel where pastor Chris Oyakhilome analysed a few lines in the Bible word by word and reached conclusions which animated the church crowd considerably. Then there was a knock on the door and room service announced its arrival.

Frank began consuming the modestly presented burger with soft fries while listening to pastor Chris and was again astonished by his phenomenal popularity.

Then he switched off the TV, put the tray outside the door and sat in the armchair with a glass of water. He wondered what to do now. He opened his laptop, checked his emails and replied to a Facebook message from Caroline in Denmark. He spent some time on various news sites, before closing down again, lay down on the bed and dozed off.

Then the phone rang … finally and Frank jumped to his feet, his heart beating. The time was 11:20 p.m.

"Yep, Mr Frank, we're ready," said an obviously fully awake colonel Chuks. "I hope I didn't wake you up."

"No, eh yes, but it doesn't matter. What's going on?"

"We'll meet down at the main entrance in ten minutes. Segun is getting his car and then we'll drive over to the minister's place."

"NOW?" Frank wanted to have it confirmed as it seemed rather late to him.

"Exactly. Ministers often prefer to meet late in the day. See you." Click and the conversation had ended.

Frank quickly went to the bathroom and put some cold water in his face. He wondered about the appropriate dress code for such a visit to his excellency, the minister, at his house around midnight. He decided to wear a jacket but no tie.

Frank met the colonel out in front of the main entrance door which an impeccably uniformed hotel staff held open for him and addressed him politely: "Good evening, sir."

"Segun is on his way with the car. He has been informed where the minister lives so we can be there in five minutes," the colonel said.

Frank thought that this probably meant that it would take about 15-20 minutes to get there but only responded with a sleepy, "Hmm, OK."

The Jeep came sprinting around the corner from the parking lot and they jumped in, the colonel on the front seat and Frank in the back seat where he sat in the middle to be able to follow the conversation in the front.

"The man called only ten minutes ago and he said that we should hurry up," Segun explained. "That's typical. We wait all day and when he has time we have to drop everything and rush there. It's always like that."

The colonel laughed. "They're all like that. They absolutely must show that they are extremely important and that we are just some small insignificant boys. Since we were the ones asking for the meeting we don't have much choice."

"Where are we going?" Frank asked. Not that names of places in Abuja would mean very much to him but then at least he would know the name of the area.

"It's out in the Ministers' Hill area," Segun replied. "You know, out IBB Way and then left into the area where all the roads are named after rivers. Where Chez Victor restaurant is situated. Frank noticed a road sign reading "Ganges Street" so the point about roads named after rivers was correct.

"Oh, OK." Frank tried to sound confident and memorised the names, so he could take note of it later and establish an overview on Google Maps.

When they had turned away from the main road and down a couple of side roads it became darker and the road narrower until they reached the end of the road with space to turn. A couple of armed policemen in black uniforms and green berets were sitting half asleep on white plastic chairs. When they saw the car, they quickly got up and held their machine guns ready for use in case it should prove necessary.

Segun rolled down his window and waited for one of the policemen to come over to his side of the car. "We have an appointment with the minister. We're from West African Motors."

The policeman frowned at Segun then bent down slightly to look at the colonel who saluted him and said, "Good evening, my friend."

Finally, he looked into the back seat where he saw Frank and lit up. "Ah, Oga, welcome Sar."

Then he turned his attention back to Segun. "Just a minute," he mumbled and went over to the large black gate which was about three metres high with spikes on top and a big "JESUS" formed in metal welded onto the gate. The policeman communicated briefly through an intercom on the wall next to the gate and then slowly began to open the gate. His colleague stood over by the chairs with his AK-47 over his shoulder swinging it back and forth while looking quite indifferent. It did not seem to be very unusual that visitors came at this time of night. They drove into the parking lot in front of the large duplex house and parked next to a new black Mercedes 500.

The entrance door was opened and an elderly grey-haired man wearing a white uniform jacket appeared, presumably the housekeeper. He looked at them suspiciously while they got out of the car.

"Good evening, Baba," the colonel addressed him in a respectful tone. "We have come to meet with "oga pata pata", your big boss." The old man stepped aside to leave just enough space for them to pass. Then he showed them into a small sitting room with a sofa settee, a bar in the corner and the mandatory flat screen TV. There was also plenty of portraits of the minister with his wife, with his children and with the entire family but on most of the pictures he was portrayed alone looking serious, almost sombre. Frank had already understood that serious portraits were necessary additions to the decor for anybody who considered himself a big shot.

"The minister will be here in a moment," the housekeeper informed them and left them alone in the room. However, it did not take long for the minister to join them. Frank immediately saw that he had not needed to wear his jacket because the minister came strolling in wearing a polo shirt, crumpled shorts and bare feet in sandals. Without much fanfare he shook hands with them, yawned intensely and bade them welcome. He did not ask if they wanted anything to drink but walked slowly and dragging his feet over to the bar and picked an almost full bottle of Martell XO cognac and four ordinary shot glasses. He apparently assumed they all drank strong alcohol and it would no doubt be shooting yourself in the foot if you asked for a Perrier, Diet Coke or something similar.

The minister fell into the armchair at the end of the settee which they had guessed that they better not sit in. He looked at each of them one by one looking very relaxed then leaned forward to pour cognac for everybody. Still no question whether cognac was their preferred drink. At least he had enough class not to ask if they wanted it with ice cubes. They sipped their glasses of lukewarm cognac and nodded acknowledging to each other. The minister scratched his head and there was a moment's silence before he opened the conversation.

"I received a visit from some representative of the automobile importers association recently. They are ambitious people who would like to be allowed to import and sell cars in Nigeria without paying duties and taxes, or at least to have the import duties significantly reduced." So, he had opened by clearly telling them that they were not the only contenders. "They are even prepared to be rather generous but, of course, we know one another, you and I." The minister looked at Segun. "And I think I'll be comfortable doing business with you," he reassured them. "You have a good reputation and I appreciate a firm cooperation based on a relationship of mutual trust. That is crucial in these matters." It all sounded quite reassuring but it was obviously not that easy.

The minister continued without waiting for their reaction. "However, I have this little request for you before we continue, or should I say before we start."

'Oh no, now it becomes complicated,' Frank thought immediately.

"My younger brother, who still lives out in Akwa Ibom State, has a good education and is doing a bit of business but he is interested in the agency for West African Motors in Uyo. There is presently another dealer but he's not doing a good job and my brother can do much better –with my financial backing and advice, of course."

Frank felt that he had to come in and make his mark. "Yes, we are certainly prepared to look at that but we would have to see a business plan from your brother. Then we can evaluate whether he is the right dealer."

This was not very well received by the minister who grabbed the cognac bottle and filled up their glasses even though they had each only taken a small sip.

"Hmm, of course we'll work out a plan but I had hoped we could agree that you give us the agency … shall we say … provided the plan is satisfactory. But we do have good connections in the state and we can do a fantastic job."

They went back and forth a few more times but it became increasingly clear that the agency in Akwa Ibom was a condition for the minister to present a proposal for extending the import duties on finished cars. He intended to fully take advantage of his position. At the same time, it was crucial for West African Motors to settle the problems around import duties on cars because fundamentally there was no cost advantage assembling cars locally. Quite the opposite, but it created employment and consequently was important to the population. However, here they were not dealing with the population but with a minister whose personal interests had first priority. Even significantly higher priority than the concern for employment. No doubt about that.

They reached the question of how – and especially by how much – they were to say thank you to the minister for his efforts. The minister waited for their offer but made it clear to them that what he expected was a sort of unofficial fee per car sold. He thought this could possibly be a fixed naira amount per car although adjusted according to each model's price level. He believed working with percentages was unnecessarily complicated. It also became clear that he expected a rather substantial fixed amount, a kind of prepaid lump sum, as a condition for spending any time and energy on the issue at all. Frank, the colonel and Segun all spoke extremely diplomatically while the minister was much more straightforward and was very blunt about his important financial expectations. He did not look troubled by the idea of doing something illegal.

Deep down inside he probably thought there was nothing wrong with demanding payment for his time and energy, which he perhaps considered a kind of consultancy work. 'It would probably be unwise to ask him about it in this situation,' Frank thought.

The discussion became more and more concrete and they were approaching an agreement while the cognac bottle emptied. This also meant that the conversation flowed more easily with time. Mathematically it could probably be expressed in the way that the negotiation flexibility was inversely proportional to the content of the cognac bottle. Just before 2 a.m. they had come far enough for the minister to consider an agreement made and he showed subtle signs that the discussions were coming to an end. But Frank would like to know how certain they were that their proposal would go through the legislation process.

"And then we hope that the passing of this legislation will be successful," he said.

"Listen. I wouldn't be sitting here wasting your time, and especially not my own time, if I wasn't sure I could handle it. I'm not a small boy, you know?" was the minister's reaction and that was clear enough for Frank to drop any further contribution to the conversation which he might have had. The minister looked at him for a while then got up as a sign that it was time to leave.

"We thank you very much for your time and highly appreciate your support, which is invaluable for us. It's been an extremely good meeting and we deeply respect your profound experience and clear views on this, otherwise complex, area," the colonel rounded up, and Frank thought it was a bit too much. The fine grammar and compliments were, however, very well received by the minister who had nothing against being treated like a big shot, Frank thought. Then they shook hands, the minister yawned openly and a moment later they were in the car on the way back to the hotel.

"Well, that's how it's done in this country," the colonel concluded. "Are you OK with this arrangement, Frank?"

"Basically, I think it is downright appalling that we have to pay him that much money but I suppose we can't avoid it," Frank complained.

"No, we can't. We simply have to make absolutely sure that the car importers do not have it their way," the colonel said.

"So, what's the next step?" Frank asked.

"Now Segun will arrange for the prepayment from his commission, right Segun?" Segun nodded. "It turned out that it wasn't necessary to give him the $20,000 so that can be included in the first payment." The colonel continued his explanation. "And then the minister will bring up the issue at the Federal Executive Council meeting where the president and all ministers and deputy ministers are present. That's where the decisions are taken and I'm sure it'll be all right."

"Gosh, I'm tired." Frank was ready to hit the sack and was also a bit intoxicated from the minister's cognac.

"But shouldn't we get back to the hotel and celebrate the good meeting with a bottle of champagne and some beautiful young ladies?" the colonel suggested. He seemed in top form.

"No, I'm too tired for that," Frank sighed, and Segun agreed with him.

"Maybe you've already been engaged?" the colonel asked and winked.

Frank just shook his head. He wondered how much they were following his private life. At least the colonel was always interested. He had to give this some more thought another day.

His telephone display showed 02:54 when he stepped into his hotel room and tumbled into bed.

Chapter Sixteen

They had agreed to meet at ten o'clock to go to the airport for an early afternoon flight to Lagos. However, it turned out that the colonel had changed his plans and Frank decided to find his way back to Ibadan himself. He called Mrs Adebayo and asked her to send the driver to Lagos. Then he went down to the mezzanine, floor 01 in the hotel, where the local airlines had their offices and queued up at Aero Contractors' counter to buy a ticket to Lagos.

"Morning, sir," said the uniformed guard outside the front door at the Hilton. "Do you need a taxi?"

"Yes please, preferably a nice car because I'm going to the airport," Frank replied, but at the same time he saw Segun come rolling his travelling bag out of the main entrance. He had also spent the night at the Hilton as he lived quite far out of town and had not felt like driving home in the middle of the night.

"Hi Segun. Are you on the way home now?" he asked, and Segun smiled when he saw Frank.

"Yes, I better get to the office and follow up on some other businesses. Are you going to the airport, Frank?"

"Exactly, I was actually just about to get a taxi."

"No, I'll drive you there. Come on – I am parked out behind," Segun said and looked at Frank. "You look a bit worn out this morning but it was of course an exhausting night with the minister."

"I'm a bit shocked that it's done this way," Frank said, and Segun chuckled.

"It is a strange system but when you get used to it and learn how it works then it's actually a crazy kind of well-organised system," Segun explained.

They reached Segun's car, threw their bags in the back and drove towards the airport while they continued their discussions about how things worked in the country. Segun was obviously an experienced businessman and had an abundance of useful connections which he used to secure good business for himself and the companies he represented. On the way to the airport Frank received many helpful hints about the business environment in Nigeria and the picture became clearer to him. Not simply a picture of total chaos but some form of chaotic organisation which required experience to navigate.

After about an hour they rolled up in front of the capital's modest airport, Nnamdi Azikiwe International Airport. Segun dropped him in front of the terminal. "Bye Frank, have a good trip back to Lagos and Ibadan. I'm sure we'll meet again soon," he said. They shook hands and Frank thanked him for the ride to the airport.

Unfortunately, it turned out that Aero Contractors had had some technical problems with a plane earlier in the day. They had, therefore, cancelled the departure at 3:10 p.m. and transferred the passengers to the following departure which in principle was scheduled for 5:50 p.m.

However, this flight also turned out to be delayed due to late arrival of the crew, as it was announced in the most carefree way over the loudspeakers. He landed in Lagos just before 8 p.m. which meant another night in Lagos as it was too risky to drive on the Lagos-Ibadan Expressway after dark. Godwin would have liked to get going the same evening, perhaps he had an appointment with a girlfriend in Ibadan, but Frank had heard enough scary stories to insist on staying until the next morning. It was another overnight stay at the Sheraton where he had had a brief night's sleep a few weeks earlier.

Frank was prepared and very determined to avoid the lobby bar and the business propositions from Happiness and Pleasure or whatever the young ladies' names were.

"Godwin, I would like to leave early tomorrow morning so be here at seven please. Then we can get out of Lagos before the traffic becomes too bad, OK?" They were parked in front of the Sheraton and Godwin confirmed that he would be there early the following day. Frank quickly checked in and decided to go for room service and an early night. He really needed a good night's sleep.

Next morning, he grabbed a cup of Nescafé brewed with hot water from the electric kettle in the room and bought two croissants from the bakery shop in the lobby before he settled the bill and left the Sheraton. It was Saturday but the traffic in Lagos was totally unpredictable. However, before traffic became too dense they were out on the expressway and passed the toilet wholesaler who still shamelessly advertised his "shit business". From there Godwin stepped on it and

Frank was in no mood to keep control of the speed and closed his eyes, leaned back and thought of other things than traffic in West Africa.

When they "landed" in front of Frank's house around nine he went into his home office to collect a few things. He noticed that some files in the bookshelf did not stand quite as they usually did. Just as some papers on the desk had apparently shifted place.

'Strange,' he thought, and called Temitope.

"Tell me, has anybody been in the house? My things are placed differently."

The cook's eyes wandered and he looked down. "No, but I cleaned the table," he explained, but Frank had seen the dust on the desk and knew for sure that it had not been cleaned.

Frank went outside to ask the security men but they had the good explanation that they had just arrived on duty in the morning. Therefore, they did not have the faintest idea of what had been going on the previous evening or during the night for that matter. Frank dropped the case and went to the office where he wanted to spend a few hours peacefully taking advantage of the fact that he would not be unnecessarily disturbed on a Saturday. He saw that George was there and asked him to come to his office.

"George, do you know this guy Segun who is our agent in Abuja. He was with us at the minister's the day before yesterday?" Frank asked him, so he could have some input from another point of view.

"I've met him. He's basically a nice guy, a very decent fellow, but as far as I know also a good friend of the colonel's. At least he came in through the colonel although I'm not actually sure how close they are any more," George said, and looked serious for a moment. "I don't know, Frank, but in any case, it always costs a fortune when the colonel goes out on his adventures and Segun Ajibola has often been with him."

"That's OK. I just wanted to hear what your opinion was, George."

"At least there's no problem maintaining a high spending on entertainment."

"All right, thanks. Let me know if you see or hear anything more which could be useful in this regard." Frank stopped and decided to speak less and listen more.

"I share your concern, Frank." George looked like he knew more than he was saying at the time but Frank let it go. Instead, he attacked the incoming mail and various internal memos, amongst others one from his human resources manager who had problems terminating the employment of some useless trainees. At 2:00p.m. he decided to close for the day to get home, maybe watch some TV and most of all enjoy the weekend.

The cook had made spaghetti with meat sauce for him in the evening but the spaghetti was overcooked and had almost turned to pasta cake. Frank ate a bit to take the edge off his appetite, drank a soda water and watched a bit of the local news when his mobile telephone rang – an unknown number.

"Hi Frank, it's me, Ifeoma … Ifeoma. We met in Lagos." She sounded hesitant and cautious.

"How are you? I hope you remember me?"

"Yes, of course I remember you. How's it going?"

"You didn't call me even though I gave you my number so I thought that maybe you didn't want to see me again. Anyway, I still decided to try to call you to hear if you're OK."

"It's nice of you to call me. I've been in Abuja for a couple of days and I was very busy but where are you now?"

"I just came to Ibadan and wanted to check if you were home. There's something I would like to talk to you about," she said, and Frank immediately imagined that there would be financially related issues involved in that conversation. He thought like crazy about how he could possibly postpone their meeting because he did not feel quite ready to see her again.

"Are you there, Frank?"

"Yeah, ... OK," he replied after all and explained to her how to find his place.

"Thank you, Frank. I'll be there in a little while. See you." He felt that he had perhaps accepted too quickly. Furthermore, he had not asked her where she was staying but he somehow assumed that she expected to spend the night with him. That thought did not seem unpleasant to him. In fact, he had to admit to himself that he had thought a great deal about her, remembering their night together at the Airport Hotel.

About 45 minutes later someone knocked on the door. The night watchman wanted to inform him that a young lady had arrived and asked if it was OK to let her in.

"Yes, yes. Just send her in. It's OK," Frank said, and thought he noticed a little smile on the watchman's lips.

He stood in the doorway watching Ifeoma come walking briskly up the driveway carrying a rather large bag. Halfway up to the house the watchman remembered that he should probably assist her in carrying it. He ran after her but only caught up with her about five metres from the house when it was too late.

She smiled at Frank as soon as she saw him and, when they got inside, she immediately put her arms around his neck and gave him a quick kiss. She waited for his reaction and then gave him an intense and wet kiss, reminding Frank about their night together not so long ago. She was wearing a skirt of exactly the right length and a tight T-shirt revealing her good proportions. She was also wearing high heeled shoes which made her almost as tall as Frank.

"I missed you," she said, and pressed her two solid advantages against his body and kissed him again.

"Hey there, come inside and sit down," Frank said, and she saw that he noticed her large bag.

"Don't worry, Frank. I'm not moving in. I'm just staying tonight, if I may. Then I'll move over to my sister here in Ibadan. Is that OK?"

"Yes, of course." Frank was relieved. He poured a glass of red wine for her which she grabbed with slightly trembling hands and emptied half of the contents in one gulp. So, her way of drinking wine had not changed since they last met.

"You seem a bit nervous?" Frank asked, and studied her.

"No, it's just because I'm happy to see you and I wasn't really sure if you wanted me to come."

Her eyes wandered a bit but then she pulled herself together and looked him in the eyes.

"Why don't we sit on the sofa?" she said, and took both their glasses and went over to the sitting room where she threw herself on the sofa making her skirt slide up her thighs. Frank could not avoid looking at her legs. "Come over here and I'll show you something," she said, licking her mouth.

He accepted her invitation and sat down on the sofa where she was now lying down. She took his hand and led it up under her skirt where he felt that she was not wearing any underwear.

Also, she was newly shaved and smooth. He wanted to pull back his hand but she held on to it and giggled. "Feel it. It's already wet." She swung one leg over him and sat up on the sofa now with one leg on each side of him. Then she pulled up her T-shirt and revealed her full breasts.

Breasts that he had fantasised about several times in the days since they had been together.

He slid down onto his knees on the floor, leaned forward and took one nipple in his mouth. She had her legs around his body and was breathing heavily. He let his mouth move down over her breast to her stomach where he licked her navel a bit. She was ticklish and let out a little shriek.

He continued slowly down her stomach and lifted her skirt to see her naked pussy which was, as he had felt it, newly shaved and smooth when he kissed her there. He moved downwards and put his tongue inside where he found her most sensitive spot and licked her more systematically. He liked the taste.

Her heavy breathing and tense body confirmed to him that she liked it and he kept going more and more intensely until she was moaning loudly and he felt her body trembling. "Oh my god, that's fantastic, Frank." He stopped and sat up still on his knees in front of the sofa and now remembered his old knee ligament injury which was given a test through such exercises. He dried his mouth and chin with his hand and smiled. He got up, limped around a bit and bent his leg a couple of time to ensure that the knee was all right.

Then he took her hand. "Come on. Let's go and take a shower," he said, and she got up and followed him without protesting. She was naked before they reached the bathroom and Frank snatched a condom from the drawer in the bedside table on the way. Not an expensive Durex in shining green packing as she had brought the last time but a simple "Prudence" which had been made available free of charge in an Ibis Hotel somewhere in West Africa. 'It usually gets the job done,' he thought.

They were in Frank's bathroom which had a large shower cubicle. He threw his clothes on the bed on the way and she was right behind him. It took a bit of time before the water was warm but after all it was not as ice cold as in Denmark. When Frank had regulated the water to the ideal temperature on the old faucet, they stood closely together soaping each other up. Ifeoma had put on a shower cap but she washed Frank's short hair and managed to rub some shampoo into his eye. They kissed and washed the soap off each other.

"What is this?" She said, and grabbed his stiffening penis. "Why is it standing out in the air like that?" She took the soap and began washing him with both hands causing an immediate effect. When she was satisfied and thought that he was ready she turned around, bent forward and slapped her own bottom hard. "Come on, take me now." He dried himself and put on the condom quickly. She was still standing with her delicious black ass in the air. "Come on, Frank – what are you doing?" He grabbed her wet glistening buttocks, lifted them up and out the sides then let them fall and admired the movement as they were vibrating back into place. He massaged them gently but when he let his finger run over her anus she stiffened – so do not touch there, he noted. Then he held her buttocks out to each side. 'Two firm and solid handfuls,' he thought. Frank slid into her and took his time. He now noticed that she had a sexy tattoo right at the point where the back becomes butt. Two lizards in the middle of the mating ritual with the male halfway on top of the female and his tail twisted around her tail. It looked a bit kinky and Frank had the impression that the male was looking at him, sort of challenging him. "We are two hotshots, right – who'll finish first?" When he was thrusting hard it looked like the lizards were playing the same passionate game and he was studying them while he increased the tempo and eventually was screwing her hard and fast.

At one point he withdrew himself, took her hand and pulled her into the bedroom where they threw themselves on the bed soaking wet as they were. She rode him with her gorgeous breasts swinging back and forth in front of his face. He tried to catch them with his mouth as they passed by, but she was up to full speed now.

They came almost at the same time and lay there for some time catching their breaths with her on top and him still inside her. Then she giggled, got up and went back to the shower.

Later they lay in bed relaxing. Frank would rather sleep but Ifeoma did not seem to be tired at all and wanted to talk.

"Frank, how is it actually going at work? I mean, is the company doing well?" she asked. "Well, it's going all right, I think. Why do you ask?"

"Because I was at that dealer ceremony, you know, and I'm interested in how things are going for you."

Her explanation sounded slightly uncertain, Frank thought. "That's understandable enough, I guess," he said.

"But I suppose you have a strong market position, don't you? I have noticed that your cars are used by many ministries and government organisations. So, you must be making a good profit. It's just because I bought shares in your company some time ago."

"Well, I suppose we do." Frank was tired and hardly heard was she was saying.

"I saw the annual accounts recently, at the annual general meeting, and the management group was mentioned. Who are the most important people in that group? Are some of them not performing so well? I mean, have you planned any changes?"

"It's amazing how curious you are," Frank mumbled, and a moment later he fell asleep, woke himself up with a violent snore and rolled over on one side.

On Sunday morning, Frank woke up the first time at 5:30 a.m. when his bladder told him that it was high time to visit the toilet. He succeeded almost without waking up, then sneaked back into bed and enjoyed that he did not have to get up early. Ifeoma was still fast asleep and looked so cute and natural as she lay there on her side with her mouth half open and messy hair while breathing deeply and regularly. Then he started thinking about work and wasted almost half an hour worrying, while he studied the ceiling's irregular pattern and the small yellow spot in the corner most likely caused by water damage in the last rainy season.

But Ifeoma's regular breathing combined with his own level of exhaustion meant that he slowly but surely was embraced by the peace of mind offered by sleep and he was swept back into dream land. Dreams were not long in coming but, unfortunately, they presented him with a continuous line of unsolvable riddles at work in a company where he had no clue what they were doing. After having tossed and turned for some time – he had no idea for how long – he suddenly sat in the cockpit of a small two-engine plane which he tried to fly. However, he could not find the correct frequency on the radio, did not know the meaning of the many instruments and eventually panicked. The plane stalled in the dream which may have been meaningful but, if so he had forgotten the meaning. He could not control his right arm's movements when he wanted to adjust the throttle and the plane started falling towards the ground. At that moment he woke up startled and saw, to his great relief, that he was still in his bed. His T-shirt was wet with perspiration and Ifeoma stood next to his bed pulling the arm with which he had been unable to reach the throttle.

"Frank. Wake up. Aren't you coming to church – it's Sunday morning?" "What?"

"It's Sunday. We're going to church. Come on," she insisted.

"You know what? I'm not much of a church enthusiast," he muttered, and closed his eyes again.

"That's up to you but I'm going to church in a little while. See you later."

"OK, bye." Frank was not seriously worried about missing church on this holy Sunday where he would rather sleep for another hour, preferably without strange dreams.

The brief debate about going to church had awoken him just enough to prevent him from going back to sleep.

He cursed and got out of bed. In front of the bathroom mirror he realized that his midriff was more stretched than he remembered it. A proper bicycle tyre was being promoted to a motorcycle tyre and Frank imagined that the Michelin man would turn up before long.

He determinedly put on his training clothes, jumped on the exercise bike and pedalled for a good half hour. His sweat formed a lake under the bike and the exercise did him good. After a long shower, a piece of toast with cheese and some quick internet surfing Ifeoma came back from church. She looked stunning, first of all physically in her colourful church dress and fancy hat but she was also glowing in another way; so relaxed and comfortable. 'Perhaps one should consider going to church next Sunday,' Frank thought, although he still felt good from the physical efforts on the bike. That was the stabilising factor in his life; physical exercise. He thought it made him more relaxed when he exercised hard on a regular basis and he had never practised any form of religious activity before. But when he now saw how balanced Ifeoma looked after having been to church he seriously considered if he should let her talk him into going the following Sunday. He postponed the final decision until further notice.

He got dressed and they went out for lunch which he liked doing on Sundays. Apart from that, there was no cook and so the choice of food at home was distinctly limited. They had Chinese at Fortune Restaurant in Onireke which absolutely was not Ifeoma's cup of tea. She just munched her way through a few small spring rolls and a bit of rice in curry sauce. The inevitable subject for the week's last day, church, was brought up again.

"But, Frank. Don't you ever go to church?"

"Well, I do… sometimes. Mostly when there is something special like weddings and such." "But not every Sunday?"

"No, you can hardly say that but I do know where the church is located near my house in Denmark," Frank said with a smile.

"But, don't you ever pray to God?" she insisted, while Frank asked himself when this inquisition would stop.

"Of course, but mostly somewhat informally I guess you could say," he replied evasively. "You know, something like; by God I hope we get this order." His smile was not returned and he understood that one did not joke about these things in this little forum.

"Next Sunday," she concluded the discussion, and he assumed it meant that he would be faced with a firm demand the following week. 'We shall see,' he thought.

They changed the subject and, not surprisingly, she wanted to know more about Denmark and why Frank had come to Nigeria.

"Are you married, Frank, or have you been before?"

"Yes, I was married and have two children of 10 and 16 but I got divorced about four years ago. My ex-wife and I have a pretty strained relationship, to say the least."

"Why did you get divorced? It's not very common here where we would rather stay together and perhaps have an affair on the side," she said. "It's also against what the Bible says – to divorce, I mean."

"Hmm, you know, we are Christian in Denmark but in quite a relaxed way. We believe in the fundamental values of Christianity, or most people do, but we generally live a rather materialistic life."

"Ha, you were the ones who sent missionaries to us and made us convert from our traditional religions and now you have forgotten about it yourselves. It's a bit strange."

"You're right about that. I suppose it's because we live in such comfortable circumstances that we don't think we need the higher powers. In fact, it is mostly older people who go to church.

How are the Danes? Is it a nice place to be? Will you bring me there one day?" She leaned forward and was speaking eagerly.

"Hey, one question at a time. The Danes are nice enough but it's not easy getting close to them – they are not very open to strangers. Most people are not actually racist, but they seem afraid that too many foreigners will come to the country and disturb their comfortable and secure daily life."

"Maybe they don't like black people," she said in a slightly provocative way and rubbed her index finger against her forearm to show the colour.

"No, we Danes don't mind Africans as such. It is more Muslims who make Danes a bit worried no matter where they come from. Gee, it's a bit difficult to explain and I have also been away from it all for so many years that even I find it difficult to understand what the Danes are thinking.

"But you'll take me there one day, won't you?" she insisted.

"Well, we'll see about that," he answered, trying not to commit himself.

"Don't worry, Frank. I won't be a nuisance for you but I would really like to get to know you better."

He nodded, made a sign to the waiter to bring the bill and changed the subject.

"What about you? Where in the country do you come from? I am guessing it must be somewhere in the south-eastern part but where exactly?" he asked her.

"I'm from Owerri in Imo State, right in the heart of Igbo-land, if you've heard about that. You've probably heard about Biafra which is the country my grand-parents dreamt of and were fighting for towards the end of the 1960s. Of course, it was long before my time and my parents were only children during the war but it is still affecting us in many ways."

"I remember my parents talking about the Biafran war."

"Nigeria felt threatened by the possibility of Biafra's independence and the army, led by General Gowon, was merciless. They blocked the entire south-eastern part of the country off and starved the Igbos until we could no longer fight. It was a horrible war."

He nodded seriously and felt how deeply affected she was by her people's history even though the war took place many years before she was born.

Chapter Seventeen

Ifeoma was sulking because Frank was not up to making love to her that Monday morning.

"Are you already tired of me," she started the conversation.

"Listen, I am exhausted and I have a technician arriving this morning to install new equipment in the factory," he explained.

She sighed deeply. "Yes, yes, I understand that but I just wanted you again," she said, and looked like she wanted to add something.

"I'm so sorry but I'm not a lovemaking machine, am I?"

The cook had set the table for two so he must have been informed that Frank was not alone. Perhaps it was because of the special occasion that he served eggs, sausages and freshly squeezed juice. They ate quickly before Frank had to get going. They left together and Frank dropped her along the way where she could easily find a taxi. Then they agreed to call each other and he focused completely on the day's work.

Jean-Pierre worked for a French company from which they had purchased some new equipment to move the factory up to a much higher level of automation.

He turned up at 8:20a.m. and had a cup of coffee with Frank during which they discussed the job at hand. He had arrived late afternoon the day before and had spent the night at a hotel in Ibadan which he was seriously unhappy with. Frank tried to explain to him that things simply worked that way in the country. The fact that the power went off several times during the night, that the air conditioning was functioning poorly and that the bed linen was slightly shabby was not at all unusual. Then Frank let him complain a bit more until he was ready to start the day's work.

They went together to the factory manager's office and Frank thought that Duncan looked more unkempt than usual. Grey stubble, slightly greasy hair, bags under his eyes and wearing a short-sleeved shirt which was at least one size too small across his belly. Frank left Jean-Pierre in Duncan's untidy charge and went back to his own office.

Frank had ordered a couple of sandwiches for lunch as he had plenty of work to do and did not want to waste time going home. While he was in the middle of the second sandwich with eggs, tomato and a bit too much mayonnaise, Mrs Adebayo suddenly came rushing into his office.

"Frank, it's terrible. We have just been informed that the car with Jean-Pierre has been hijacked by armed robbers. He's been kidnapped," she rattled off.

"What? Say that again." Frank had heard the message but thought it sounded too crazy to be true so he had to have it confirmed that he had got it right.

Mrs Adebayo was rather agitated. "It was Samwel in the HR manager's car who saw it. They were in a queue at the railway … the railway crossing." That explained everything because everybody would refer to a specific railway crossing this way. So, he knew where it had happened. She continued and was now speaking even faster. "It … it was a minibus with robbers carrying machine guns. Samwel is outside. Sam, come in and tell the boss what happened. Come on."

Sam seemed less shocked even though he had witnessed the incident. "Yes, they threatened the driver and two of them jumped into the car and they drove away."

Frank tried to get a clear picture of what had happened. "So, the robbers jumped out of the minibus and then they threatened the driver of the car driving Jean-Pierre. Two of them jumped into the car and they drove away. Who was driving the car?"

"One of the robbers did. He pulled the driver out of the car and hit him with the gun. Then they pushed him into the backseat. He was bleeding," Samwel explained calmly. He might as well have been telling them what he had for dinner the day before.

"Which driver was driving for Jean-Pierre and which car was it?" Frank asked. "John in pool car two." No unnecessary chitchat from Samwel.

"Just a moment." Frank sat with his head in his hands and looked into his desk. In moments like this it was crucial not to panic. Keep calm now and think. "Go and fetch George, the colonel and Funmi," he said, and Mrs Adebayo ran off and tore her dress when the sleeve got stuck on the key in his door.

George and the colonel were there in a minute and Frank summarised the situation to them. He was less upset than Mrs Adebayo and he was guessing that, on a scale for the level of anxiety, he would be between her and Samwel, who seemed ice cold. Frank tried to get a plan in place.

"Colonel and George, you know the commissioner of police, don't you? You are members of that Police Officers' Mess, right?" Frank knew they were, because the company had just paid the subscription which was rather convenient in this situation.

"Yes," they answered simultaneously.

"Who will call him to explain what has happened and hear him what he is able and willing to do about it?"

'We probably won't get a lot out of this,' Frank thought, but it was something they absolutely had to try. However, he did not lose his energy.

"I think we, you and I, should go there to speak to the commissioner," the colonel suggested. "I'll just call him first to make sure he's around."

"OK, we'll do that as soon as we finish here," Frank said.

Then Funmi turned up and she looked very disturbed, almost in deep shock. Frank once again went through the quick summary of the problem and Funmi's complexion had now turned greyish.

"What you will do now, Funmi... are you OK, by the way?" Yes, she thought she was. "You'll call everybody you know in the area and in neighbouring states. Distributors, private customers, friends and acquaintances and you give the particulars of the stolen car and the people kidnapped. They are to be on the lookout, send people into the street and talk to the police."

Then he leaned back and closed his eyes. "What else can we do, George? Is there anything more we can do?"

"I'll call the people I know in Ogun State and I also know a policeman who is stationed near the border to Benin Republic. Otherwise, I don't think there is much we can do except pray to God. With his support anything is possible," was George's qualified input. The need for prayers to the higher powers had seemed to circulate around Frank ever since he arrived.

"Yes, we'll have to do that," Frank said, and hoped it would be sufficient. "I'll wait for a couple of hours before I inform Jean-Pierre's company but I can't wait any longer than that. Then they'll have to decide when his family should know."

Funmi still looked extremely shocked and was leaning against the door frame still with a grey complexion. She did not make any significant contribution and Frank just hoped that she would not faint.

"And then you keep me informed. If you can't get in contact with me then tell Mrs Adebayo what is going on, OK?" Frank instructed them, and he was himself slightly surprised about his own drive. The situation was bad enough but the episode with the snake had, after all, been much worse – at least for him personally.

"Well then, shall we go and see the commissioner?" Frank asked the colonel who simply nodded.

Police headquarters for Oyo State were located less than ten minutes' drive away and the colonel knew the way into the commissioner's office where he seemed to have a close relationship with the secretary in the front office who showed him deep respect. She got up and he quickly gave her a tight hug and a kiss on the cheek.

"Oh, my colonel," she beamed.

The colonel introduced Frank as, "my new managing director". She looked up and down at Frank but did now show any significant enthusiasm or any awe at meeting the company's managing director.

"Is he in?" the colonel asked without specifically mentioning the commissioner and the secretary quickly got up.

"Just a moment. I'll tell him you're here." She disappeared through the door to the commissioner's office. It took only a moment before she came out and showed them with a gesture that they could enter the office.

The colonel walked straight over to the commissioner and they shook hands – the commissioner held the colonel's upper arm with his left hand and smiled. They did not talk but it was evident to Frank that they knew each other well.

The colonel introduced them. "This is my new managing director. His name is Frank Grabowski and this is commissioner of police, Idehen." The commissioner had a firm handshake, a warm hand and an ice-cold gaze. Frank noticed his impeccably shining shoes and knife-edge creases in his black uniform trousers.

"It's an honour meeting you, sir," Frank said, and the commissioner made a gesture indicating that they should sit on his flowered sofa in the corner of his spacious office.

"Yes, Mr Frank. Colonel Chuks here has briefed me about your little problem and we shall of course do whatever we can. That's what we are here for." He paused while staring intensely at Frank. "But I had sort of hoped that you would have come to see me much earlier. It is, after all, normal courtesy – in this country in any case – that you, as a newly arrived guest in our country, come and greet the police." Another short pause to see which effect this had on Frank who did everything possible to look composed. "It's not good to ignore important people and then later come to ask for their assistance when you are having problems. Don't you agree?" Idehen asked, while his ice-cold gaze pierced Frank who fully agreed with the commissioner's statement. "But perhaps you expected to be able to do without the police just like your predecessor did?"

"No, no, not at all," Frank said. "I am very much aware of the importance of the police but I have not been here for very long and certainly had the intention of coming to see you."

The commissioner looked briefly at the colonel and then back at Frank. "Very well, we'll handle the case but make sure you come and see me from time to time." He put emphasis on the word "see" and concluded in a tone of a headmaster. "Do we agree on that?"

Frank did not disagree at all and even if he had he would not have said so.

The commissioner stood up which meant that the meeting was over. They shook hands without any further conversation. Frank was sweating but had cold hands from the pressure of the situation. Idehen's hand was still warm; his eyes arctic.

After the meeting with the commissioner, Frank went back to the office but it was almost impossible to concentrate on anything. Poor Jean-Pierre. Frank tried to ignore it but could not help imagining ugly pictures of violent and unpleasant scenes. John was a calm fellow so he was not the worst driver to be with when things got ugly. He wondered if there was any other reason for this kidnapping than simply stealing the car? Jean-Pierre was not known in the country so it could not be personal. Was anybody after Frank himself? Why was he so unlucky? The thought raced around in his head and blocked any logical line of thinking. He felt like having a beer or even better a whisky but he could not go anywhere now. So, he checked the latest international news on BBC Africa and read that a church had been blown up in Maiduguri, way up in the north-eastern part of Nigeria towards the border with Cameroon and Chad. Boko Haram had once again taken responsibility for the action and it did not exactly improve his mood. Time dragged on and it was stressful just waiting without any news.

At 4 p.m. he called Jean-Pierre's boss in France who at first reacted to the dramatic news with absolute silence. Then he started a tsunami of incomprehensible comments and questions. Frank was grateful that he, early in his career, had had the opportunity to learn French, because he had heard the Frenchman speak English on one previous occasion and it had reminded him of a British TV comedy. But even in French it was necessary to pay attention to be sure that the man had understood the seriousness of the situation. They ended the telephone conversation when Frank believed they had agreed that he would keep the managing director of Jean-Pierre's company informed about any new development and that they would inform Jean-Pierre's family. So far, so good.

Twenty minutes later the colonel came to his office to say that he had heard no news although he had contacted the commissioner of police again. Frank imagined what the newspaper headlines would look like the following day if they lost Jean-Pierre and the driver. He walked around in his office, sat down and got up for another round with his brain on the road to panic mode. At 5:30 p.m. he did not see any reason to hang around the office and went home where he had a large whisky with no ice or any other form of dilution. Nothing happened. There was no news whatsoever. The world was on stand-by, at least the part of the world in which he was operating. It was actually not much fun at all but he imagined that it would be much less entertaining for the two kidnapped colleagues or their relatives for that matter.

At 7:45 p.m. his mobile rang.

"Bonjour, it's Jean-Pierre here," a slightly shaky voice said. "We were attacked. Now they let us go. I don't know where we are. The driver found a police station. We have borrowed their phone. I have no clue where we are." Jean-Pierre's voice was trembling more and more.

"Phew, thank God," Frank said with a sigh of relief and thought that perhaps the prayers had made a difference after all. "Is the driver there? Then let me speak to him please." "Hello, sir. John on the line." The driver's voice sounded stable enough.

"Hello, John. Do you know where you are?"

"Not exactly, sir but I believe we should be near the border to Benin Republic, sir."

"Frank was reassured and now knew that they were safe. "OK, find some transport. Agree on the price and come straight to my house in Ibadan. Then I'll pay the taxi – I assume that you don't have any money."

"OK, sir." No superfluous chatter from John. He knew exactly what needed to be done. How lucky it was that the robbers had taken him along so Jean-Pierre was not alone.

"Excellent, John, we ..." Frank continued but John had hung up. There was no need for unnecessary courtesy when you were in a crisis and had to get on with things.

Late in the evening they arrived at his house in a battered old Peugeot 505. Frank settled the bill and he also had to give the driver some petrol from his drum in the garage. There was "fuel scarcity" which was the standard expression in Nigeria when you had to queue up for eight to ten hours to fill the car with petrol. It was almost more important for the driver to have the petrol than the cash.

So there they were, the two released "prisoners of war". Jean-Pierre wearing a very tatty shirt, some strange-looking shorts and with wide-open eyes. Obviously not the same clothes he had been wearing in the morning. John had a large band aid on his forehead under which some blood had seeped down into his left eyebrow. He was, incredibly enough, dressed even worse than Jean-Pierre. John wanted to head for home right away and Frank invited Jean-Pierre in for a whisky to calm him down.

"My God, have we been worried about you - you can't believe how much," was the best opening Frank could think of. "What the hell happened to you?"

Without any further encouragement Jean-Pierre started spilling his guts. "They took everything, my money, my ring, my mobile, my pen, my glasses ... everything." He took a couple of deep breaths. "It was bad. I was so scared. They hit the driver in the head and threatened us.

They … they … they were extremely aggressive, threatened us with their machine guns they groped me and forced us to get undressed when they left us. We just stood there in the middle of a field completely naked." He started crying, sobbing in convulsive fits. Frank decided not to interrogate Jean-Pierre but first of all to calm him down. He was shocked himself just hearing about what had happened.

"You know what? I'm going to find some clothes for you which you can borrow from me because what you are wearing is really disgusting. Then you can take a hot shower as well," he said, and Jean-Pierre's sobbing became slower and less violent.

"But the whole thing seemed like it had been planned. I don't know why but they asked me who I was and somehow, they were surprised that I had just arrived and that I had nothing to do with the company. It looked like they had a plan and that everything did not go according to their plan. Then they got really pissed off and that's when they threw us out of the car and took our clothes," it was pouring out of Jean-Pierre.

It sent shivers down Frank's spine. Could all of this really have been planned – and why? He was wondering if it had been an attack against West African Motors, perhaps even against him personally but, somehow, he found that hard to believe. He just could not see the logic in it and that type of carjacking, where driver and passengers were taken along, was not unusual at all as far as he had heard. Often the robbers wanted to carry somebody along in case there was a security device which stopped the engine after a few minutes. If they were spotted, it could also be an advantage to have hostages so it happened often. Furthermore, Jean-

Pierre had probably been too shocked to really grasp the situation fully.

"But did they harm you in any way? I saw John's head," Frank asked.

"They tied our hands." Jean-Pierre showed him his red and swollen wrists. "And they said they would rape us and they drew lots to decide who was going to be first." He started breathing heavily again. "But then they got angry and threw us out of the car. The leader was very aggressive and threatening. There was something wrong with one of his eyes. He looked very scary."

Frank poured a couple of large whiskies. "Would you like to call home and tell them you're safe? I informed your company about what happened this afternoon."

"Yes, but I'll wait a little while." He took the whisky glass with a shaking hand and emptied it in one gulp. "I just need to pull myself together first," he said, while he took the bottle and poured another large whisky for himself.

'It's probably natural that he wants to have some booze,' Frank thought.

Chapter Eighteen

Ifeoma was at her sister's place when her mobile rang with a reggae-inspired ringtone. She answered it quickly.

"Hello, my dear Ifeoma. How now? Are you OK, my lovely?" He never introduced himself but she knew the colonel's voice anywhere, anytime. She shivered. "I don't hear anything from you.

What's going on, my dear?" he continued.

"Well, there hasn't been much to report," she started but he immediately interrupted her.

"Come to my house so we can talk. Now." "But it's almost ten p.m. and ..."

"NOW." And then he had pressed the red button.

She did not like it but did not feel that she had any choice. Shit, how difficult it was dealing with him. She put on her shoes, found the car keys for the Civic and hurried off. She had not used the car when she visited Frank because she did not want him to know that she had a car. Now when she was going to the colonel's place it made no difference. Twenty minutes later she honked the horn in front of the gate at the colonel's house and saw a couple of armed policemen when it was opened. She drove inside and parked the car.

He opened the front door when she got there and smiled. "Hey baby. You're looking good."

He grabbed her butt when she passed him and gave it a hard squeeze. "Haven't we put on a bit of weight there? You're becoming a real mama." They went into the sitting room where the colonel immediately closed the door and took the offensive. "Why the hell don't I hear anything from you, my little friend? What's going on?"

"I'm doing the best I can but I have to get to know him a bit before he will open up to me," she said.

"You have to pull yourself together, you know. Didn't I tell you that you had to find out what he knows and what his plans are, which changes he wants to make and so on and so on. Or are you too stupid to understand such a simple assignment?"

"I'm doing everything I can, but ...," she tried but was not allowed to finish.

"You're too slow. Why do you think I gave you a car and the money? So you could have fun with him and fuck him for your own pleasure, you little bitch?" He walked over and sat next to her. He grabbed her thigh and let his hand slide up to her crotch. He tried to kiss her but she turned her face away which obviously annoyed him. He removed his hand, then gave her a hard slap in the face and grabbed her hair. "You said you could help and I've paid you well for this job. Now you have to do something about it, OK?" He pushed her away. "Remember! You obey me. Is that clear? Otherwise I'll have you sent home to Enugu or wherever the hell it is you came from."

She felt like crying but did not want to give him that pleasure and remained calm.

"I know and I'm really doing my best," she said.

"I want some more information so I can follow what's going on," he snapped. "You have to make sure he has complete confidence in you and that you talk about what is going on in the company, his opinion about colleagues, about me. I hope you have understood that for Christ's fucking sake?" he shouted into her face. "I recommend that you do something about it. You'll call me in a couple of days. Understood?"

"Yes, yes." She tried with a little smile which became slightly forced. She wanted to leave but he grabbed her arm.

"And then you have to be a bit more willing in the future. You're a sexy woman and I want to take advantage of that before you get too old and fat." He let her go and she started walking towards the door.

Then she remembered her friend, Chioma, who had been going out with the colonel. She turned around and wanted to say something.

"What is it now?" He beat her to it.

"Well, it's just that I wanted to hear how Chioma is. I haven't heard from her for some time," she said.

"Oh, her. No, I'm not seeing her anymore. I got fed up with her and threw her out. I guess she has gone back to Port Harcourt. She was a little spoiled brat and became completely impossible in the end. So I didn't want to waste my time with her."

If only Ifeoma had known how he really was before she had been tempted into this affair. If only she had not been so naïve but he had been so generous, pleasant and charming at the time. Some nasty shit to get involved in but she had needed the money to move on with her life and she really wanted to finish her studies. He had been going out with her friend, Chioma, who had told stories about him, but Ifeoma did not really believe her. He had seemed completely different; more pleasant and charming than he was now. Now she had no idea where Chioma was and she very much doubted his explanation.

He sat down again and turned on the TV so she turned around and left, worried about her friend and in a bad mood at the situation she found herself in. He deliberately turned up the volume on the TV and did not even glance at her when she left the room.

Chapter Nineteen

Jean-Pierre had recovered, at least to some extent. Having drunk his brains out the night before, today the biggest problem seemed to be his hangover.

"Well, what a mess. I am so sorry that you had to endure this," Frank said.

"Yes, that was the worst experience I've had in my whole life." Jean-Pierre looked ten years older than when he arrived. The shock caused by the kidnapping, and followed by the whisky had been a bad combination for him.

"Have a pleasant trip back home and I hope you're not so shocked that you won't come back to Nigeria again," Frank said, but he seriously doubted that they would ever see him again.

"Oh no. I don't think so," Jean-Pierre said, but did not sound very convinced himself.

Frank thought he saw the trace of a tear in the Frenchman's eyes and, in any case, his hands were still shaking.

"But have a good trip home. Have some red wine on the plane, watch a movie and try to forget what has happened. And then try not to be kidnapped," Frank said, and he immediately regretted it. It was an inappropriate joke and it certainly did not look like Jean-Pierre was amused. They got up, Frank followed him down to the car and waved as they drove out the main gate.

'We'll never see him again,' Frank thought.

On the way back to his office Frank met George who was waiting for him on the landing.

"Hello, George. How are you?"

"Fine thanks. And you've now sent off the unlucky hero?" George sounded a bit quiet. "But could we meet in your office," he added.

"Yes, of course, George." They walked together to Frank's office and sat down.

Mrs Adebayo brought a cup of coffee for Frank and tea for George. The system now worked, she knew more or less when he wanted coffee, it was the right strength and, most importantly, it was without sugar. The only point remaining was whether it should be normal coffee or decaffeinated which she believed was much less unhealthy than real coffee. Frank could not see any point in drinking coffee without caffeine, as he had explained it to Mrs Adebayo. She, however, insisted on running a smear campaign again non-decaffeinated coffee as she called it. She made coffee sound like a narcotic.

They sat and drank coffee and tea for a couple of minutes. Frank glanced at his email on the laptop and thought about the unlucky Jean-Pierre. Then George was ready to bring up what he had wanted to see Frank about.

"Frank, I've thought a great deal about the problems we are currently experiencing. I have also gone through some files and studied the costs of various purchases."

Frank thought that he had more wrinkles on his forehead than he used to.

"Yes, George, and have you found anything of interest?"

"I have made some observations but I would actually prefer if we could meet somewhere outside the office. Perhaps tonight if you're available?"

"Yes, that's fine with me but where would you like to meet?" Frank was slightly surprised about George's suggestion.

"I have a little watering hole where they serve cold beer and snacks. We can sit there and talk undisturbed.

"That sounds great. What is the name of your so-called watering hole?" Frank asked. "You know, I'm still new in town."

"I suggest we meet in front of Kokodome at eight? But it's better if you drive yourself so nobody sees us. You know my car and then you can follow me from Kokodome. It's not far from there."

"Yes, I believe I can find that." Frank had been to the restaurant which was situated next to Ibadan's tallest building, Cocoa House in Dugbe. The only building in town that you could call a skyscraper. The first of its kind in West Africa, as Frank was informed by proud Ibadan inhabitants. As much as 24 floors, he had been told but the building had burnt out sometime in the 1980s and to Frank it looked like it had never been fully refurbished. It still gave a slightly miserable overall impression.

"OK, Frank, I'll see you later then." George got up and left his office. Strange that he wanted to meet at a bar and not under more formal settings. He must have discovered something and most likely he did not want anybody to know how much they discussed the issues. However, Frank thought that this arrangement seemed a bit too much like playing secret agents.

Frank decided to go home and exercise a bit before he went out to drink with George so he left the office at 5 p.m. on the dot. He went straight to his bedroom, changed into training clothes and put a CD of The Doors on the stereo at full blast. He warmed up by skipping rope for ten minutes and then rode intensely on the exercise bike for 20 minutes before he finished up with some push-ups and a couple of sets of sit-ups. The rapid pulse and sweating felt good when he stopped and went to the shower where he took his time. The scale stopped at 96 kilos and that was at least 4-5 kilos more than it should have shown. He would do something about that as soon as possible with a more balanced diet, including the liquid intake, and some more exercise. These best intentions were not always lived up to and sometimes postponed until further notice.

He put on a pair of jeans and a polo shirt, assuming that the dress code would be casual when meeting George, and took a small bottle of mineral water from the fridge while he checked his emails once more and then he left the house. The watchmen looked surprised that he drove himself as they had never seen him driving himself in the evening. He had done it on a Sunday afternoon but never a weekday in the evening. Anyway, they could think what they wanted. He drove carefully as he did not wish to be acquainted with the local police officers and he found Kokodome without problems.

Frank saw George's grey Avensis as he drove into the parking lot and went over beside it. George made a sign that Frank should follow him and started driving. The entire situation reminded Frank a bit of the scene in The Godfather II where Michael Corleone is to meet with Hyman Roth in Miami and drives himself from the central railway station while following Roth's right-hand man, Johnny Ola, to Roth's house.

Frank followed George while they drove slowly through some narrow streets that Frank did not know at all. George stopped in front of a simple building with a rusty aluminium roof. Above the door hung an almost horizontal wooden sign with the word "Sadelicious" painted in large letters and a precisely copied Guinness logo with the name as well as the harp reproduced in every detail. He assumed that the brewery, which had a strong market position in Nigeria, had sponsored the artwork.

'So, this was George's watering hole then. Well, the man did not exactly have extravagant habits,' Frank thought. George walked into the bar first and got a big smile and an even bigger hug from a happy heavyweight lady. She was sincerely happy to see George and after the hug she also gave him a wet kiss on the mouth. Frank wondered if he would also get one but had to content himself with a solid handshake, a smile and a, "Welcome to Sadelicious, I'm Mama Sade."

They went to the back of the room where George apparently had his regular table. The entire interior was simple but looked clean and neat. Frank smelled food but was mainly thirsty.

"So, Frank, are you also a Guinness-drinker like my friend George here?" Mama Sade had her arm around

George and smiled happily so Frank got the feeling that they had something going on between them. It made him think about Ifeoma for a moment and he caught himself hoping that she would soon visit him again.

"No, I prefer a Star," Frank replied, and she fetched the drinks for them. They poured their beers and touched glasses.

"OK, Frank, listen." George went straight to the point. "There are problems with the purchase of parts, diesel, tyres and many other things. Everything we buy locally. There is something very wrong."

"What do you mean? What is happening exactly?" Frank asked.

"It's a complex system of fraud as far as I can see. We pay too much for what we purchase. On paper there are many different suppliers but in reality, there are very few people involved who control it." It looked like George had much more to say but he paused briefly and took a large gulp of his Guinness before continuing. "There's possibly also something fishy with the quantities we receive and most likely also with the quality. It's all one big game and you can probably guess who's involved in it."

"The colonel?" Frank asked.

"Exactly, but you have to be careful. I don't know how much you've heard about him but he can be a dangerous man." Frank noticed that George said you and not we, so George did not envisage the possibly dangerous measures to be taken as being group work.

"Dangerous man. In what way?" Frank asked.

"I heard a story from one of the companies where he worked before. The managing director had apparently taken bribes and the colonel knew about it or perhaps he had even arranged it.

The managing director was found hanged in his garage," George explained.

"HANGED!" That sounds like absolute madness," Frank said. "Are you sure about that?" "I have a friend who worked for the company then and he told me some scary stories."

"Yes, but hanging himself. Goddammit." Frank was shocked.

"Yes, he did apparently. There was a farewell note where he admitted to a lot of fraud and said that he could no longer go on – it all sounded very mysterious. The police investigated the case but concluded that it had to be suicide and closed the case rather quickly. Nobody felt like questioning the investigation and conclusion."

"What the hell can we do about this? If the colonel is so unscrupulous, he is capable of just about anything," Frank said, and shook his head.

"I think you should ask for a meeting with the chairman of the board, Chief Adeyemi. Maybe he can help you and give you some advice on the best way forward." So here we were back to you and not we. George was obviously afraid of becoming too deeply involved in the affair even if he was responsible for the company's finance and accounts department. Frank thought that it was a bit weak of him but did not want to criticise. He had, after all, been open about the problems he had identified which was a great help to Frank.

"Yes, I think you are right. I'll call in the morning and ask for a meeting with Adeyemi," Frank said.

"In the meantime, we have to be very discreet." George looked nervously around in the room. "Here's my private email address. I don't like using the company's mail for private correspondence. Somebody could have access to the mail system and I also suggest that you send private mails via your mobile modem and not through the company's server.

Frank raised his eyebrows but, at this point, no longer rejected any theories after what he had heard since his arrival only a few weeks earlier.

"I'll just write down my private email for you as well. And then please send me documentation confirming what you have just told me," he said. "I highly appreciate your loyalty, George."

"Of course." George leaned back and signalled to Mama Sade that she should bring another couple of beers. The order was quickly executed but this time she brought two Guinness and one Star and she pulled over a chair to their table. So, their body language had apparently shown her that they had finished the more serious and confidential discussions.

"So, Mr Frank. What do you think about Nigeria? I hope you already found a girlfriend so you're not too bored here in Ibadan. Not a whole lot is happening in this giant village," she said, laughed and winked at George. "George, you have to arrange a fine young lady for him or do you want me to find one?" She gave Frank a light punch on the shoulder. "Or maybe you prefer big mamas like me?" she laughed, took a grip of her large breasts and moved them around a bit so Frank felt himself blushing. "Oh, don't be shy, my dear friend." She put her arm around him and kissed him on the cheek.

"No, Sade. I think Frank is capable of finding a girlfriend himself, if that's what he wants to do," George said.

She relaxed and apologised if she had been too rude but also said that Frank was always welcome. "A friend of George's is also a friend of mine," she said, and winked at Frank.

They talked about this and that for a while but Frank felt more like finishing his beer and getting home. He was no longer in doubt that George and Mama Sade were more than just friends. There were other customers in the bar and she served drinks for them from time to time but in between she always came back to their table. Frank finished his beer and thanked them for a nice evening.

George remained seated. "See you tomorrow, Frank," he said, while Mama Sade followed him outside.

"Come again soon," she said, and waved goodbye as Frank walked to his car.

Frank noticed the special African new moon lying down like a banana with the ends in the air, jumped into his car and drove home.

Chapter Twenty

When Frank had left, Mama Sade called a young girl who was washing the dishes in the kitchen. "Stay here and serve the other customers," she said, and went with George to the small apartment behind the bar. They often did that when he came to visit.

It was an old love for George and he was very happy both about their friendship and the intimate relationship they had. None of them were young any more but he was still attracted to her and enjoyed it when they lay in each other's arms after having made love. He was married and had four grown-up children but the relationship with Sade was something he really appreciated. When they had made love, he lay on the side with his hand under his head and looked at her voluptuous body.

"This guy, your boss … Frank," she said, and looked at him. "He seems to be OK. I hope nothing will happen to him. Like with his predecessor."

"I hope so too."

"You have to help him. Otherwise it won't work. You know that and you also know where the problem is, right?" she said. She knew the company well and he had told her about what had been going on for the past few years so she fully understood the dynamics of it.

"Yes, I know that."

"Look after yourself but you have to help Frank so he doesn't break under the pressure."

George knew that she was right and he was deeply concerned.

It was almost midnight when they kissed goodbye and George walked to his car. He was tired but, as always, he felt good when he had been with Sade. The children had moved away from home, two of them were in university in the UK and two had already finished their education. Over the years his wife had completely lost interest in sex which made the arrangement with Sade perfect for everybody. He thought that his wife might have a hunch about what was going on but she accepted it as long as it did not affect her own stable life and especially that it did not threaten her financial security. Apart from that, she often went home to Osun State to visit her family and was currently on one of such trips. That suited him fine.

He unlocked the car with the remote and drove away in no hurry at all. Slowly through the streets of Dugbe which were now almost deserted compared to when he had arrived with Frank.

Frank was a decent and competent guy but George thought that he had difficulty fully understanding how Nigeria functioned, which was no surprise. Most other Africans had difficulty understanding Nigeria and many were downright scared of visiting the country. Even many Nigerians lost their bearings in Nigeria where personal relationships across society made systems work in an odd unpredictable way. Money was everything at all levels. To be rich was the most important for most people – not how you made your money but how much you had. George did not like it. He was not rich but he had a good salary and was able to offer his children a good education. He lived a good life based on his salary and some lucrative investments he had made over the years. Now he did not need so much anymore. He had a company car and had bought and paid off his house many years ago. He did not keep expensive girlfriends but had a solid and deeply satisfying relationship with Sade. She never asked him for money and, furthermore, they owned the bar together from which she made a decent living. He did not regret never to have enriched himself at the cost of the company or other people. Therefore, he felt bad about the way things were going in the company and how difficult a situation Frank was in with little chance of help. He had to stand shoulder to shoulder with him or at least advise and support him but he had to do it in a discreet way in order not to risk everything himself.

On the way home he passed Cocoa House again where he noticed a Toyota double-cabin pickup with two young guys in the front seats come out from the parking lot. They drove out after him and followed at a distance with the same low speed he was driving. He found that odd as young men in a pickup would normally have overtaken him at high speed considering the very limited traffic. He was approaching his house and decided to take a little detour but the pickup was still following him although further behind now. Finally, he could no longer see it. George drove up in front of the gate at his house and honked the horn. The watchman began opening the gate and he drove inside but at exactly that moment the pickup appeared around the corner of the small street. It came at high speed behind him, the watchman tried to close the gate behind George's car but the pickup smashed into the driveway and hit the gate which resulted in the watchman being thrown back and rolled over the ground. The pickup braked hard next to George's car and the two young men jumped out of the front doors. One pulled out a gun and pointed it at George through the side window in his car while the other man closed the gate. Two other young guys got out of the pickup from the back seat. They were all wearing camouflage pants and military boots. They looked around inside the compound and went over to the watchman who was getting back on his feet. They violently pushed him into the small gatehouse and George could no longer see what was happening to him. He also concentrated more on the man with the gun which was pointed at him.

The man opened the car's front door and grabbed George's arm. "Get out, old man," he said, and pulled George out of the car so violently that he fell down on one knee. He received a hard knock in the back of his head and felt dizzy. Blood was dripping down on the gravel in the driveway. George was afraid of what was to come but did not panic.

George was pulled to his feet and pushed forward towards the front door.

"Unlock the door," shouted one of the men. They all four stood around him and George felt threatened. The leader of the group was tall with a shaven head and a small beard. He had a scar through one of his eyebrows and there was something wrong with that eye but George did not manage to see it clearly. The man had a flat cigarette in his mouth, maybe a joint – it definitely smelled different from an ordinary cigarette.

"Open that door, fool," he shouted. It was not good and George fumbled with the keys, got a knock in the back and dropped the keys. Then the leader picked up the keys and unlocked the door. They pushed him inside and locked the door behind them.

Inside the house they switched on the lights and yanked him into the sitting room, pulled over a chair from the dining area and sat him down on the chair. The leader had a roll of gaffer tape and taped George's forearms to the chair's armrests and his feet to the front legs of the chair. Then they emptied his pockets, took the battery out of his mobile telephone and looked at the bundle of naira he had had in his pocket.

"Eh? Small money, old man. We want everything you've got. So, where do you hide your money?" It was still the leader speaking. One of the others gave George a hard slap in the face. "I'll give you everything I have but please don't hurt me. Please. I haven't done anything to you," George begged them.

"Drop all the small talk. Just tell us where the money is. Then we decide what we do with you," the leader said and poked a finger into George's chest. "Remember! we're in charge here." He passed the flat cigarette on to one of the others who took a strong puff from it.

"There's a safe in the bedroom. The code is 736148. In there is all the money I've got at home." George had no desire to argue with them. He knew that he had to give them everything they demanded but he also remembered that there was very little money in the safe. He was worried about their reaction when they found out that this robbery would not make them rich.

The leader signalled one of the others to go in there. After about five minutes he came back with an envelope and gave it to the leader. He took it with a frown and turning the corners of his mouth downwards.

"This is a fucking joke. You must have more than this – big oga like you. Aren't you the Finance Director?" he snapped. He held a little bundle of dollars and a package of 1,000-naira bills in the air and let them fall on the floor. Then he hammered his fist into George's face which made George dizzy and blurred his vision. George was now certain that this would be really unpleasant and was afraid that he may not survive. He felt blood running down his chin.

"Wait a minute. Please don't hit me again. I'll give you everything I have," he said desperately, as best he could with a split lip.

"Where's the rest, idiot?" The leader grabbed his throat and pressed so hard that George could hardly breath. Then he loosened his grip slightly and opened his eyes wide. "Well, come on then. Or shall we shoot your toes off first? Or pull out your fingernails?"

"No, no, no. In my briefcase, in the car, there's some money." George desperately tried to remember which other valuables he had that could interest them. The leader signalled one of the others who left the room.

"I hope you're not making fun of us?" He held George by the throat. "Otherwise we'll be back tomorrow. Understand, old man?" The thought was unpleasant but George could not speak with the robber's fingers pressed against his throat.

The other man came back from the car with the briefcase. They did not even bother asking him for the combination but simply broke open the locks. There was an envelope with around 200,000 naira which was not a fortune and George was afraid of what they might do.

The leader found the envelope and went berserk. "This is fucking too much, man." He pulled out the gun from his belt and fired a shot into the chair George was sitting on just a few centimetres in front of his crotch. "Now I advise you to think very carefully or I'll shoot your balls off. Understood?" George understood very well and if he had had any more money or other valuables he would have given it to the robbers right away.

"I don't have any more here. I just don't have any more. If I had more ..." he tried but was interrupted.

"Chris, bring the tongs. We have to make him remember," the leader said to one of the others who had, so far, hung back. He smiled and brought out a large pair of pincers from his pocket which he opened and closed a couple of times.

"No, I don't have any more. You can take everything I have but there's no more money. I just don't have any more money. Oh my God." George imagined the worst and feared that unbelievable pain was headed his way.

The leader cut a piece of tape from the roll and placed it over George's mouth while he desperately tried to pull his arms free of the armrests. They did not even ask for money again when the man with the pincers just went over, placed it on George's middle finger and pulled off the nail. The pain was indescribable and he almost lost consciousness. He had his eyes shut, shaking uncontrollably and tried to scream but could not because of the tape over his mouth. The leader tore off the tape and George was gasping for air. He tried to talk but could only mutter a few incomprehensible moans.

The leader grabbed his throat again. "Now, listen very well, my friend. Now we take your nails one by one until you tell us what you have for us. Because these peanuts are a complete joke," he whispered in George's ear.

They pulled out another two nails and George was dizzy, almost unconscious, when they stopped. The leader waited a moment while George became slightly clearer in his head. "We don't want to waste any more time on you now but you have to remember two things. First of all, you must have more money next time we come." George nodded, completely exhausted.

"Secondly, be careful who you associate with. The guy you were with tonight is not good company for you. OK?" George nodded again.

The leader stood up. "Come on boys, let's get out of here," he said to the others. Then he pulled out his gun again and shot George in one knee. At first, he most of all felt the shock from the bullet's power shaking his leg and almost pushing him over backwards. Then the pain came as an explosion and George lost consciousness.

Chapter Twenty-One

Next morning, Frank was having breakfast and a strong cup of coffee when his mobile phone rang. He saw on the display that it was Mrs Adebayo.

'Unusual,' he thought. 'She never calls me in the morning.' "Good morning, Mrs Adebayo," "Frank. Something horrible has happened. George has been attacked by armed robbers and shot."

"What! That can't be true." Frank almost added that they had been together the evening before but stopped himself. "How serious is it?" he asked instead.

"They shot him in the leg. He's at the hospital – the university hospital, UCH. They just called. It's serious but that's all I know," she rattled off.

"OK. Does my driver know how to find the hospital? Then I'll go there and visit him right away," Frank said.

"Yes, Godwin knows the hospital but it's very big so I'll call him now and explain at which department George has been admitted."

"Thank you, Mrs Adebayo. See you a bit later." Frank looked at his toast with cheese but had lost his appetite. He fetched a pack of cigarettes from the bar which he had placed there hoping that he would stop smoking again. However, events had accelerated so wildly that he felt like smoking almost all the time. He lit a cigarette and sat down to finish his coffee. The bad luck they had experienced lately was shocking, but was it really just bad luck? So much had happened that now he was becoming convinced that certain people were unhappy about his arrival. How else could so many things go wrong in such a short period of time? He got up and walked around the sitting room and dining area a couple of times while smoking the cigarette. He put out the cigarette when there was still about a quarter left but regretted it immediately and lit another one. Another round of the sitting room. He looked out of the window but saw nothing. Then he looked at the cupboard in the bar and noticed the bottle of Danish bitter which he suddenly felt an urge to drink. He took the bottle from the glass cupboard and filled a small glass, sniffed at the bitter and suddenly did not feel like drinking it after all. He went to the guest toilet and poured it into the sink.

"Is everything all right, master?" the cook asked from the kitchen door.

"Yes, I'm just not very hungry," Frank said distantly. He finished his coffee quickly and put out his cigarette, then took his briefcase and went out of the front door. "OK, Temitope, I'm off," he shouted to the cook.

They arrived at the hospital and Frank noticed the large sign, "University College Hospital" above the entrance. Godwin found the right building, stopped in front of the entrance and gave Frank a note with the department and room number.

Frank got out of the car and noticed how worn out the building was, with peeling paint, broken tiles and a mess of electric wires between this and the neighbouring buildings. He found the Accident & Emergency reception where he asked for George Akinrogbe. The receptionist, in a shabby light blue coat with at least two different types of buttons and one missing, searched on the computer for some time. She then had to ask a colleague for assistance.

There was a strong smell of hospital and Frank felt unwell. A central air conditioning system was blowing air into the room which was only marginally cooler than outside. A drop of sweat ran down Frank's chin and landed on the reception counter. Finally, they located George and gave him the room number.

"But he can't receive visitors now," the nurse at the reception said. "He is much too sick and will be operated on a bit later today."

"Is anybody from his family here?" Frank asked "His son is there."

Frank thanked her and walked down the corridor towards the room. He was depressed about the whole situation and miserable at being in a hospital. The room numbering was illogical and he walked down the wrong corridor before coming back and finally found George's room. A young man was sitting on a rusty metal chair in front of the room. He got up as Frank was approaching.

"Hello, sir. Are you Mr Frank?" he asked. "Yes, I am. Are you George's son?"

"Yes, my name is Femi, sir. I talked briefly to my dad this morning and he's in great pain."

Frank judged Femi to be around his mid-20s. He seemed mature for his age but also looked very serious – almost grim, understandably enough.

"How serious is it?" Frank asked. He was worried and had reason to be.

Femi's eyes were wet. "They shot him in the knee and it doesn't look like his leg can be saved.

They may have to amputate just above the knee. It's completely smashed." He looked like he wanted to add something but dropped it and closed his eyes. Then he looked at Frank and shook his head.

"Was it a robbery? Did they steal anything?" Frank asked.

"They opened his safe and they stole the money he had but they left my mother's jewellery.

They stole the car too," Femi said. "My dad said something about you but he was in so much pain that I really couldn't understand what he said."

"About me?" Frank was shocked.

"Yes, it seems odd but you probably can't speak to him now. Try to come back tomorrow, sir,"

Femi said and sat down again.

"Thank you, Femi. I'll come back tomorrow then."

"Mr Frank. Those people, who did this to my father, we have to get them. They must not get away with it. Please promise me that. I'll help as much as I possibly can. You can count on me." "Of course, Femi." Frank shook hands with him and walked back the corridor. He was shocked by what had happened to George and would really have liked to talk to him but it would have to wait. What could George have said about him? The son was very bitter and determined to do something about it but he had not mentioned the police. As Frank had learned, people often did not take the police into consideration when criminal cases needed to be solved.

Frank walked too far down the corridor once again and had to turn around. The nurse at the reception was still there. He politely said goodbye and asked around what time the following day he could meet a doctor.

"Five o'clock," she replied, without looking up from her computer screen. Frank entered the back seat of his car.

"Where are we going, sir?" Godwin asked and looked at him in the rear-view mirror.

"To the office, Godwin." He was still pondering the situation and Godwin had understood that it was not the time for conversation. There had been a snake in his bedroom, which could happen in Africa, but how did it get inside the house? Jean-Pierre had been kidnapped by armed robbers, which was not that unusual, but he was under the impression that the robbers had a plan, why? And now it had hit George. There seemed to be a lot of unfortunate incidents and he began doubting that it was all a run of bad luck or sheer coincidence. George had warned him about the colonel and was attacked the same evening they had been out together. Something was very wrong.

He went to the office where he had a brief talk with Mrs Adebayo about what had happened.

A couple of the heads of department, who had heard about it, came to know more but he could not tell them much more than they already knew. Everybody seemed shocked. He tried to get some work done for a few hours but made very modest progress and was mostly spending his time considering which steps to take to solve the problems and, not least, protect himself. He decided to ask for a meeting with the chairman as soon as possible. He would also have a serious conversation with the colonel to get a better understanding of the man, how much he knew and get a feeling of how much he was involved in all of this. Of course, without letting him know that he was under suspicion.

But first he would call Ifeoma and ask her to come and visit him that evening. He needed female company and he needed to talk to somebody who most certainly did not have anything to do with it all. However, he was still a bit in doubt how to judge her. From the beginning it had been a wild affair, mostly about sex, and he had thought of her more or less as an escort girl but then they had been together again and it went well. He felt they could talk about more serious matters – she was eloquent and reasonable and apparently wanted the best for him. He had to admit that he still did not know her very well but he felt good about having her in his life. She had just appeared out of nowhere and he only hoped that she did not have any ulterior motive. He would feel a bit exposed if she should start becoming difficult, perhaps coming up with financial demands, but he pushed the thought aside.

In any case, he looked forward to seeing her again.

Chapter Twenty-Two

Ifeoma noticed, with pleasure, that the display read "Frank" when her phone rang.

"Hi, Frank. You are calling early. Where are you?"

"I'm in the office but I'm going home soon. Something happened to one of my people last night. He was attacked by armed robbers at home." He sounded depressed.

"Oh no. I hope it's not too serious. Did anything happen to you? Are you OK?"

"Yes, I'm OK. That is, nothing happened to me but I felt like seeing you. Are you in town?" he asked.

"Yes, I'm still at my sister's. Shall I come over to your place later, honey? Then I'll take very good care of you," she replied quickly.

Ifeoma arrived at Frank's place a couple of hours later and saw Godwin walk away just a few hundred metres from the house. So Frank had sent his driver home. As soon as she entered she saw, to her annoyance, that there was an almost empty bottle of red wine on the table and Frank looked both tired, half drunk and disillusioned.

"No, Frank, you idiot. Have you been drinking alone?"

"No, no, I just had a glass of red wine. It's not much, but everything is shitty and I missed you.

"Yes, a bottle of red wine is what you drank. What's wrong?" she continued complaining. He did not answer but went to get another bottle of red wine and poured two glasses while he began telling her the story of what had happened to George. She was shocked but tried not to show it too obviously. She got up and walked over to the window towards the back yard where she stood with her back to Frank but without really noticing anything outside. She turned the wine around in the glass and spilled a drop on the floor.

"Why don't you leave? There is too much going on and I don't like that you may be in danger," she said, while standing behind him and placing her hand on his shoulder. She walked around the chair, put the glass on the little side table and kneeled down in front of him, placing her head on his stomach.

"Why do you say that? Who says I'm in danger?" he asked.

"I can see what's happening and I can see that it could be risky for you. Besides, it's my country and I know how things work here. Maybe it's difficult for you to understand but, believe me, it's better that you leave." She lifted her head and felt a tear in one eye. "I have come to like you and I don't want anything to happen to you." Then she smiled. "But if you want me to, I'll come with you no matter where you go."

"I've not always had great success with the challenges that I've thrown myself into," he said. "This was a huge opportunity – to come to a company with possibilities. A company with problems I can solve … I'm convinced I can solve, have success, establish a good reputation within international management in Africa. That is what I always wanted but it's difficult to explain why it's so important." He looked thoughtful before continuing. "My mother always said that I was stubborn but I don't think that's why. I just don't want to give up so easily. They won't take this opportunity away from me in this way," he said, and she saw that he clenched his jaw firmly.

"I think I understand you," she said, and put her head on his stomach again. She smiled to herself when she felt that it was slightly softer than the first time she had placed her head there.

She did not tell him that because she knew it would annoy him to know that he had put on weight.

"But nothing must happen to you, Frank," she said, trying to express her sincere concern.

"Remember, this is Nigeria and it is wilder than most other countries. People are so greedy. They only think about money and many would do just about anything to become rich. You can't be sure that everybody has the same interests as you and your adversaries may be ruthless. Maybe they are desperate. If you stand in the way of people enriching themselves they may do anything to get rid of you.

She stayed like that, with her head on his stomach, and neither of them spoke for a while. Then she pulled up his T-shirt and kissed his stomach. She moved a bit closer and bit his nipple and it startled him. She climbed up on the sofa so she was sitting across his lap and kissed him, lightly at first, then more and more passionately and felt how it aroused him. She let her hand slide down to his crotch and felt it. Yes, it was working – his body reacted the way she wanted it to. Now he was hers and she wanted to give him the physical pleasure he was waiting for.

"So, I can still arouse you," she said, and let her fingers run through the hair on his chest.

"Close your eyes, honey and I'll make you think of something else," she whispered.

She took her time, caressing him slowly and meticulously while he began breathing heavily with a relaxed and content expression on his face. She played with him and tried to keep him just on the edge of coming, then let him relax a bit until she tightened her grip and let him explode.

He lay completely naked on the sofa with her hand around his penis. She was kneeling beside the sofa and smiled at him.

"Was it good?" she asked.

"Jesus Christ, yes. That was great. Where did you learn tricks like that?" he sighed.

"We learned that in year one at the Academy for Relaxation Therapy in Owerri so if you liked it, you've been lucky meeting a true expert," she giggled.

He tickled her gently on the neck and on her shoulder, she shivered and had goose bumps on her arm.

"Oh, I love to be caressed that way," she whispered. "I hope you'll do that to me now and then."

"You are beautiful," he said, and closed his eyes again.

"And you're a really nice guy," she said, knowing it was a compliment without being a declaration of love but hoped it was good enough for Frank. She took his hand and looked at it, turned it around and studied the palm of his hand and his fingers.

"Is something wrong with my hands?"

"No, on the contrary. You have soft, almost magical hands. It feels so good when you touch me," she replied, and he looked at his hands with a slightly bewildered expression. It probably was not a real compliment for a man to have soft hands.

Then Frank apparently remembered the cook and looked towards the kitchen.

"Ha, ha, I've locked the kitchen door and you didn't even notice," she laughed.

"Now you'll go and take a shower, I'll wash my hands and then get the cook started preparing some food," she said, and stood up.

"When he had finished his shower and came back to the sitting room, she had put the TV on a channel showing a Nigerian movie.

He stood and watched for a moment. "That woman is pretty good looking," he commented – the layman's spontaneous expression of opinion.

"Her name is Stephanie Okereke. She's a big star and has been for many years." She knew her Nollywood thoroughly. "Do you think she's prettier than me?" she asked mockingly, but he did not take the bait and said nothing. "I know that I'm not as slim as Okereke," she insisted.

"There is nobody as wonderful as you," he said, and she realised that he enjoyed the teasing exaggeration and gave him the finger without any further comments.

That evening, after they had eaten, they sat in front of the TV until Temitope had finished washing the dishes. He came in and said, "Goodnight, master."

Then he stood in the doorway to the kitchen with a little smile on his face.

"Goodnight," Frank said, but the cook stayed there for a moment as if waiting for something.

"Yes, is there anything you want to say?" Frank asked him.

"No, but I have filled the thermos with hot water. Do you need anything else?" Ifeoma thought that he was probably just curious.

Temitope left but a moment later he opened the door again. "Come and lock the door, master," he said.

"Yes, yes, bloody hell. I'm coming." Frank stood up and followed the cook into the kitchen, locked the door after him and they were finally alone in the house.

Frank brought two cups, the Nescafé and the thermos into the sitting room together with a bottle of cognac and two glasses.

"So, you want to get me drunk and take advantage of me sexually, eh? I know you men. The only thing on your mind is sex," she said, trying to look completely serious.

"But that's the only way I can get laid. All women reject me unless they are completely stoned." "Then we'll just have to see if you can get me drunk enough. Otherwise you may have to tie me up," she said, and winked at him.

She changed the channel on the TV again. This time to one of the local stations showing a programme where a happy woman apparently explained to the programme's host about cooking. It was one of Ifeoma's favourite programmes and she sat and giggled from time to time.

"What on earth is that programme about and which language are they speaking? I can hear some English words but have no clue about the meaning."

"But they speak Pidgin English. A kind of local English which all Nigerians speak to some extent. The programme is called "Na so I see am" and the guy running it is Smart Oshoko. He's extremely popular. The lady is married to an important businessman in Port Harcourt and she is explaining how she makes sure that he eats well to cope with his busy schedule."

"Oh, that sounds interesting," Frank said, and sounded like he meant boring.

"It's quite funny to watch actually," Ifeoma replied.

A bit later in the programme they showed a clip of the man, and his physique certainly showed that he ate very well every day, suggesting the wife's mission was a success. Ifeoma enjoyed watching Smart Oshoko for some time while Frank dozed off and only woke up now and then when his own snoring woke him up.

"My neck is hurting me," she said when the programme was over and turned her head with some loud cracking as a result. "Could you give me a massage please?"

"You can go to the bedroom and get completely naked. Then I'll join you and give you a super massage with heavy massage oil ... all over your body." "Sounds delicious and then what?" she asked excited.

"Then, when you're all oiled up and well massaged, I'll lick you until you scream and beg me to take you. Then I take you hard and fuck you until you come." He was still sitting back in the armchair with his eyes closed but continued slowly. "Are you drunk enough for that or shall I bring the handcuffs?"

She got up, went into the bedroom and hoped that he would follow her. She was wet and really wanted him to do what he had just described.

"Come on, baby. Hurry up. I can't wait any longer," she shouted, but he did not come and she thought that he purposely let her wait.

Then he came strolling into the bedroom and went to the bathroom to brush his teeth and took his time. He brought the massage oil to the bedroom and deliberately placed it on the bedside table, still taking his time.

He gave her exactly the treatment he had described in such detail except for the handcuffs. It proved unnecessary to tie her up. Later, when they had both come, he lay on top of her completely covered in oil. They were both out of breath. Frank pulled out of her and their oiled-up bodies separated with a little plop. She hoped that he had understood that the massage oil was very welcome. If not, she would tell him as soon as possible.

Chapter Twenty-Three

Frank called the chairman of the board the following morning, explained briefly that he had some issues which he would like to discuss and asked for a meeting. The chairman sounded rather cold but said that he had just arrived in Ibadan and if they were to meet it would have to be that evening at 9.45 p.m. He did not ask if the time was convenient for Frank, and it did not seem to be up for discussion, so Frank confirmed that it was all right with him. He did, however, wonder what would have happened if he had said that the time was inconvenient. He was already a bit tired of the important personalities and their gigantic egos who always had to demonstrate how important they were. He tried to remember the exact wording of the old proverb; "modesty is a virtue" and thought there was a second part of the proverb which he could not recall. It was not a proverb high on the agenda in this country. Frank knew that he had no choice and planned to go to the chairman's house in the evening as that was apparently the only time the man could see him.

He asked Godwin to stay because he did not want to bother concentrating on driving when he also had to be well-prepared to explain to the chairman what was on his mind.

'And what exactly is it I want to discuss?' he asked himself when he had come home and sat with a little notebook. He had to play with open cards and tell the chairman everything he thought had gone wrong. He had to get the chairman's advice on what to do about security. He could, after all, be in serious danger but it was impossible to plan how a meeting would go when you were dealing with these big shots. Frank thought about their first meeting in London and did not look forward to the meeting later in the day.

Ifeoma was still at Frank's place. Neither of them had said anything about how long she could or would stay. Somehow it seemed obvious that she would stay at least a couple of days. They had both enjoyed the evening before and she wanted to repeat the success as soon as he came home but he had to keep a clear head. He had explained that to her as well as he could but she was now sulking in front of one of these trivial local movies. He ignored her and planned to make it up to her when he came home again later.

He left the house early and went through his notes for the meeting in the car. It was the first time he saw the chairman's house and it was, not surprisingly, an impressive building.

Architecturally not very charming, almost like a two-storey concrete block, a large parking lot in front of the house, a massive entrance door – and, not forgetting, four heavily-armed guards who did not look exactly welcoming but scowled at him suspiciously. The security measures here seemed to be even tighter than at the minister's house in Abuja.

There was no well-dressed butler as in London, only a young lady who said, "Welcome" and asked him to sit on a sofa in the hall. He had arrived ten minutes early and prepared himself to wait for a while before being invited into the inner sanctum. After a couple of minutes, a young man came to the hall and asked Frank to follow him into a small sitting room where a flat screen on the wall was showing CNN but with the sound very low. He sat there and went through his plan again and became slightly nervous about the intimidating atmosphere in the house.

The small sitting room was full of photographs and paintings – all with the chairman, his wife, children and, if Frank was not mistaken, also his mother in various combinations, situations and dress code. On all the pictures the same confident smile was seen on the chairman's face. No wide smiles or laughs. No fooling around. No fun and games, only the same serious smile. Frank wondered whether the chairman had any sense of humour and thought that perhaps he should tell him a couple of jokes involving nuns and sailors or a blonde joke just to ease up the tension. On second thoughts, he decided that it would probably be a bad idea. Maybe it could be saved for the day when he had decided to resign but not now that he needed advice from an ultra- serious Nigerian businessman who was also his boss.

Frank had made himself comfortable on a large soft armchair but immediately thereafter the servant showed up. "That's the chairman's place," he said with awe in his voice. Frank struggled to get out of the soft cushions, moved over to the sofa next to the large armchair and glanced around the room. The servant stood like a statue and watched him.

Frank tried to look questioningly because the servant was apparently waiting for an instruction. He was unsuccessful and added a careful, "Yes, eh … yes?"

"What may I offer you until the chairman comes? Coffee, tea, coke, water or beer?" he said stiffly and there seemed to have been a slight frown at the last option so Frank chose a cup of coffee.

Some impatient waiting and two cups of coffee later the chairman appeared in his loose local robe, a little matching hat worn at a jaunty angle and an expanded version of his serious smile.

The servant was still present but now had a more fearful look in his eyes.

"Give me a coke," the chairman snapped while studying a CNN commercial for Zenith Bank.

The servant was so tense that he did not realise that the chairman was talking to him and did not react immediately. The chairman sharpened the tone unmercifully. "A coke, a coke, I said!

Wake up useless boy," he barked. Chief Adeyemi looked at Frank and shook his head. "It's impossible to find good people nowadays."

As in London, the volume on CNN was turned up and down, mobile phone conversations took place, questions were asked but answers not listened to and not least servants were yelled at.

It took quite some time before Frank had the opportunity to explain his concerns to the chairman. However, it was not until he mentioned his worries about the colonel that he really caught the chairman's attention. Then he listened carefully but quickly started shaking his head.

"Are you accusing one of your heads of department of being corrupt or perhaps even a direct threat?" the chairman asked and took a few deep breaths before continuing.

"Because, if that's the way you see things, I certainly hope that you have evidence of what you're suggesting."

"I'm not accusing anybody but so many strange and unpleasant things have happened since I arrived, and …" He was interrupted by the chairman.

"Now, perhaps part of the problem is that you don't know Nigeria well enough yet. As I mentioned in London there are many risks, perhaps even dangers, in this country. It is therefore crucial to negotiate your way through it all with strong diplomacy, willpower and most of all solid management principles."

"I understand that very well, sir but …" Frank tried.

"You will have to gather your team and make them all pull in the same direction if you understand what I mean." At that point there was something interesting on CNN and the chairman increased the sound, then heard that it was a repetition of news from earlier in the day. He reduced the volume again and continued, "and I can't imagine that your comments about Colonel Chukwuemeka are correct. I am aware that he has his own way of working – a very independent way – but it also has its advantages to have such a person on the team. In any case, you will have to hold a meeting with him and discuss the issues if you don't agree on how the company should be run. After all, you are the person in charge and you have to show strength and determination. This is important. Your team – the entire team – must understand who is at the helm and they must respect you. They have to understand that there can be only one captain on the bridge and that's you. This is crucial."

Frank did not feel like saying anything else because it was clear to him that he had been lectured about how to run the company and his team. The chairman had talked to him like a schoolboy and he understood that he could not count on much support from that side, at least not to get rid of the colonel. It made him very concerned about his own safety but it also created a slight doubt in his mind whether he was right in his assumptions about the colonel's involvement in everything that was going on.

It seemed like the chairman had read his mind. "If you're nervous about security then have a meeting with the police commissioner. I'll write a little note to him so he knows that you're coming from me." At that point Frank did not want to mention that he had in fact already met the commissioner, and certainly not that the meeting had been less than successful. So he thanked the chairman for his time and would give some thought to whether he should meet the commissioner again. In view of the good relationship he had observed between the colonel and the commissioner, it would probably be shooting himself in the foot if he tried to discuss these issues with the commissioner. He did not feel that a little handwritten note from the chairman would be stronger in terms of loyalty than a solid personal relationship.

"Remember that Nigeria is a bit of a rough place but rarely as dangerous as it looks and certainly not as bad as all the dramatic stories would suggest. Come back and see me if you still have problems. I'm in London for a week from tomorrow but I'll be back in Ibadan for a few days after." That was the end of the meeting. The chairman stood up and put his arm around Frank's shoulder. "I'll see you when I get back," he said, to round up the meeting and shortly thereafter Frank stood in front of the house and waited for Godwin to start the car.

Frank was almost depressed. There was no doubt that the way the meeting had gone was a disappointment to him and his mood had dropped several degrees. It had gone much worse than he had hoped for. Clearly that the chairman considered him a beginner, did not take the situation very seriously and wanted him to solve the problems himself. Perhaps everything was not quite as serious as he had thought … but then again; snake, kidnapping, shooting and so on. Hell, it was not normal and he now remembered the text message which he had received shortly after his first meeting with the chairman in London. Had it been a warning to him not to venture into this job? Was the chairman just such a big shot that he could not take Frank's tiny problems seriously? Or could he even be directly involved in some of the things that were going on. At this point, Frank could not rule out any of the possibilities.

Frank jumped into the car in his usual seat, the back seat on the right-hand side, which was popularly called "owners' corner", from where you could easily communicate with the driver without distracting him too much.

Godwin did not usually ask any questions but when Frank entered the car he looked at him in the rear-view mirror. "I hope everything is OK, sir?" he asked. Perhaps he had, after all, noticed from Frank's body language that everything was not quite right.

"Yes, it's all right, Godwin. Let's just go home," Frank said, and Godwin had another quick look in the mirror before concentrating on driving.

At home Ifeoma was still watching TV, this time a movie with an actor Frank did not know and he did not bother asking. She was still sulking and they did not exchange many sentences before he said goodnight and went to bed.

"Please switch off the light and the TV when you come to bed, OK?" he said, and she just nodded without looking at him.

'No sex tonight,' he thought, but he was not in the mood after meeting the chairman.

He lay in bed and went through the meeting in his mind. What could he have done differently and what should he do now? He would definitely have to have a meeting with the colonel and confront him with some of the problems, perhaps take the bull by the horns and reduce his area of responsibility enough to make it easier to control him. But how would the colonel react to that? And what could he do to improve his own safety? There were, after all, many things indicating that he was in a dicey situation.

Frank had tossed and turned in bed for about an hour when Ifeoma came and slid into bed next to him. At first, she said nothing then she moved closer to him and kissed his shoulder.

"Sleep well," she said, and a few minutes later he heard from her breathing that she was already sleeping. That also calmed him down and shortly after he fell asleep.

"Frank, Frank. There's somebody in the house," Ifeoma whispered in his ear.

Frank felt that he had just reached the peaceful place where sleep takes over. "What?" he mumbled, still not fully awake. He had heard what she said but not completely understood it.

"I heard something from the sitting room. I think there's somebody there," she whispered into his ear. "Somebody pushed a chair across the floor – definitely. What are we going to do?"

"Be completely quiet for a moment," he said, and they waited for a few minutes in silence.

Frank was almost falling asleep again but then heard a weak sound, metal against a wall he guessed.

"Stay here. I'll check what it is. Be quiet and, no matter what happens, stay in here. He got slowly out of bed, put on a pair of shorts and sandals. He opened the bedroom door very slowly and carefully – she had forgotten to lock it so he could open it without the faintest sound. He looked into the hallway leading to the sitting room but could not see or hear anything as the security door between the bedroom section and the sitting room was closed and locked. A little light came through the curtain from the lamp on the terrace but it was quite dark inside the house.

Frank unlocked the security door very carefully and opened it slowly. He hesitantly moved into the sitting room, waiting for his eyes to adjust to the darkness. He began dimly seeing the shape of furniture in the sitting room but there was no sign of anything unusual. He walked with small steps towards the dining area and began relaxing since everything appeared to be in order.

Perhaps he was just too stressed by everything that had happened. Should he check the kitchen as well? Yes, he'd better do that. He realised that he had been walking in a bent over position and was very tense, almost without breathing. He straightened up and let out a sigh of relief. Phew, it was false alarm. Then he registered a faint smell of mothballs – what was it they were made of again? Oh, yes, naphthalin.

The blow to the back of his head was hard.

Chapter Twenty-Four

Frank fell forward onto the floor – stunned, perhaps more from the shock than from the effect of the physical knock. But he was dizzy.

The light was switched on and blinded him while he lay on hands and knees. He turned his head upwards and saw the boot moving towards his face just in time to turn his head and avoid being hit in the mouth. However, his head was forcefully turned to one side and he felt a sharp pain in his neck. He was close to losing consciousness but stayed on the floor with his arms around his head while waiting for the next knock or kick. It did not come.

"Get him up," he heard a low raspy voice say. Not a voice he was familiar with. He was pulled to his feet and his eyes were now getting used to the light. Two men were holding his arms and the third man stood in front of him, hands on his hips. The latter made a movement with his head and they dragged him over to the dining room where they threw him on a chair. Frank placed both arms heavily on the dining table, his head hanging. A few drops of blood dripped out of his nose and landed on the table. The third man sat down next to him while the two other were busy at the bar from where he heard jingling of bottles and glasses and some chuckling from the two men. They had lost interest in him.

"We want to have all the money and valuables you have or we'll tear you apart before we shoot you. Is that understood?" the third man said. He was very dark and had a shaven head. He had a deep scar through his left eyebrow and the left eye was discoloured and had a squint. His features were rough and he had strong, sour breath. He bit a cola nut and spat out a small piece on the floor. "So, we'll start with the money. Where do you keep it?"

Frank had become more alert and knew that he absolutely needed to go along with them. Opposition would be much too risky because the threats were probably real enough and they could easily beat him up or simply shoot him. Also, Ifeoma was in the bedroom and he wanted, at all costs, to avoid them discovering her. It was easy to imagine what they would do to her if they found her. Hopefully they had no clue that she was there.

"I have some money in my briefcase in the office. You can have all of it but please don't shoot me, I beg you," Frank said, and tried to sound submissive even though he felt like breaking their necks one after the other. Perhaps not a realistic scenario.

The two others came from the bar with glasses, a bottle of whisky and what was left of his cognac. He doubted that they would appreciate any of it but that did not matter in his present hopeless situation. They slammed the bottles and glasses hard on the dining table. One of the glasses fell over, rolled over the edge of the table and smashed on the floor. More chuckling from the two, who behaved like a couple of naughty school boys. They were obviously intoxicated and must have been drinking before coming to his house. One pulled the cork out of the cognac bottle, threw it over in the corner of the sitting room and drank straight from the bottle.

The other roared with laughter and did the same with the whisky. The third man, the one with the scar and the damaged eye, who was no doubt the leader of their little gang, looked at them and shook his head. That just made them laugh even louder. They were drunk, very drunk, Frank concluded. The two concentrated on drinking and entertaining each other in a local dialect which Frank did not recognise but it did not sound like Yoruba.

The leader focused on Frank again. "Now the two of us will go to your office and get the money without any trouble, OK?" he said.

"Yes, of course," Frank said, but then held one hand to his head where he had been kicked and grimaced in pain. "Arh, my God," he said, and bent his head to gain a bit of time so he could think about what to do. "Just a second," he said, stood up and assessed the situation. Two drunk idiots who were mainly interested in drinking, both with AK-47's placed against the wall. A leader who had not been drinking and looked much sharper, with a gun in his belt in addition to the AK-47 which he had placed on the dining table.

"Cut out the bullshit and come along," he snapped at Frank, sounding annoyed as he took a step forward. Frank let his legs shake a bit and stood with one arm firmly on the table to support him, swaying back and forth.

"Jesus Christ, come on now," snarled the leader, pulled Frank's arm and grabbed his AK-47 from the table. They left the two drinking buddies at the table and went to the office in the bedroom section.

'Oh God, please don't let him find out that she's in the bedroom,' Frank thought.

Frank went into the office first and switched on the light. "My briefcase is there on the bookshelf. I am going to open it. Is that all right?" he asked the leader. Better ask once too many than once too little.

"Yes, dammit, but hurry up."

Frank looked around him and noticed the paper knife standing in the pen holder from the clearing agent. He went over and took the briefcase, set the combination and opened it. He turned to the leader and showed him the contents.

"Here it is. The envelope is there." The leader took it and tore one end of the envelope.

"I hope this is not what you call money?" he shouted and held out the bundle of naira, which he had just removed from the envelope, close to Frank's face.

"I have more in one of the drawers in the desk. It's locked and I have the key in the pocket of my shorts." He did not want to be shot by mistake, moved slowly and explained what he was doing. There was no reason to die now, certainly not by being shot by a mad burglar. If at all possible, he wanted to avoid it by behaving as they told him to.

"Then find the damned key and open the drawer, idiot!"

Frank took the keys out of his pocket and turned around to go to the other side of the desk. Then he did something which was not planned nor well thought through. He had no idea where it came from but he grabbed the paper knife from the pen holder. In one movement he turned around towards the leader, swung the knife in a curve from knee level and hammered it into the jaw of the robber. His mouth slammed shut with a loud crack and a piece of his tongue was bitten off and fell on the floor. The blade of the paper knife was halfway into his jaw and he was bleeding profusely. The AK-47 slid out of his hands and fell on the floor and he took a step backwards with his hands trying to pull out the knife from his jaw. He was screaming as loudly as he could with his mouth closed and while struggling with the knife which had created much more damage than Frank had dared to hope for.

Frank picked up the machine gun, turned it around and hammered the butt into the man's face. He fell backwards against the wall. His legs wobbled and Frank took a quick step forward and hit him again as hard as he could, with the butt of the AK-47 driving into the guy's ear. Blood sprayed up the wall and he sincerely hoped that he had neutralised one of the enemies. However, a major part of the problem remained unsolved; the two drunkards in the dining room. "What'sch going on in there?" one of the them shouted from the dining room. Frank looked at the AK-47 in his hands. He clicked out the magazine with a little tap in front of the trigger. It was full and he put it back in place. Then he checked the lever on the right-hand side of the weapon – it was secured. He pushed it down into the automatic firing position and was ready for action.

'Thanks, Okafor, for your instructions. It comes in really handy now.' "Hrallo," one of them shouted from the living room.

Frank took three long strides into the sitting room and saw one of the robbers standing in the middle of the room with a bottle in his hand. His eyes were wide open and he looked like he wanted to say something but stopped when Frank fired a burst in his direction. Oops, the AK-47 did not shoot as precisely as he had expected. It had pulled upwards and to one side and only one shot had hit the robber in the forearm. He adjusted his grip, concentrated and then fired again. A series of six or seven bullets which hammered into the upper body of the robber, one of them in the throat. Unbelievable how much noise such an AK-47 made, especially when fired inside a relatively small sitting room. A deafening noise in fact. The other robber had grabbed his weapon from the other side and came around the table with it in his hand but he hit a dining chair with one foot, stumbled and dropped the weapon which slid across the floor.

"Leave it," Frank shouted at the robber who was now lying on his knees on the floor. Frank took a couple of steps towards him. "On your feet and OUT." The robber was, fortunately, very drunk. He was still on the floor, looking over at his AK-47 a few metres away. Then he looked at Frank and made a resigned gesture.

"OK, OK, then I'll go," but he stayed on his knees. Frank clicked the lever to semi-automatic and sent a single shot into the kitchen door behind the robber. He now struggled to his feet, swayed back and forth before taking some wobbly steps towards the door.

"Get OUT," Frank shouted, and thought to himself that he sounded more desperate than he really was. He felt in control of the situation. He followed the man out of the door and while he stumbled down the driveway towards the gate.

The nightwatchmen had been awakened by the noise. They would no doubt claim that they had not been asleep at all, despite the fact that three robbers had entered the house without their knowledge – it demanded a more thorough investigation. Frank fired two shots in the air. "Now you take this guy and tie his hands and feet. He's stone drunk so you should be able to handle that," he shouted. The three nightwatchmen took a couple of quick steps towards the man who wobbled. They jumped him and overpowered him with excessive force.

Frank walked back inside the house and into the office. There was a large dark pool of blood under the head of the robber and it was running in one of the furrows between tiles. He was still alive so Frank went to the kitchen storeroom and fetched a roll of brown tape. He tied the robber's hands behind his back with the tape and also gave the feet a couple of rounds of tape for the sake of good order.

Then he went to the hallway and knocked on the bedroom door. "Ifeoma, are you awake. I hope that I didn't make too much noise."

'If she's not awake she has to be severely hard of hearing,' he thought.

She pulled open the door and looked around. "Oh, baby. You're OK. Sweet Jesus, what happened here?" She looked at him with open mouth and wide-open eyes. "And what has happened to you? Look at you. Your nose is bleeding and look at your T-shirt, it's wet with blood.

Did they shoot you?"

Frank wiped his nose with his sleeve and looked down himself. He pointed at his T-shirt. "This is not my blood, I think." He paused a bit. "I knocked down the guy in the office and then shot the one in the sitting room. The watchmen have tied up the last one outside. He was pissed." That was the best summary Frank could give with short notice immediately after the battle. They went to the sitting room, he put the AK-47 on the bar and they did an assessment of the battle field.

"Damn it, those bastards drank all my cognac and whisky." Frank tried to joke because he was too shocked to think seriously. Then he went to the bar and took out his Danish bitter bottle. "But they left this one. Try to taste this stuff, honey. It has been brewed to drink immediately after dramatic and shocking events … or when you go hunting in the Danish autumn cold. He took two glasses at random and poured the dark-brown elixir generously. Dr Grabowski has prescribed a double "Gammel Dansk" bitter, there you go." He pushed the glass towards her. She shook her head but still took the glass, tasted it and, with a grimace, showed her opinion of the traditional Danish drink. It was just after 4 a.m.

Frank went to the bedroom to pick up his mobile phone. He called the colonel who answered it quickly and did not sound drowsy. "Yes, Chuks, Colonel Chuks, it's Frank here. I have just knocked out a robber and shot another one. I think we're going to need the police," he said. There was a moment's complete silence in the other end. "Can you hear me?"

"OK. I'll get the police and come over immediately," the colonel said, and hung up without asking Frank how he was feeling.

Frank took the AK-47 from the bar and looked at it. "Fantastic weapon, this one. Did you know that it is the most commonly used weapon in the whole world? And it's unbelievably reliable. You can drag it around in mud, sand, anything and it will still shoot. That I have only read, not tried myself," he said.

Ifeoma shook her head again. "How do you know how to use it?" she asked.

"Well, you know, I didn't really, but when I arrived I was talking to a policeman while waiting for the colonel. It was in Lagos. He showed me how it works and it's rather simple actually."

Frank clicked out the magazine and put it on the bar. He then went to look at the robber he had shot. He lay in a pool of blood and was dead. It was a terrible mess. There would be quite a bit of extra cleaning up to do for Temitope. Ifeoma stood shaking with one hand over her mouth.

Frank was in overdrive from the adrenalin, in a state somewhere between trance and euphoria.

He looked at his right hand and noticed that it was only shaking very slightly.

"Honey. Go and get dressed before the police and the colonel arrive," he said.

"And drink this quickly. It will calm your nerves." She frowned and went to the bedroom.

Someone knocked on the kitchen door. 'Probably Temitope,' Frank thought, because he only used the kitchen door. He must have been awakened when Frank fired the machine gun earlier. The cook looked shocked when Frank opened the door.

"Sorry, master. Eh, I heard gunshots," he said, and looked around him.

"Yes, we are still alive but this guy is not feeling well," Frank said, and pointed at the dead robber on the floor in the dining room. "There will be some cleaning up to do later when the police have taken him away."

Then Frank heard some moaning from the office and remembered the leader of the gang. He went there and saw that the man was still alive. He rolled some extra layers of tape around his hands and feet because he wanted to be absolutely sure that he did not suddenly escape. The pool of blood around the man's head was dark and massive and Frank was surprised that he was still alive. On the other hand, he was not overly worried about the man's health. They had got what they deserved so his conscience was clear. He was still shocked about having been in such great danger but he would not have sleepless nights over what he had done to the robbers. Right now, the most amazing thing was the confidence with which he had surprised and dealt with them. It was suddenly completely surreal, almost unthinkable, that he had just rolled some tape around the legs and hands of the wounded robber and that another robber lay dead in the dining room. Had he really dealt with them in such a violent and ruthless way?

A car drove fast and braked hard in front of the house. Frank looked out of the window and saw the colonel's car from which he and two police officers stepped out. Typical that the police did not come in their own official cars but were driven by the people who needed them. Later they would almost certainly request a smaller, or perhaps a significant, "motivational incentive" to follow up on the case. These officers obviously did not come directly from the police station but more likely from the colonel's house, because Frank recognised his AK-47 instructor, Okafor, who seemed to be some sort of permanent bodyguard for the colonel. 'No doubt on the company's account,' Frank thought.

"Hi, Frank. We came as soon as we could. Where are the robbers?" the colonel said on the way into the house.

"One is lying down at the gate house, their leader is wounded and tied up in the office and the third one is dead. I shot him, thanks to your excellent lesson down in Lagos a few weeks ago, Okafor," Frank said, smiling at the colonel and Okafor who smiled back and saluted him.

They looked at the dead robber in awe, stood inside the door for a moment and then slowly approached him. "Did you shoot this guy here?" the colonel asked with doubt written all over his face.

"They had broken into the house and knocked me down when I came in here. Then one of them took me to the office to steal my money. I knocked him down and took his machine gun.

And well ... what then? Yes, then I went into the sitting room and shot this guy here. The other one was so drunk that he fell over and dropped his weapon so I sent him to the watchmen who overpowered him. That's the short version, I believe," Frank told them, not without a bit of pride in his voice.

"Jesus Christ, Frank. You're a real killing machine," the colonel said, and shook his head while Okafor nodded acknowledgingly. The colonel looked at his watch. "Around 6.30 I'll call the commissioner and tell him what has happened. Normally you would have to go over there to give your explanation but I think we can manage with Okafor and I going there to talk to him."

"Will nobody come to investigate the crime scene?" Frank wanted to know.

"Let's see if we can arrange things so it won't be necessary," the colonel said and then whispered to Frank: "But remember to "see" the commissioner very soon." He rubbed his index finger and thumb against each other to remind Frank what they were talking about.

Ifeoma came out from the bedroom, now wearing jeans and a T-shirt but still with ruffled hair and bare feet. She looked a bit tense when she saw the colonel and Frank noticed that her gaze flickered slightly. The colonel seemed to think it was quite amusing.

"Oh, so you've found one of the local beauties, I can see. I hope she takes good care of you," he laughed.

Frank did not comment on the remark but addressed Okafor. "How do we get rid of these two robbers? One is still alive but we can't have him lying around here."

"No, of course. Okafor, we'll take the one who's alive and drive him to the hospital, right?" the colonel said, and Frank thought he saw a little wink but did not mind. He just did not want to have a seriously wounded robber, tied with tape, lying around in his house and especially not if he risked dying there. Frank was not crazy about having a dead body lying on the floor in his dining room either. Okafor called the other policeman who had been waiting outside the door. They got an old bedsheet which they used to carry the body out to the car where they put it in the boot.

Okafor went to the office and they heard some moving around and a weak moaning after which he came out again and made a gesture with his arms. "He was already dead. Probably lost too much blood. I don't think he would have made it to the hospital anyway. Do you have another bedsheet, Mr Frank, so we can bring him along?" Frank did and then both problems were solved in one go.

"I'll put some handcuffs on the other guy down at the gate house, and then we'll pick him up later," Okafor said, and a few minutes later they had gone again. Frank was suddenly exhausted and felt dizzy. He poured another Danish bitter and swallowed it in one gulp. Then, without warning, he had an overwhelming feeling of nausea and ran to the bathroom where he emptied his stomach in several violent thrusts. In the end he lay on his knees with his arms on the edge of the toilet with strong stomach cramps but there was nothing more to throw up except some bile.

Ifeoma came, helped him onto his feet and supported him while he washed his face and brushed his teeth. Then he fell onto the bed and she switched off the light. He heard her give some instructions about cleaning to the cook before he fell into a deep sleep.

Chapter Twenty-Five

II Good morning, Mrs Adebayo," Frank said, when
he stepped into the front office and wondered if it
was still relevant to say good morning when the time
was approaching noon. Frank was feeling far from fine
after the dramatic events of the night. He felt almost
like he was walking beside himself. The world around
him seemed like a movie which he was watching from
a seat in the first row of a large cinema. It was a strange
feeling and he was asking himself if it had all actually
happened.

Frank hoped that Mrs Adebayo would not begin to
question him about what had happened and why he
had not come to the office earlier, but she was usually
very discreet.

"Ekaro," she said. "Hmm?"

"Ekaro, good morning. I thought you had learned a
bit of Yoruba by now," she giggled.

Oh well, but Frank thought that he had been busy
enough having snakes killed, overpowering burglars
and managing intimate relationships.

"Ekabo," he tried which made Mrs Adebayo giggle
even stronger.

"No, ekaro, it means good morning. Ekabo means welcome."

"Yes, I probably better get started on some Yoruba lessons soon," he said distantly and continued into his office where he noticed a large pile of papers in his in-tray. Unbelievable how fast things pile up. He threw his briefcase on the bookshelf behind his desk and sat down, thought about what to do and then got up again.

"Mrs Adebayo, is the colonel in the office today?" "Not yet, but I think he'll be in later."

"OK, but there are some things I would like to discuss with him. So, when he comes please ask him if he can come to the office tomorrow, even though it's Saturday. I have to go to the hospital to see George today and I don't know how long it will take so we may not have time to meet today. Tomorrow the office will be quiet."

"Of course, Frank."

"Please send me a text message when it has been confirmed."

He sat down again, opened his email and began working on the incoming mail: internal memos, reporting from accounts where they seemed completely lost without George, sales figures for the previous month, statements of accounts from the banks, letters from smart business people who wanted to become suppliers to the company – everything from tyres to copying paper. An hour and two cups of coffee later he had cleared enough to be able to leave for the hospital to visit George.

Service at the reception of UCH had not improved significantly and, as he was no longer in the same room as during the first visit, it took some time to locate

George again. Frank wondered if they sometimes lost patients – simply misplaced them somehow. When the reception staff had finally located George, and Frank found the room, it turned out that he had been given a bigger single room and that several of his family members were present. Frank greeted the son, Femi, whom he had met the first time and was introduced to George's wife. He now understood the man's relationship with Mama Sade much better as she had quite a bit more charm than the wife. Oh, and Sade was also much more physically attractive. The mood was very low and when Frank reached George's bed he understood why. George was in bed with a kind of tent built over his legs, was hardly conscious and definitely not clear in the head.

"Hello, George, how is it going?" Frank sat on a small chair next to the bed. He touched George's hand and felt that there was contact but also saw great pain in his eyes. "George, are you OK?"

George was moving his mouth but Frank could not hear what he was trying to say. When George tried again Frank thought that he could read his lips and saw "my leg". His worst fears were confirmed. Femi had mentioned the risk of George losing his leg the first time Frank came to the hospital. Frank had, however, hoped that it would be possible to save it after all, ignored the possibility and thought they would somehow manage to patch him back together. He turned towards the son who just nodded and Frank understood that the leg was gone.

There was not much more conversation but he remained seated for a while until he felt that it would be appropriate to get up. He nodded at the family, received a grave smile from the wife and Femi followed him out of the room.

"He doesn't look very good," Frank said.

"They have amputated his leg just above the knee. He is in incredible pain and he is very depressed about it all."

"Yes, I can understand that but the hospital must be able to give him some more medicine to reduce the pain."

"They can, but they have this idea that they should not give him too much analgesia because it means that the recovery is slower," Femi said, shaking his head.

"Holy shit," Frank said. "That's ridiculous. You have to insist that they give him more pain relief. It's unacceptable to let him suffer this way."

They continued talking on the way to the car and the son voiced his concern repeatedly. First of all, over his father's health, secondly over why it had happened. "We never had robbers before and my dad never has much money at home," he said. "There must be something else behind it."

"It has crossed my mind and I consider this an extremely serious case," Frank said. "But please keep me informed about how your father is doing. Here is my card with my mobile number. Just send a text if I don't answer the call and I'll call you back."

Frank was miserable as he walked to his car while wondering how much Mama Sade knew about what had happened. He decided that he would drive by her restaurant as soon as possible, assuming he could find the place again. She must have heard about what happened and was probably extremely worried. Then he had to make the unpleasant decision about who should carry out George's work until he could return. That is if he would ever be able to return to work. In any case it would not be soon.

Chapter Twenty-Six

Somebody knocked on Frank's door but before he could answer, the door was opened resolutely. A smiling colonel entered the office and closed the door behind him.

"Hello, Mr Frank. How now?" They both hesitated for a moment then shook hands. They sat down and there was another moment's silence before they started speaking at the same time. There were tense smiles and Frank considered how they could open up the discussions. He was well prepared and yet he now found it awkward.

"Perhaps we should go to the meeting room," he suggested. "There's a bit more space than here."

The colonel thought that was a good idea so they got up and went through the door from Frank's office directly into the meeting room. Frank felt that it would ease the tense atmosphere and make it easier for them to get started if they sat in a neutral environment instead of him sitting behind his large desk.

"Well, there's no Mrs Adebayo to make coffee on Saturdays," Frank said.

"No problem, let me make the coffee," the colonel said and got up.

Frank had brought his laptop, a set of management reports, a calculator, a paper pad and a pen for the meeting while the colonel had only brought his calendar. Frank had noticed that many Nigerians used these as notebooks. Nothing had been written yet and there was no formal agenda but Frank knew that it was up to him to run the meeting in order to maximize the outcome.

"What exactly is it you want to discuss today?" The colonel had taken the initiative but a least it opened up the meeting. He looked relaxed and it reminded Frank that he probably had no idea that Frank suspected him of being behind the, more or less, direct attack against him. It was absolutely crucial to keep this meeting completely professional and not give the colonel any impression of how much Frank really suspected him.

"Well, I believe there are many things which do not work as well as they should. Specifically, our cash flow is not nearly as good as it should be. We're always short of cash despite the reasonably good sales," Frank began.

"Now, we shouldn't forget that the country's economy is weak and the government, in many ways, are postponing important decisions because the president is sick and out of the country most of the time. Furthermore, the new budget has not been approved by the national assembly yet," the colonel said. It sounded like a quick excuse before Frank had explained what he thought the problem was.

"Yes, I know, and we should not forget that but let us not get distracted by external factors," he said. "We have a healthy market share and sell quite well, as I just mentioned." Frank paused for a moment. "Also,

I believe that the government is rather busy spending this year's budget before it's too late. So it should be to our advantage, not the opposite." A gulp of coffee and a quick glance at the colonel who was frowning. "But when I look at our bottom line and our liquidity I am worried," Frank said, and let the colonel speak.

"Many of the customers, who have extended credit terms, especially the large governmental organisations, pay much later than the agreed terms," the colonel argued.

"Yes, that obviously affects the liquidity but not the bottom line. At least not before interest. It is quite important to understand the difference between fundamental accounting terms." Frank thought that the colonel did not have a clear picture of the difference between cash flow and profit and loss.

"No, but if the customers don't pay on time we are short of the money," the colonel tried. "Yes, that is precisely the cash flow, the liquidity. So if they pay faster, our liquidity is improved.

However, we register the sale as revenue when we have signed the contract and delivered the car, regardless of when it is paid," Frank insisted. "But that is a minor detail in the big picture. There are many other factors causing the company to make less money than it should."

"I don't quite understand where you're going with this," the colonel said.

Frank had taken the initiative and felt he was on safer ground – the discussion was moving in the right direction. He brought out the management reports. "See, in these reports the accounts people have analysed the development in various expense accounts and it is shocking reading."

The colonel looked at him and shrugged. "That's difficult to comment on as I haven't seen the reports."

Frank ignored the last remark.

"In the last three years our revenue has increased by 27 percent annually on average and since inflation has only been about 12 percent that's a very healthy development," Frank explained. He did not have a finance and accounts education but over the years he had acquired a good understanding of fundamental principles and he had always been good with numbers. "But when we look at the bottom line, the result drops by four percent during the same period. So something is wrong."

"I know that George is in the hospital but I believe he should have been in this meeting or, in his absence, some of his people. They must be experts when it comes to accounts," the colonel objected.

"No doubt about that but George is not available and I have received all these figures from his people. Furthermore, a lot of this is related to your area of responsibility and that's why we need to discuss it." Frank felt that he had the wind behind him and continued energetically.

"So, that's my fault, or what?" the colonel said as he felt where the conversation was going. "Did you plan this meeting, with all these numbers and reports, to hold me responsible for the company's problems?"

"No, I'm not saying it's your fault but there are some specific issues we have to discuss," Frank said, and deliberately avoided the direct confrontation too early in the meeting.

"What exactly is it we're talking about?"

"OK, you're responsible for procurement, stores and security matters. That means watchmen, contact to the police and that kind of thing," Frank said. "Correct."

"So, when we now look at a few of the important purchases, we have for instance changed the supplier of tyres three times during the period and we are now paying 74 percent more for the tyres than we did three years ago." Frank watched the colonel and awaited a reaction.

"We negotiate hard with all our suppliers and when we can't get the best terms from them we change to another. That is why we have changed supplier of tyres several times." The colonel was on the defensive now. "And then it is important for safety to use the best tyres because accidents can be fatal especially when driving on bad roads in a hot and humid climate. An exploding tyre can cost lives."

"Yes, but I'm just drawing your attention to this dramatic increase, which is significantly above inflation." Frank felt the need to park the issue of tyre purchases in order not to get lost in the details, so he let it go and attacked another issue. "Then there is this supplier of windows, Nigerian Glass. I believe his name is Okonkwo, isn't it?"

"Yes, I think that's him."

"We are paying him twice as much as we did three years ago. Does that sound correct?" Frank asked.

"I don't think it's that much but, oh well ..." the colonel began.

"It is," Frank interrupted him and he was now up to full speed and controlled the discussion. "We are paying exactly 96.4 percent more now than we did three years ago. In my books that's almost twice as much, right?"

"Yes, but to a large extent it is also new models where more complex, and more expensive, windows are required."

"Absolutely correct, but we've taken that into consideration and it only explains an 18 percent rise so there is still a dramatic increase."

The colonel looked unhappy and under pressure. They both took a gulp of coffee, the colonel with a loud slurp as if the coffee refused to leave the cup.

"Then there are the diesel purchases for our generator. That price has also increased. Apart from the fact that the consumption is considerably higher than three years ago. We consume 184 percent more diesel now than we did then. That is almost three times as much. That is crazy ... completely crazy," Frank said, and studied the colonel's reaction which was difficult to read.

"Maybe we are paying a higher price for diesel but it is extremely important to have the right quality. Otherwise we risk receiving bad diesel which can ruin the generator. That's why we only buy from suppliers we know. Apart from that, there has been scarcity for long periods of time and that's why the price is high. You are aware of that," the colonel defended himself.

Frank thought about this argument which was difficult to contest. The market price was affected by artificially created scarcity situations. Was he prepared to take a risk on the diesel and destroy a generator costing a fortune? Could the colonel be cynical enough to put some shit in the diesel and have the generator bust up just to prove a point? Frank could not rule out that the man was calculating and ruthless enough to do so. However, he had to make sure, at all costs, that the colonel did not pick up on his suspicions. No one spoke for a couple of minutes.

The discussion between Frank and the colonel continued for more than three and a half hours. It took a long time for them to agree how the purchases should be handled and how to ensure the best prices. They dug into procedures around receipt of purchases in the stores, how this was documented, the risk of fraud and possible improvements in internal procedures.

Finally, they reviewed the issue of security which Frank purposely had left for last on the agenda, as he knew that the colonel's arguments would be difficult to dispute. Generally, the colonel's idea was that if you did not spend large sums on unofficial payments to the police you exposed the company's managers to serious threats. If Frank was prepared to take a risk on this, the colonel had no problem reducing the costs, even quite considerably, but he strongly recommended not to take any chances on security. It was hard to argue against this.

"We have to put in place some tighter systems to control these things better and keep the costs down," Frank concluded when they were approaching four hours' discussion.

"To control me better, isn't that what you mean?" the colonel said. "So, I have less influence and to keep me down, or what? You have listened to rumours and now I must be put under administration. You, white people always have some fancy solutions to everything. You come in and expect to change everything in five minutes while the rest of us, who have been fighting for the company for years, are kept at a certain level and never have a chance to be promoted to managing director." The bitterness glowed from the colonel's eyes with such power that it shook Frank. It made him lose some of his momentum.

"It's not personal against you. It's a question of internal procedures unrelated to personalities," Frank said, but he heard that it sounded artificial.

"I think it looks personal when you suggest that my purchases are too expensive, I cheat with the stores and pay too much for police protection," the colonel said. He was winding himself up. "But remember, we're in Nigeria and many things are done differently here from what you're used to in Denmark or other places. There are things you can do at home that you can't do here," the colonel warned him. "You can put yourself in great danger if you don't listen to advice from people like me, who have experience in this part of the world." It sounded almost like a threat but Frank tried his best to consider the colonel innocent until proven guilty and not the opposite.

Frank did not feel quite comfortable with the situation as they were approaching the point where he had to explain to the colonel how the procedures should be tightened. His plan would mean that the colonel's responsibilities would be reduced and more decisions would have to be approved by Frank than previously.

"So, let us try to conclude at least the main points. From what we have discussed, I see the situation as follows," Frank said, and the colonel moved uneasily back and forth on his chair. "I would like to be more involved in all purchases made locally. We have to establish guidelines to ensure that prices and quality are compared according to an agreed system. I will ask the internal auditor to come up with a proposal for these guidelines."

'So far, so good,' Frank thought.

"But I hope that I'll still be responsible for procurement," the colonel said.

"Sure. We're not changing the organisation as such but we have to obtain and compare prices as well as work out a recommendation for purchases. Only when the amount is above a certain limit, of course." No further objections from the colonel. "As far as the stores are concerned, I would like to see a copy of the inventory very regularly. We must also go through all the documents that are completed in connection with goods entering and exiting the stores or transferred to production. I will also ask the internal auditor to prepare an overview of this." Frank almost felt that he was attending a debate in the House of Commons. "Last but not least, I would like to have a list of all the payments we are making for security measures. Amounts, persons and frequency, so I can have a clear picture."

"We can't do that, Frank. We have to be extremely discreet with these things. It is, in many case, unofficial payments to the police."

"I fully understand that and it has to be completely unofficial and confidential statement, only for internal use – in fact, only for me. It could even be a hand-written note. I don't ask for documentation or receipts. We consider it deeply confidential – I just want to know what we are paying, to whom and for which services."

"You are removing almost all of my responsibility and demoting me to an ordinary middle manager," the colonel complained. "It's regrettable that you have so little confidence in me." He shut the calendar hard and slammed his pen on the table.

"Let us try to run it this way. We can always loosen up again when we see that results are improving."

"Excuse me for a moment, I need to go to the gents," the colonel suddenly said, and left the board room.

Frank waited for almost ten minutes before the colonel came back and sat down at the table again. He somehow looked more relaxed now than before he left the room.

"OK, Frank. Let's try what you suggest then. I am, of course, also interested in the company making a profit," the colonel said. His mood had completely changed during the ten minutes he had been away. Now he seemed to accept the changes Frank had suggested.

By now it was getting dark outside, and the colonel suggested that they should go out for a drink – a reconciliation drink as he called it. Frank had not seen that coming and really wanted to get home but he found it hard to refuse and accepted the suggestion.

"Where should we go then? Preferably not too far away," Frank said.

"Hmm, we could go to Kakanfo Inn. There we can sit in privacy and continue discussions. We can also eat something Nigerian or Indian," the colonel suggested.

"That sounds fine. I just have to check my emails and make a couple of calls. So, let's leave in about 20 minutes, OK?"

That was a deal.

They arrived at the same time at Kakanfo Inn which was not familiar to Frank. He had heard that it was one of the reasonably acceptable hotels in town; probably half a star above mediocre, he guessed. It should be adequate for some Indian food and a couple of beers. They went to the restaurant together and here as well the colonel was a well-known person to whom the staff showed extreme respect with nervous gazes from some of the waiters. They sat down at one of the tables and were almost alone in the restaurant. However, after a little while a couple of young ladies, whom the colonel also knew, showed up. He got up and went over to their table to greet them, spoke to them for a few minutes and came back.

"It's a couple of my little sister's friends who are out for some fun, I think," he explained.

The two ladies sat at a table at the other end of the restaurant but kept an eye on Frank and the colonel while drinking Diet Coke and smoking menthol cigarettes.

A couple of large Star beers were served and Frank was thirsty after a long and exhausting day, so they quickly needed a refill. They continued the discussions where they had left off at the office but were going around in circles, except that the colonel now seemed to feel much better about the conclusions.

'Incredible,' Frank thought. He had limited the man's responsibility significantly yet he now seemed in high spirits. Perhaps because of the two young ladies who he kept throwing glances, smiling and winking at. So, it was obvious that he wanted them to stay and maybe join them at their table.

Frank had ordered a Chicken Tikka Masala with white rice while the colonel had stuck to a well-known Nigerian dish, pounded yam with a green gluey sauce. They were both hungry and ate fast, after which Frank had imagined that he would find an excuse to leave. First of all, he wanted to end the meeting with the colonel while they were still on good terms. Secondly, he really missed Ifeoma. When the waiter took their plates out they ordered their third beer but the colonel also wanted to venture into something slightly more exotic and went to the bar.

Frank had to go to the gents to get rid of some of the liquid. When he came out of the toilet he bumped into one of the girls from the restaurant who was looking the other way.

"Oh, sorry. I didn't see you," she said, and looked up and down him making it too obvious that the collision had not been coincidental. She moved closer to him and took his hand.

"I like how tall you are?" She smelled strongly of smoke and perfume. She put a small piece of paper in his hand. "Call me when you feel like it. I'd like to know you, OK?" She winked at him, turned around and went towards the ladies but stopped again, turned around and had a quick glance at Frank. He put the note in his pocket without looking at it but thought that he had to remember to throw it out before getting home so Ifeoma would not see it. They were not exactly married but she would certainly not approve, if she should find a note with a girl's name and a mobile number.

When he came back to the restaurant, the colonel had ordered a couple of cognacs which had already been served. There was also a packet of small cigars and the colonel offered Frank one which he accepted. Then they touched glasses and tasted the cheap cognac of unknow brand. It reminded Frank of a holiday in Spain with some class mates from high school and lots of cheap booze many years earlier. The cognac burned in his throat. Beer, cognac, cigars and, Frank was guessing, female company at the table would not be long. Absolutely right, a couple of minutes later the two princesses came waltzing over to their table bringing their small handbags and cigarettes, obviously to stay. The colonel showed with a hand gesture that they were welcome to sit down and the girl whom Frank had met in front of the toilet showed signs of feeling some kind of ownership as she sat next to him and moved her chair close to his.

"So, what can we offer two fine girls like you?" the colonel asked, comfortably reclining and with a smile on his face. "I think you need a real ladies' drink – something like a Bailey's with ice, isn't it?" They both smiled and nodded approvingly and the colonel signalled the waiter who came running right away. "We need two double Bailey's with ice for these two young ladies and then two more cognacs and double this time. The last ones we got were too small."

"No, I don't really think … I need to get going," Frank tried half-heartedly but he could see that it would be difficult to get away at that point. He decided that this would be the last cognac. They were smoking and drinking and the girls started giggling to each other. The girl next to Frank had now moved her chair even closer to his and had taken a firm grip of his thigh. He was getting drunk and feared that before long he would begin to feel like getting to know the young lady showing such interest in him.

At the same time, he also felt the smoke bothering him and suddenly felt sick. 'We haven't had that much to drink,' he thought, but it was rapidly getting worse.

He had to go to the bathroom where he felt dizzy and fell on his knees in front of a toilet and the horrible stink did not reduce his nausea. He threw up violently several times and coughed for a while before getting back on his feet but he felt even more dizzy and his sight was blurry. Very strange feeling. He staggered back to the restaurant where the three others looked at him mystified. Frank almost fell down on his chair and leaned forward with his elbows on the table. Their mouths were moving but he could not hear anything except a strong buzzing in his ears. Then everything went black.

Chapter Twenty-Seven

Frank slowly regained consciousness and the first thing he sensed was a sharp light in his eyes. He struggled to remember what had happened and work out where he was. He felt terrible. He lay on one side with his face towards the light and tried to open his eyes, with the result that the world turned upside down and everything was spinning around. He could just about see that the light came from an opening in the curtain – so it was daytime. He scratched his chest and discovered that he was naked. Then he felt a hand on his stomach and was kissed on his neck while the hand moved down towards his naked crotch and took a grip of his hardening dick. The kisses moved to his cheek and the hand started masturbating him. He was incredibly dizzy, completely exhausted and unable to do anything physically demanding, such as opening his eyes. He rolled onto his back, still with his eyes closed, and was now kissed on his mouth. The taste was unfamiliar, strange and he tried to free himself but was weak and being held firmly. He felt beard stubble and the shocking reality that he was kissing a man manifested itself in his unstable world. Frank tore himself loose and rolled over the edge of the bed onto the floor where he threw up immediately – a cascade of what looked mostly like muddy water. He coughed a bit, got his breath back and stumbled up on shaky legs.

"Oh, Frank. Don't you like it? Last night you were having such a good time. Don't you feel fine this morning?" said the young man who had just kissed and played with him.

Frank did not answer but walked away from the window where he hoped to find a bathroom.

On the way, he stubbed his toes on a table but reached the bathroom just in time to vomit again. He had to kneel in front of the toilet to empty his stomach until there was nothing left except cramps and a severe stomach ache.

He kept hanging on the toilet edge for a while before struggling to his feet and into the shower cubicle, where he had difficulty adjusting the old and rusty taps to have water the right temperature. The shower only improved Franks condition marginally. He saw no signs of toiletries nor drinking water and he did not feel like getting tap water into his mouth so he spat a few times and wiped his mouth. Then he put a large towel around his waist and went back to the room where the man lay naked on the bed. Frank could not avoid noticing how impressively equipped the man was and his stomach confirmed its unstable nature. He dragged himself over to an armchair and fell into it with heavy moan.

"Who the hell are you and what's going on here?" he stammered exhaustedly.

"You know that, Frank. Why don't you come over here? It was so nice last night."

"Shut up." Frank sat on the chair crouching and shaking his head. "And put on some clothes – it makes me sick."

"But yesterday you said ..."

"Shut the fuck up about yesterday. I can't remember anything and I feel like shit," Frank shouted. "And put some clothes on and get out of here."

"OK, if that's the way you want it, I'll just get lost." The man dressed hurriedly while Frank recognised his own clothes in a bundle on a chair. He avoided looking himself in the mirror.

"OK, Frank. I'm off. Do you want my number?"

"OUT." The man looked offended, left the room and slammed the door behind him. Frank got up and stood there swaying in the middle of the room, then picked up his clothes. Only then did he notice a thick brown envelope with his name on it. He tore it open and poured the contents, which was a bundle of photos, onto the table. He gasped when he saw himself in several very compromising situations.

He remembered nothing and must have been unconscious. The pictures were generally taken from an angle behind Frank where his eyes were not visible. On one of the pictures the young man sat on the bed with Frank on his knees in front of him and with his erect cock in his mouth.

On one of the other pictures they both lay naked on the bed, apparently kissing each other but this picture was also taken in such a way that Frank's face was only partly visible. He flicked through the pictures and had to take another trip to the bathroom to empty his stomach of the very last contents.

It was clear that he had been drugged the evening before even though he had no idea how it had been done; maybe in the food, maybe in one of his drinks. He imagined the pictures circulating in the most problematic places and he knew that it could cost him dearly.

He put on his creased clothes – the same as he had worn the day before. His phone was on the table and he now noticed the 14 missed calls from Ifeoma who had to be extremely worried about not being able to contact him all night.

He sent her a text message as he did not feel like talking to her right now: "Hi honey. So sorry! I'm coming home now and will explain what happened. Love Frank." She did not answer it.

Upon leaving the room, he ran into the colonel who, at the same time, came out of another room together with the two young ladies from the night before. When he saw Frank, he smiled and whispered something into the ear of one of the women, gave them both a slap on the butt and then they wiggled away down the corridor to the stairs at the end.

"Oh my God, Frank. You look terrible today. What happened to you last night? You were so wild." Then he looked up and down the corridor, where there was obviously nobody, and whispered to Frank: "If you prefer men you should just have said so. Then I could have helped you organise it. You know, these things are not accepted here in Africa. People think it's wrong, almost criminal, to be gay. You risk getting into serious trouble if this becomes known."

"Hell no. It's not like that at all. I have no clue how that guy got into my room," Frank said desperately.

"You don't need to explain anything to me. I'm not saying anything – you can trust me. We all have our little secrets but take my advice and be very discreet about it." The colonel winked at him and left the same way as the girls. Frank waited a moment and then went down to the reception where he paid his bill in a hurry. He was still dizzy.

When he got home, Ifeoma was not there and he found a little handwritten note on the night table in his bedroom: "Frank. I was worried sick. Where were you all night? Hope you have a good explanation. I have gone to my sister's. See you. Your Ifeoma."

He understood that she wanted to punish him by leaving for her sister's place and he was sad that she was not there. On the other hand, it suited him well because it gave him some time to recover and, not least, prepare what he wanted to say to her. He would have a hard time telling her what happened.

Frank was pleased that it was Sunday and he had the house to himself. It was particularly an advantage when one was completely wasted and ready to go to bed, which was precisely what he did. A couple of pain killers, a glass of water and a couple of hours' sleep later he felt a whole lot better. However, he still desperately tried not to think through the entire scenario around his waking up. His stomach now felt much more stable and he made a couple of fried eggs and some sausages which he devoured with generous amounts of salt, pepper, Tabasco and Dijon mustard.

Now he just needed to do one thing; call Ifeoma and ask her to come back as soon as possible.

"Hi, Ifeoma, it's me. I just wanted to see if you can come over so we can talk." The silence lasted a few seconds too long.

"Frank. You bastard. What the hell is it you're doing. I was so scared." "It's a long story but please come over. I miss you."

"I really don't know. Give me a couple of hours then I'll call you back." She had never sounded this cold in the time he had known her.

Exactly two hours later he heard the gate open and saw Ifeoma walk up the driveway. He gave a sigh of relief.

She only offered a quick kiss on the cheek when she came inside and seemed somewhat cool. They sat down and looked at each other for a few moments. Then she spoke.

"Frank. When you didn't come home last night, I was extremely worried and you didn't even call. I tried to call so many times but you didn't answer. Do have somebody else?" She seemed afraid of hearing the answer.

"Honestly, Ifeoma. I wasn't with somebody else. I don't have anybody but you. Believe me." There was more to tell but Frank had little desire to tell that story. "The story is really painful and I can hardly bring myself to tell you." He sighed and looked down at the table.

"But Frank. That sounds awful if you can't even talk about it."

"I think I was tricked into an ambush by the colonel. We went out for dinner after a long meeting in the office. Suddenly I felt bad and I can't even remember how it ended. I just blacked out completely." She looked like she had a lot of questions but he held up his hand to show that she should wait. "The next morning, that is today ... So, this morning, when I woke up in the hotel room, goddammit, there was another man in the room. They had also taken some disgusting pictures which could have consequences for my career if they use them against me." He took a deep breath of relief and resignation while shaking his head slowly. He raised his head and his eyes met hers.

"It's obvious that it was arranged and that you were drugged," she said. "Somebody took that kind of picture to have something on you so they can use it against you if it becomes necessary. It can hurt you seriously if they use them." They both pondered the situation before she continued. "We are up against some really bad guys, Frank. You can see that, can't you?" Of course he could but he said nothing.

"But I hope you don't get a taste for other men and dump me," she said, trying to cheer him up. He did not find it funny – his sense of humour had got lost somewhere along the way.

The next morning Frank had just sat down to have breakfast when he heard Ifeoma's phone ring. She had, apparently, left it on the bar the previous evening. He went to pick it up and bring it to her in the bedroom but it was still ringing when he got there.

He could not help but see that the display read "Colonel".

Chapter Twenty-Eight

Frank's heart skipped a beat when he saw that it was the colonel calling Ifeoma. Did she know him, and if she did, how? Did they have something going together? Was it a conspiracy against him? He was overwhelmed by anger, disappointment and feelings he could not yet define. He clenched his jaw, went into the bedroom and knocked on the bathroom door. She opened the door with a towel wrapped around her head. He handed her the phone without speaking.

"Did my phone ring?" she asked.

"Yes, it did but finish in there and get dressed. There's something we have to discuss," he said.

"OK, just a minute," she said cheerfully.

He went to the kitchen and put on the electric kettle for a cup of coffee. He looked out of the window to the front yard and the driveway. He saw the cook sitting on a chair in front of the boys' quarters with eyes closed. He was waiting for Frank to open the door for him but Frank did not want him inside until he had talked to Ifeoma. He stepped back as the cook opened his eyes and looked towards the house. The water was boiling and he made two cups of coffee. Then he went to the dining room and sat down at the table. While waiting for Ifeoma, Frank sent a text message to Mrs Adebayo informing her that he would come to the office later.

Ifeoma came from the bedroom wearing shorts and a large loose T-shirt but no make-up. She had clearly dressed in a hurry as she must have felt that something was wrong. She came over to kiss him but he turned his cheek.

"Morning, my darling. How are you this morning?" she said smiling. "Hmm, well ... actually, not very well, you know," he grumbled.

"Oh, is something wrong. You don't look happy."

Frank did not really feel like having this unpleasant conversation about the colonel's call but he knew it was unavoidable and decided to get straight to the point.

"Listen. We haven't known each other for very long. I'm not quite sure how we ended up being together but I have started liking you, and the sex, well, the sex is just amazing." He paused for a moment, drank some coffee and swallowed again before continuing. "A little while ago, when you were showering, your phone rang and I couldn't avoid seeing that the display said "Colonel". His mouth was dry and he drank some more coffee. She began to look uncomfortable and wanted to say something but he raised his hand to stop her. "I also want to say this: Since we met, a lot of strange and very unpleasant things have happened to me and around me. I have a suspicion that the colonel is behind some of it and I'm trying to find out what's going on. You never told me that you knew him but now I discover, by chance, that he's fucking calling you." Frank took a deep breath, got up and walked around the dining table. "Please explain to me what the hell you're running around doing," he said, raising his voice. He sat down again and looked at her.

She sat with her head bowed and said nothing for a while. "Answer me for Christ sake," he shouted, and hit the table hard. It startled her and she looked up with tears in her eyes, still not speaking. "Oh no, don't give me that bullshit. Don't sit there and act hurt. I just want to know what the hell is going on."

"Frank, I'm terribly sorry about this but please let me try to explain. Please try to listen to what I have to say." "I'm all ears."

"It wasn't a coincidence when we met," she began hesitantly. "I didn't even have anything to do with your dealer convention. I was asked to come ... no, wait, I'll start from the beginning." She dried her eyes and took a deep breath. "The big man, the dealer from Port Harcourt, is not my father but I know him from before. I was his girlfriend for a few years and he was good to me.

He was kind of my "sugar daddy" as we call it. Later he found a new girlfriend and dumped me. He likes very young and slim girls. I had become too old and fat but we were still friends and he helped me with money when I moved to Lagos and needed a place to stay." She paused for a while and sighed. She looked at him to see how he reacted to all of this. Frank tried not to react at all. He had promised to hear her entire story.

"The man knows the colonel and I think he owes him a favour or maybe the colonel has something on him. So, it's difficult for him to say no when the colonel asks him for a favour. He called me and explained that one of his friends, the colonel, needed help to get some information. It was all about getting to know a man and make him talk about certain things related to his company. Maybe not company secrets, but information the man's friend would pay well for. That's the only explanation I got. I was not very keen on accepting that kind of thing. I didn't want to do it but I really needed the money so I said yes. I took it as a job and hoped that it would be over quickly. The dealer invited me to his office in Lagos to meet the colonel, and the colonel was very kind and charming in the beginning. He promised that what I needed to do would not be illegal and that I would be paid well for it. First he gave me a car and promised me money when I started giving him information." She looked at Frank but quickly looked down again.

"Shit, what a mess," Frank said bitterly. "So it was all arranged?"

"Yes, I was told who you were and that I should get to know you as soon as possible. Then I could begin finding out the things the colonel wanted to know," Ifeoma said.

The slap hit her right on the cheek and was so hard that her head swung all the way to the other side and her mouth sent a piece of saliva through the air.

"What the hell do you think you're doing, you little whore. You come here and pretend that we have something together. You play on my feelings and make me like you and then it turns out that it was all because of money. For all I had with you, I might as well have paid a hooker. At least then I would have controlled it myself. Now I pay a much higher price."

"Frank. Try to listen to me, let me explain … please?"

"That's enough. OUT," Frank yelled and pointed at the door. "Go and pack your stuff and get lost."

"Frank," she said softly and looked at him for a moment before dropping her eyes. He saw a tear drop on the table.

"OUT," he shouted again. He knew that if he hesitated he would start becoming soft and trying to understand her. He did not want to give himself time for that now because she had humiliated him, treated him like shit. He had to get rid of her before she tried to talk him round.

She got up slowly and went to the bedroom, then turned around and looked at him.

"I'm sorry, Frank," she whispered. He looked away.

Five minutes later she came out from the bedroom with her bag and walked to the main door.

"I'm so sorry," she said again. "I love you and didn't want to hurt you. I would very much like to try to make it up to you, if you want me to."

He stood in the same spot at the dining table where he had hit her. From there he saw her walk out of the door and down the driveway where the watchman opened the gate for her and closed it behind her. He felt the pressure in his chest and felt like running after her to ask her to come back and talk about it. He stayed there and watched the closed gate. His anger began to evaporate, turning into deep frustration and in the end desperation. He pulled himself together, ran out of the door and shouted to the watchmen at the gate.

"Hey, you." He did not remember the watchman's name and it did not matter. "Go and get her … run." He showed with a hand gesture that the watchman should get moving after Ifeoma.

The watchman looked confused for a brief moment but then got the message and ran out of the gate as fast as he could.

Almost ten minutes passed while Frank stood and stared at the closed gate. Then it was opened and the watchman appeared. He held the gate for Ifeoma who walked slowly, her head bent, up the driveway towards the house.

When she got to the door, he took her head in both hands and gently wiped away a tear from her cheek with his thumb.

"Come and sit down then we'll talk about it," he said. She followed him to the dining table and sat down, her purse in her lap.

"I'm so sorry I hit you. I shouldn't have done that no matter what happened," Frank said. "It's OK, Frank. I deserved it," she replied.

"You must understand how difficult it is for me to accept or understand what you have done."

It took a moment, then she sat up and looked at him.

"Frank. Listen to me. It's true that I was paid to get to know you. And I understand if you're mad at me or if you don't believe what I'm telling you now." Her voice was trembling slightly but she stayed composed. Slightly wet eyes but no tears, no panic. "When we started seeing each other I came to like you – very much. It began from the very first time I saw you. And the first night you were so nice to me and seemed like a good person. I liked you. I looked forward to being with you, not as an assignment, but as a friend, a lover."

"You are absolutely right. It is damn difficult to believe what you're now saying. So, you took this assignment where you should get to know me and collect information from me. Then, out of nowhere, you suddenly liked me and now you are almost innocent," he said.

"No, I'm not innocent but honestly, believe me, I really do like you. I just wish we could be together for our own sake just because we like each other. Can't you feel it? We've got something together and that's also why I couldn't ask you about everything I needed to, because … because I just couldn't do it." Now her eyes were a bit more wet.

"I'm struggling to believe some of what you are telling me now," he said and shook his head.

"And how did you imagine this would end?"

"I don't know, Frank. I thought it would only be for a short time, relatively easy to do. Then I could get my money and move on with life. I would never have done it if the dealer hadn't asked me to. He had been so good to me and he owed the colonel a favour. It became complicated," she said.

"But I still don't quite understand," he wondered. "You haven't been able to get very much information. So, what have you been telling this colonel who wants to know so much?"

"No, I haven't and that's been a huge problem and he has become really mean lately. He is threatening me with all kinds of ugly stuff if I don't tell him about everything you do and what your plans are," she said.

"Yeah, no wonder if he's given you a car and money and then you don't deliver," Frank said. "And what do you think he will do if he doesn't get what he paid for. He's not exactly an angel?" "He's evil all the way into his soul, the devil himself," she said. "Frank, let's run away from here. Let's get away and start over somewhere else. Or, if you don't want me to come with you, then go alone. You're in too much danger here."

"I can't. I just can't," Frank said. "There's no way I can run away from this. Can't disappear with the tail between my legs. If I do that, I'll never be able to look myself in the eyes again. I would lose all trustworthiness. No, I can't run away. I have to finish this." He got up and took the cups to the kitchen, then he walked around the sitting room as he often did when something was on his mind. He looked at his watch and it was only nine o'clock.

'Oh, to hell with it,' he thought and went to the bar to get the Gammel Dansk bottle. He poured two glasses, carried them to the dining table and put one in front of her.

"So, you insist that I should be addicted to your Gamle Dask," she said, and he could not help smiling at her pronunciation.

"Gammel Dansk," he said slowly and clearly.

"Gammel Dalsk," she tried again. He shook his head and smiled but gave up further pronunciation lessons.

"Well, Ifeoma, I don't know. How the hell do we move on from here," he said, and looked at her. "What do you want to do about this? I suppose you have to go and report to the colonel, don't you?"

"I have to pretend like I am giving him information but I don't want to do anything that can harm you." She sniffled and suddenly the facade cracked, she broke down sobbing and lay down over the table. "Oh, Frank, I want so much to help you but he's a mean person," she stammered out through the sobbing.

Frank got up, fetched the Gammel Dansk bottle and filled his own glass – she had not touched her own. Then he walked behind her chair and put his hands on her shoulders to comfort her.

She sat up and he could see her nipples through the T-shirt so he let his hands slide down to touch her full breasts. She stiffened slightly and he took his hands back to her shoulders. He massaged her shoulders a bit.

She turned her head from side to side and he sensed that she enjoyed it.

"I don't mind that you touch my breasts, Frank. I was just a bit surprised," she said, and he let his hands slide down to her breasts again but let go, sat down on the chair next to her and looked her in the eyes.

"I can't right now, Ifeoma. You are beautiful and everything but it just doesn't work for me today. I'm sorry."

He went to the bathroom and undressed to take a shower hoping that she would join him. She did so a few minutes later. They stood closely together and washed each other without saying a word. They kissed a little and he rubbed her back and buttocks. Somehow it was a timeout, not an end to their discussion but a break, regrouping before they had to continue. However, Frank had no clue how they would be able to reach a conclusion or in which tone their conversation would be held when they came out for the second half. He just knew that they had to come to an agreement; either to part ways or to continue, but they needed some kind of agreement. It had surprised him when he almost felt disgust for her and thought of her as a simple prostitute. He had meant it when he said that he might as well have bought sex instead but now he was uncertain what he really felt.

"We haven't finished talking about this," he said to her while they were drying themselves. "I'll go and open the door for the cook and have him make some early lunch for us so we can have an uninterrupted discussion."

"OK, Frank. I'll get ready. Just give me five minutes," she said.

"Five minutes. Does that mean half an hour or are you quicker than most women?" he asked, and was sure it would be a least half an hour. She did not reply but was already busy in front of the mirror.

Frank was dressed in two minutes. A pair of jeans, a T-shirt and bare feet in sandals and he was ready. He went to the kitchen and opened the door for the cook, drew the curtains in the sitting and dining rooms and switched on the TV. It started at Africa Magic but he quickly changed to SuperSport 3 where they were showing a repeat of an English Premier League match from the previous weekend. He had already watched the game and switched off again. A bit of music was perhaps better inspiration for the conversation they needed to finish and he chose Barry White. "What am I gonna do with you" had to be a suitable way to resume the conversation. Then he asked the cook to get started on some lunch and found a reasonable wine from the bar.

Ifeoma came out from the bedroom and looked stunning wearing a stylish dress in green and black that stopped just above her knees and was sufficiently low-necked to show off her breasts but without being vulgar. Just as he liked it. A pair of long earrings matching the dress and her own short hair gave her a sporty look. All of this completed by a pair of medium high-heeled shoes. In short, classy.

"Ah, Barry. I love Barry White," she said.

"But he must have died almost before you were born," Frank said. "No, Frank. I'm not that young and everybody knows Barry White."

"You look amazing," he said.

"Thanks, baby," she said, and leaned forward so he could kiss her cheek. He took a wineglass and poured the red Zonnebloem Pinotage for her.

Barry was singing: "Oh, what a groove? Love how you do it. Ain't what you got babe. Girl, it's how you use it."

"Let's go and sit at the bar. The cook has to set the table in a little while," he suggested.

She sat on one of the bar stools and he went inside the bar behind the counter to stand in front of her.

"So where do we go from here? And more importantly; can I trust you from now on or will I be castrated or murdered in my own bed one day?" he said.

"I have been thinking and would really like to help you. We have to agree what I should tell the colonel so it doesn't hurt you but also in such a way that he doesn't begin to suspect anything," she said, and held up her glass. "Skål, isn't that what you say in Danish." They touched glasses and he confirmed that her Danish was impeccable.

"Are you sure you dare to continue. What happens if he finds out?" Frank asked.

"He won't find out. I'm a good actress. Also, we'll prepare ourselves. I'll tell him that you're a bastard and that you hit me." She pointed at him. "And actually, you did."

"Well, yes, but he can see that I didn't hit you really hard."

"You're wrong, because you will, of course, hit me properly so I have a swollen eye or split eyebrow. It's not more complicated than that," she said, and gave him a sly smile. "And maybe you really want to hit me, right?"

"Hell no, stop it. I can't fucking hit you so you get hurt. I already felt so bad about the slap I gave you," he said, shaking his head.

"Don't worry. I'm tough so I'll just hit my head against the wall to make it look real. Just take it easy." She said, and giggled a bit.

"Shit," was all he could say. "You're really a tough cookie."

"Things have not always been easy for me. I've become hardened with time but I have survived by the grace of God."

"Does anybody know about your agreement with the colonel?" he asked.

"The dealer knows that the colonel wanted me to help with something and he arranged our first meeting but he doesn't know the details. I haven't told anybody else. Maybe the colonel has, I don't know."

"First of all, you have to try to avoid meeting him or talking to him in the next couple of days, OK? And if you can't avoid it then explain that you have been trying your best but that I am completely out of balance and impossible to talk to after the robbery," he explained. "And then the thing about me going bananas and hitting you so you've become afraid of me and have to lay low for a little while."

"Understood, boss. I am quite good at lying."

The cook looked hesitantly through the half-open kitchen door. "Eh, master, should I serve the lunch now?" he asked.

"Yes, of course," Frank replied.

They sat down at the dining table and had a quiet lunch while discussing the strategy for handling the colonel. Frank remembered George and felt bad that he had neglected him with everything that had happened. He decided that he would deal with all the other problems the following day and then show up at the office on a more regular basis.

Late afternoon he went to his home office to check his emails. A few rolled into the inbox. However, the first one that caught his attention had the following heading: "Leviticus 20:13", which did not mean a whole lot to Frank. He hesitated for a moment, then opened the mail and saw a short text with no further explanation and no signature. It simply read:

Leviticus 20:13

> If a man goes to bed with a man as with a woman, both of them have committed an abomination; they must be put to death; their blood is on them.

Frank felt it like a punch in the guts. He read the text a couple more times and knew for sure that it was a reference to the ambush he had been lured into. A malicious ambush which his enemies now intended to use against him.

Chapter Twenty-Nine

Frank had had some busy days after having recovered from the heavy sedation and the shock of his unpleasant awakening at Kakanfo Inn. In George's absence it was a major task to prepare all the documentation required for a board meeting of the company. Since this was his first formal meeting with the entire board, it was important that he gave a good impression.

The accounts department was led by a chief accountant who was unbelievably slow and Frank had asked for the same things repeatedly before anything happened. He had lost his temper a couple of times during the week but felt that it had only led to a marginal improvement from the chief accountant.

The invitation letters for the board meeting had been sent out by the company secretary long ago, together with the minutes of the last meeting which took place before Frank's arrival. Now Frank had completed the whole package of reports about the company's performance, monthly results and a number of observations which he wanted to share with the board.

The day of the meeting had come and he felt clear signs of nervousness.

He thought of the episode at Kakanfo Inn again and especially the email with the quote from Leviticus. He cursed to himself for having ended up in such a bad situation, could not sit still and felt a need to move. He decided to walk around the factory, something he had neglected during the period of all these unforeseen events, meetings and now preparation for the board meeting.

He got up and walked briskly out his door. "I'm going to the factory," he said to Mrs Adebayo, who nodded while continuing to type on her computer at high speed.

The factory area was large and Frank decided to do a round as far as he could, starting with the main store where all the CKD cars and other parts were kept in stock. The entrance to the warehouse was a 10-12 metres-wide rolling gate which was usually open but this morning it was almost completely closed. He walked there and squeezed through the narrow opening between the gate and the wall. Inside, he stood for a moment while his eyes adjusted to the change from sharp sunlight to the artificial and insufficient light inside the warehouse.

One of the stores people came driving on a forklift and braked hard when he saw Frank. He looked around, whistled and shouted at the storekeeper, "Hey, Paul, the boss is here." Then he drove down to the other end of the warehouse.

Paul now came running and looked surprised when he approached Frank. "Hello, sir, what can I do for you?" he asked slightly out of breath.

"Well, I just wanted to do a round because it's been a long time since I was here in the warehouse. What are you up to down at the other end?" Frank asked, and began walking further into the warehouse where he looked at a stack of plywood boxes. Paul almost blocked his way and was smiling anxiously.

"We just received a container with tyres from Pirelli which we are stacking properly so they don't take up too much space," Paul explained.

"Let's walk around so I can see what we have in stock for the time being," Frank said, and noticed Paul's hesitant reaction.

"Yes, yes, of course." Paul said, turned around quickly and glanced down towards the other end of the warehouse where the forklift had just loaded a rather large wooden box. While they were walking down the warehouse, the forklift came racing past them and Frank saw that "Nigerian Glass" and an address in Ghana was painted with large black letters on the box. Paul noticed and quickly explained. "It's faulty car windows which we are returning to Nigerian Glass." That was the unpleasant Okonkwo's company whom Frank had not heard from since their first encounter. He thought that it would be worthwhile to investigate the matter in more depth. He had never heard about wrong or faulty deliveries of car windows before and certainly not windows to be returned to Nigerian Glass in Ghana. He just had to find a way to enter the warehouse when nobody else was there so he could investigate it properly without interference. Even in the morning, before the storekeeper arrived, the watchmen would see him if he went into the warehouse – same in the evening. Besides, how would he get the key to the warehouse?

He had to ask George as soon as possible. Maybe there were other ways into the warehouse.

After about a half hour's tour of the factory, Frank went back to his office and read through his reports once again to be on top of all the matters he wanted to bring up with the board. The first impression was important and he would be remembered by most of the board members for the way he handled his first meeting.

West African Motors' board member from Kano, Alhaji Abdullahi, was the first to arrive, half an hour before the meeting was scheduled to start. They had not met before and had a brief introductory conversation before Abdullahi went to the board room. Then they arrived one by one; Mr Osita from Imo State was the next arrival and he presented himself as the company's Igbo-representative and seemed proud of it. The company secretary had arrived early. The two representatives from the new Saudi Arabian owners arrived shortly before the meeting started. It surprised Frank that they had not found it useful to arrive a day earlier, possibly to be shown the factory and have a better understanding of the company's activities. Apparently, they had complete confidence in the chairman, Chief Adeyemi.

The chairman was actually the last to arrive. He sat down at the table in the board room two minutes late, when everybody else was already seated. He did not find it necessary to apologise for his late arrival.

Frank recognised the chairman's strong aftershave which he could still smell on his hand after the handshake. The chairman took off his hat, put it on the table and closed his eyes. "Let us begin with the opening prayer," he said, and started praying. "God Almighty. We thank you for your mercy and we pray that you will forgive our human weaknesses and errors." Frank lost concentration and began wondering how he would possibly be able to make it through such an opening prayer, should he be asked to deliver it. Or what if the chairman planned to check his prayer competencies by asking him to do today's closing prayer, provided there was one on the agenda? "We pray that you will help us in our challenges to make this company successful and profitable to the benefit of all employees, shareholders and other stakeholders."

'Oh, this is quite a practically-oriented prayer,' Frank thought, while practising a possible closing prayer in his mind. After a few minutes the chairman finished the prayer, put on his hat and cleared his throat.

"So, Mr Company Secretary, let us go through the minutes of the last meeting page by page and I would ask the board members to comment and make suggestions of any amendments. I assume that everybody has read the minutes thoroughly," the chairman said, and looked around, turned to the secretary and gave him the word. Under the strict guidance of the chairman they spent ten minutes amending details in the wording of the minutes of meeting which, in Frank's opinion, was mainly completely academic just as minimal spelling errors were debated far too thoroughly.

Thereafter the chairman took the floor mainly to welcome the new owners' representative. "Gentlemen, since our last board meeting major things have happened, including a dramatic and tragic incident, but today I wish to focus on the more positive changes." He paused for a moment while tasting his tea. It was apparently not sweet enough as he grimaced, pushed the cup towards Frank showing two fingers – so, two pieces of sugar in the tea. "We have, first of all, new investors whose representatives are present here today. I welcome Prince al-Mansour and Mr Faisal. It is a pleasure to welcome you and be your host during your stay in Nigeria. I look forward to a long and mutually beneficial cooperation in years to come."

This was news to Frank but he guessed that the chairman had insisted that the new owners should stay with him during their short stay. This way he could politically strengthen his position.

The prince acknowledged the chairman's words with a little nod and a hint of a smile while Faisal kept a straight face. It seemed like he had come along to carry the prince's bag and possibly handle other practical details. He looked like a bodyguard.

"Furthermore, we should not forget that we have a new managing director. He is sitting here beside me and we'll have the opportunity to go through his management reports in a little while.

Welcome to Frank Grabowski, to whom I wish the best of luck in the management of this company," the chairman continued.

Then it was Frank's turn to present his management report to the board. He started with a short presentation on himself and his experience over the past 15 years. Thereafter, he went through the tables in the report which showed the company's performance year-to-date compared with the previous year and with the budget. Frank had also studied the budget thoroughly and had prepared a list of details in the budget which he thought were unrealistic, both positively and negatively. It was, after all, his predecessor who had prepared the budget and had it approved by the board but Frank was responsible for living up to it. He wanted to make sure that certain concerns were noted as early as possible. This suited the chairman well and he gave Frank an appreciative nod.

Frank was still so new that nobody on the board could blame him for the fact that the performance left something to be desired. Several of them had heard about his problems and wanted to hear how he looked at the developments since his arrival. On this point the chairman cut in and assured the board that he supported the new managing director fully and that he would do everything in his power to assist him. He would also put in place all security measures to avoid the risk of something happening to the managing director. There was a discreet reference to the accident Frank's predecessor had had although it was not specifically mentioned. The chairman's clear comments also meant that the other board members did not feel like digging into the questions around Frank's problems and the issue was closed there.

The meeting ended without the prince having said very much apart from an expression of his deep gratitude for the chairman's hospitality. His henchman, Faisal, as far as Frank had observed, perhaps did not speak much English. The chairman closed with comments about the importance of the entire team working together and how important it was to the success of the company that Frank proved to be the man who could gather the troops and ensure that everybody was pulling in the same direction. Nobody from the management team was mentioned but Frank was convinced that the chairman made reference to their meeting about the colonel and in his own subtle way reminded him to cooperate. Then the formal part of the meeting was over and they adjourned for lunch.

During the entire lunch it was clear to everybody how strong a personality the chairman was, and how little anybody wanted to disagree with him. At one point during the discussions they touched upon football and, not surprisingly, they immediately focused on the English Premier League. This led the chairman towards a former star, Justin Fashanu, about whom he had recently watched a TV programme. Fashanu had Nigerian roots and was a huge talent whose career got off to a good start from his youth. However, his career derailed when he later came out of the closet as being gay. When he was accused of sexual assault on a 17-year old American man it went from bad to worse for him and it ended with him committing suicide. The programme had apparently inspired the chairman to some considerations about what was right and wrong.

"But think about it! What is it that makes men sleep with other men? There are so many beautiful women in the world and then some men, incredibly enough, prefer to be with other men. I mean, it is very strange. Wrong quite simply." He stopped his speech shaking his head while pouring a glass of water. "When you buy a lawn mower it comes with a manual. So, the manual for life would be the Bible, isn't it?" Nobody seemed to feel like commenting on the chairman's wise words and he continued. "And according to the Bible it is despicable to be with people of the same sex. Well, apart from the fact that it is gross." The chairman's disgust showed in his face and Frank felt his gaze pass across and stop at him for a brief moment but he felt no desire to comment on the chairman's remarks. Frank obviously had his opinion on the matter but he had long ago realised that, to a very large extent, it was not acceptable to be homosexual in Africa and would not be in his lifetime. However, he had more or less given up being a spokesperson for human rights in this respect.

The attitude seemed archaic to him. On the other hand, the chairman's little speech indicated to him that what had happened in the room at Kakanfo Inn had perhaps, partly or fully, been communicated. Frank felt that the chairman's speech had been directed towards him but probably, and hopefully, none of the other participants had had that thought.

After the meeting there were various informal conversations in smaller groups for about 15-20 minutes before, one by one, they said goodbye to Frank, thanked him for a good meeting and wished him good luck taking the company forward. As Frank had guessed, Faisal carried the prince's bag and during the farewell formalities still did not prove that he possessed the power of speech.

Frank went to his office, sat down and sent a text message to Ifeoma as he had not spoken to her for a couple of days and missed her. "Hi baby, am through with the board meeting. Still alive. How about you, are you OK?"

The answer beeped in on his Samsung phone shortly after. "Am OK. Will go the colonel tonight." Frank did not like it. He was afraid something would happen to her and could not see how she could get out of the trouble she had gotten herself into.

Frank sent her a short reply. "Take good care of yourself." He had a strange uneasy and tight feeling in his chest, a sense that something was wrong, or perhaps rather that something was right – with Ifeoma. Something between them, something with her in his life and the other way around. It was the first time he had this feeling or at least the first time he admitted it to himself. She had not come into his life like a princess in a Hans Christian Andersen adventure, far from it, but her presence had affected him. She had begun meaning something to him, much more than just the physical pleasure.

'I just hope nothing happens to her,' he thought.

Chapter Thirty

George felt that things were improving, at least physically. He still found it difficult to keep track of the days but it had to be around two weeks since he was attacked by armed robbers. The pain was still bad but now at least it was sufficiently under control that he could sleep properly. Actually, he lay most of the day floating back and forth between being half awake and asleep. Perhaps they had started giving him more painkillers because he felt weak and drowsy all the time. He was now fully aware of the fact that his leg had been amputated above his knee. He felt terrible about it and he still could not get himself to look at it. Most of all he felt like screaming out loud but he did everything possible to maintain his composure.

While he lay pondering, and getting depressed by his dark future, Sade came through the door with a bouquet of flowers and a big smile.

"Hey, honey," she said, and came straight to him and gave him a big kiss. "How are you doing, baby?"

"Hi, my love. I'm better but I still seem to feel pain in the leg I no longer have and it's very unpleasant."

"Femi called and said that your wife had been here but that I could come today so I hurried out here. I missed you like crazy."

"I missed you too but I would rather have met over a Guinness at Sadelicious than here in this godforsaken place."

"Don't worry, George. It won't be long before you're out of here."

"There was something else I was thinking about, Sade," George said, and tried to collect his thoughts. He was suddenly in doubt about how well Sade knew Frank. Perhaps she had only met him once, the evening when he was attacked.

"You remember Frank, don't you," he asked.

"Yes, of course. You came to Sadelicious together that night when you were attacked. He also called me a few days later to hear if I was aware that you had been shot. That was sweet of him but why do you ask?"

"Because I think he could be in danger and we have to do whatever we can to help him." "You're probably right, George but what exactly did you have in mind?"

"Maybe you could give him some advice and warn him about some of the people in the company again. Also, I don't think he has a weapon and that could be useful for him to have, don't you think?"

"Just take it easy, honey. I'll talk to him and help him," she said, and George felt lucky having such a beautiful and wise lady by his side.

Sade sat on a chair next to George's bed holding his hand while softly humming "Abide with me" to him. At the same time there was a knock on the door and Frank turned up.

"Hello, George. It's good to see you and you look like you're feeling better," Frank said, gave George a firm handshake and held his hand with both hands.

"Thank you, Frank. Yes, I'm a bit better now. It still hurts like hell but not so much that I can't live with it. I think they have started giving me some more painkillers but I'm just so tired."

He saw Frank greeting Mama Sade politely and shaking hands with Femi. They seemed to have met before, although George was not aware of when and where.

"Listen, Frank. I know that it's very inconvenient that I can't work for a while but I hope you won't throw me out. As soon as I feel a bit better, I can work from home and soon after that I can start coming to the office from time to time." George was seriously worried that the company would retire him now that he had become incapacitated for a long time, so he made a huge effort to seem as fresh as possible to Frank.

"No, take it easy, my friend. There's no rush. As soon as you feel a bit better and come home we can arrange some brief working sessions with your accounts people so we don't lose anything along the way. Don't worry about this – just concentrate on getting well again," Frank said, and sounded as if he meant it. Perhaps he was just being considerate to George as long as he was in the hospital.

They sat there for a while without speaking but Frank looked like he had something on his mind.

"Oh yes, George, by the way, there was another thing I wanted to ask you about. I went to the warehouse the other day and it looked like the people panicked when they saw me. They were clearly not comfortable having me running around. I would like to snoop around but preferably without anybody knowing about it," Frank said. So that was what he had been mulling over. George immediately knew what he had in mind.

"So, you would like to know how to get into the warehouse without anybody seeing you, isn't it?" George asked.

"Exactly, George. Can you think how I can get in there without being seen by the stores people, watchmen or anybody else for that matter?"

"Listen," George said, and noticed Frank's wide-open eyes. "In the small kitchen in your section on the first floor there is a hatch in the ceiling. Up there in the loft there's enough space for you to crawl on hands and knees across to the warehouse. It must be about 12-15 metres away, I would think."

"So there's no direct access from the office block into the warehouse?"

"No, you have to get up into the loft. I have never been there myself but I have looked up there and it should be possible without too much trouble. Then when you get to the warehouse there's another hatch where you can get out and climb down. You can also see it from inside the warehouse and it is placed quite high up. There are metal steps in the wall so you don't need rope or mountaineering equipment.

"Perfect, George."

"But you'll have to do it in the evening when people have left the office and the warehouse. "Yes, I'll find an excuse to stay a bit longer one of these days," Frank said.

"Be aware, though, that it is probably filthy up there and there could be rats. I believe that I've heard them move about up there when I'm in the office late in the evening." "I hope there's no alarm in the warehouse, is there?"

"No, there's no alarm. The watchmen walk around the entire office and warehouse building from time to time during the evening and the night but they don't have a key to the warehouse. So, just avoid making noise and if you carry a torch be careful where you direct it."

"Excellent. I'll find the right time and then be careful not to fall down from the loft and into the warehouse," Frank said, and looked enthusiastic.

George was tired and no matter how desperately he tried to seem fresh he was dozing off. Frank noticed because he tapped George's hand and said, "Well I better get going. We just had a board meeting so there's a lot of follow-up."

"Yes, OK. I hope the board meeting went well and that you received everything you needed from the accounts department," George said. He sensed a strong feeling of powerlessness.

Frank had needed his assistance to prepare properly for a difficult board meeting and he had not been there. It was a terrible situation for him.

"The meeting actually went quite well, I must say. He's a tough guy, the chairman, but I survived," Frank said with a smile.

"But, Frank. There's something I haven't told you," George said, and noticed that Frank's expression changed from enthusiastic to insecure. "The night I was shot, the robbers said something about me being in bad company. They must have meant you because we had just been together at Sadelicious."

"That's a strange thing to say. Do you think it was more than a robbery?"

"I don't know, Frank, but it surprised me that they would say something like that."

"Anyway, thanks for mentioning it," Frank said, and started getting up but George took his hand.

"Frank … be careful." Frank nodded and George let go of his hand.

When Frank got up, Mama Sade followed him out of the room and George assumed that she would suggest a meeting with him as they had agreed.

Chapter Thirty-One

Frank arrived at Sadelicious around 8 p.m. as he had agreed with Mama Sade and looked around before entering. The last after-work guests were on their way home and the late rush had not started yet, so the place was almost empty. Mama Sade sat at the bar with a beer, got up quickly and came to greet him as he entered.

"Hi, Frank. Thanks for coming. Do you want anything to drink?" she asked, and gave him a hug and a kiss on the cheek.

"Yes, why not. Let me have a gin and tonic," Frank said, and looked around for a suitable place to sit down.

She shook her head and took her beer from the counter. "No, come with me in the back," she said, and instructed the young girl behind the bar to send a gin and tonic and some peanuts there.

In the back, she sat down at one of the small tables and Frank could not ignore her voluminous bosom when she bent forward to sit down. He almost felt like he was being sucked down between her breasts where he treaded water to avoid being absorbed by bottomless quicksand. Oh, what a death. She noticed, smiled and adjusted her blouse to cover her breasts marginally better.

"I am really very sorry about George," Frank began. He was not sure what she wanted to talk to him about and he wanted first of all to express his compassion.

"I know, Frank. You don't have to tell me. I came to know you through George and I know how much he respects you even though you've only worked together for a short time." She put her hand on his forearm. "And that's why he is so worried about what could happen. Do you understand?" She looked him in the eyes and gave his arm a little squeeze. "You're a good guy, Frank but there are things going on in that company and it could all become very dangerous if you prevent them from continuing with what they are doing."

"I know that something is going on but I have not been able to get the full picture yet. It's clear to me that there are some bad people involved in the management of the company," Frank said, while he took her hand in his. It felt reassuring to talk to her although he did not know her that well.

"Listen to me, Frank. Power and money do strange things to people and they are involved in some criminal stuff and making a lot of money out of it too. I only know what I hear from George and a couple of other people that I know in the company … yes, and then what I have been able to figure out myself – because I'm not a silly bimbo. I actually worked for the company some time ago and that's where I met George. I had a central function in the procurement department but when Colonel Chuks came in, my work was quickly made redundant. He brought in his own people and didn't want me to know how they operated. In the end it became unbearable. So, I quit, got my gratuity and opened this bar – together with George by the way but that's confidential."

Dammit! She had worked for the company. Frank had not been aware but now understood much better how she knew George and how she could have so much inside knowledge about the company's operations and employees.

"But, Sade, what is it they're doing and who's involved apart from the colonel?"

"I don't know all the details, Frank, but one thing is for sure, the colonel is the key figure. I assume you know that he tried to put himself forward as a candidate for the job when the former managing director died?"

"What!" Frank now remembered Simon's comments at their meeting in Copenhagen. It was, of course, the colonel he had been talking about as the head of department who was interested in the job. The colonel had seriously hoped and tried to become managing director of the company which logically made him an adversary, perhaps even an enemy. Frank suddenly remembered a comment made by the colonel during their recent meeting when he had said something along the lines of: "You white people think you know it all and the rest of us never get a chance," or something like that.

"It's true and I heard that there was a time he was even bragging to his friends about taking over the job," she said. "You also have to be aware that his people in the procurement department and the store are almost all completely loyal to him. They all get something out of it and they are as thick as thieves. Some suppliers as well, amongst others the guy who supplies windows but maybe also suppliers of tyres and other parts purchased locally."

Mama Sade patted him on the cheek and smiled before continuing. "But I wanted to make sure you understand how dangerous this could be. We're not talking about peanuts and we're dealing with totally ruthless people here." She paused for a moment while the young girl served Frank's gin and tonic. Then she got up, locked the door and went behind a desk where she opened a large safe. After a couple of minutes, she came back with a plastic bag and placed it on the table.

"It's important that you can defend yourself and I heard how you took care of the robbers at your house so you can probably also handle this one properly." She pulled a shoebox out of the plastic bag, opened it and took out a handgun. "This is a Glock 17, nine-millimetre pistol with 17 shots in the magazine. A neat little thing, easy to use and incredibly popular all over the world because it's so reliable and weighs very little. It's a nine-millimetre, so you can't shoot through an engine block but it can easily do damage to the bad guys if need be."

Mama Sade handed him the gun but Frank hesitated a bit before taking it.

"Hello, wake up. You swung around an AK-47 and shot a robber with it so this little toy pistol can't scare you." She burst into a loud laugh and pinched his cheek. She quickly showed him how to load and take out the magazine, how to ensure that there was no round in the chamber and how to operate it generally. Then she pulled out a couple of boxes of ammunition from the shoebox. "Here are the bullets. Let me know if you need more. There's an extra magazine in the box that you need to fill but it's better that you do it yourself so you get the feel of it. This is the permit for the gun. It's in my name so I'll have it changed to your name through a connection in the police tomorrow." She looked at him while he sat and played with the gun, inserted the magazine a couple of times and weighed it in his hand. "It's a fine little gun, the Glock, isn't it?" She pushed him with the elbow and laughed. "It costs 500 Dollars, is that OK? And that's with the permit, Frank."

'She's a hell of a woman, this Mama Sade,' Frank thought.

"Yeah, I'm not a simple bar mama, am I?" she laughed. Then she became more serious. "But there's something else, Frank. This, your girlfriend." Frank wanted to interrupt her but she made a gesture with her hand and continued. "Yeah, yeah, I'm aware that you have a local girlfriend but I don't know her. Is she trustworthy? Maybe she's nice and pretty but money is everything to a Nigerian woman, and she may sacrifice you for some quick money. Maybe she's even part of a conspiracy. You don't have to explain anything to me but think about it. Generally, you should be very careful who you talk to about your problems. You can't trust anybody 100 percent, except me and George of course. And for God's sake, be careful in everything you do."

Then she packed the gun and the ammunition back in the shoebox and the plastic bag, got up, unlocked the door and looked outside.

"Patience, bring one gin and tonic and a Guinness in here now now."

"Sade, I really appreciate everything that you're doing for me. I really do. It would be great if you let me know if you hear anything else that could be helpful."

She grabbed Frank by the neck and pulled him closer thus pressing her voluminous femininity against his shoulder. She surprised Frank by giving him a big kiss on the mouth.

"OK, my son, watch yourself, OK?" she said, and smiled at him. "And then I don't think you should come back here again. You never know if they are following you. It's OK that you've been here tonight but you should not be seen here too often. When you're leaving, I'll send one of the girls with you. You hold her hand when you leave and she will carry this bag. Then it looks like you came for a pick-up, OK?" Frank nodded and took a gulp of his gin and tonic.

They finished their drinks and he left the bar accompanied by the girl, as Mama Sade had arranged, and drove home.

Chapter Thirty-Two

II Hello, Colonel Chuks. It's Ifeoma." Her voice trembled slightly but she had decided that this was the only way to handle the matter; to take the initiative and call him.

"Ifeoma, my little friend. How nice of you to finally call me. I have been waiting to hear from you for a long time. When are you coming to visit me again, my dear?" She shivered just from hearing his voice and considered hanging up but was afraid to do so.

"But it's actually very convenient that you are calling now because I have something you must do for me. Why don't you come over to my place tonight at 7 p.m.?" As usual, he didn't waste time on courtesy and hung up without waiting for her to answer.

Ifeoma prepared herself and sent Frank a text message. "Going to the colonel now – wish me luck." She put on a discreet makeup and made sure not to dress too sexily because she feared how he would treat her when she saw her. She was ready, jumped into the car and drove off to the colonel's house.

The house was, as always, guarded by heavily-armed mobile police with green berets and AK-47s. They were waiting for her and waved her inside through the gate and she parked next to one of the colonel's cars and a black Chrysler 300C with tinted windows, which she had never seen before. One of the policemen opened the car door for her and showed her towards the entrance. A female employee opened the door just before she reached it. The employee showed her through the hall and into a small sitting room where she sat down. She was not offered anything to drink. A few minutes later the colonel entered the room together with an elderly man. "Ifeoma, this is Okonkwo from Nigerian Glass, who we are working with at West African Motors, and this is Ifeoma who assists me with some practical matters. Isn't it, honey?" The colonel laughed and slapped Okonkwo on the back. "Well, my friend, I guess you need to get going. I have something I need to take care of with Ifeoma here so I'll see you soon, buddy."

They shook hands and the colonel winked at Okonkwo who nodded at Ifeoma and left them.

The colonel waited until Okonkwo had left, then he closed the curtains in the glass doors, smiled at Ifeoma and slapped her hard in the face. His hand came all the way from his hip and hard enough to make her fall over onto one of the couches in the room. "Now, I'm fucking tired of you. Who the hell do you think you are, eh?" He grabbed her hair and pulled her onto her feet while she spat a bit of blood. "Haven't I told you that you have to cooperate and haven't I explained that I'm in charge here?" he shouted into her face.

He pushed her back onto the couch where she struggled to sit up.

"But I'm doing everything I can ..." she tried, but he interrupted her.

"Shut your bloody mouth and listen to me once and for all." She nodded slightly and he sat down in front of her.

"This guy, Okonkwo, and I have some business together that I don't want disturbed. That's why I need to know everything your boyfriend is doing so he doesn't get in the way. Following me so far, honey?" She nodded again and he continued with his finger lifted. "First of all, you must make sure he trusts you completely which I'm sure you have already done, OK? And secondly, you must report all important information to me. That means who he meets with, who comes to his house, what they talk about, EVERYTHING."

The colonel slapped her in the face again – not as hard this time, only as if to make sure she was paying attention. "Here's another mobile phone which you hide from him and from this you send me texts when there is anything interesting. My number is coded in as "Oga". Still understandable to your chicken brain?" He took a little envelope from his inside pocket. "And here is some white powder that you put in Frankie Boy's drink when I give the instruction ... if it becomes necessary."

He grabbed her arm and lifted her up while she tried to keep calm and not look too weak. He held her out at arms' length and looked her up and down. "You look fine, my love, except that you're getting a bit chubby, aren't you?" He grabbed the skin on her stomach between his forefinger and thumb, squeezed hard and pulled it out. "Fortunately, our Danish friend seem to like fat girls like you," he said laughing. She was humiliated and felt like doing something desperate but kept control of herself.

Apparently, it was a hobby of his to treat women like shit, but the colonel had not finished yet. "Next time you wear something sexier, all right? Then we can have a good time and I'll give you a good ride to make you scream for more." She looked down. "Oh, well, that'll be next time because I'm busy now but there's something I want to show you in the guesthouse out in the back yard, something I collect."

He pulled her with him out of the sitting room, through the kitchen and out of the back door towards a large garden where she had never been before. A paved path twisted through the garden to a little hut placed in the far end of the garden and invisible from the driveway or the parking in front of the house. She was afraid and tried to avoid following him to the hut but he took a firm grip of her arm and pulled her along. Then he took out a bundle of keys from his pocket and unlocked the door to the hut. "Take it easy now. I just want to show you something so you know what we're talking about. You have nothing to fear … yet."

He pushed her into the hut which was dark and damp with closed blinds in front of all windows inside the hut. It only had one room. She stood for a moment to let her eyes get used to the darkness. After about ten seconds she could make out the details in the room and gasped when she saw some kind of altar against the end wall. A couple of large candles were lit and on the altar was a skull, or rather a human head which had reached a state of decay making the teeth visible and the eyes appear wide open. Ifeoma now knew where the foul smell, which she had noticed when entering, came from.

What shocked her most of all, what gave her a mental hit like a sledgehammer, was the hairband on the half-rotten head. She recognised the material from the hairband her friend, Chioma, often wore. She became completely limp and fell onto the floor and emptied her stomach out on the cold tile floor. Her vomit ran along the floor, a rat peeped out, sniffed it and ran away again. She heard the colonel's footsteps behind her and felt his brutal hand around her neck.

"OK, I think it's over, honey, and you don't look like you're feeling very well, are you?" She was moaning loudly but he pulled her to her legs. He held one arm around her neck, took her chin with the other hand and forced her face in the direction of the awful sight on the altar. "This is a sacred place for me and a few other initiated people and you don't talk about it to anybody else. Understood? From now on you know where you'll end up if you give me any more wahala, and you'd make a fine decoration up there next to your friend, don't you think?" He let go of her face and let his hand slide down her breasts and down to her crotch. She was too weak to resist and just wished it would all end now. Then he turned her around and showed her out of the hut. "Now you go home and make yourself really hot and then you call your friend and tell him that you're coming to see him tonight because you really want him. Then you fuck his brains out so he doesn't think about whether he can trust you. That's what you're best at anyway, I heard."

Ifeoma stumbled to her car on wobbly legs that felt like overcooked spaghetti, without paying attention to the policemen's looks. She drove from there to her sister's house to recover and think about how to handle the situation in view of the latest unpleasant turn of events.

Chapter Thirty-Three

Frank had gone to the office early the day after his meeting with Mama Sade because he wanted to prepare the mission into the warehouse. He wanted to avoid wasting time in the evening. It was only 7 a.m. when he opened the door to his office and at that time there was nobody else in the management section of the building. The entire first floor was quiet and he expected to have at least 25-30 minutes before the first of his colleagues would show up. He quickly left his briefcase in his office, locked the door between the managing director's section and the rest of the managers' offices and left the key in the lock to make sure that nobody could surprise him. Then he went to the small kitchen where George had told him about the hatch in the ceiling. As expected, it was there but did not look like it had been opened for years. He brought a guest chair to the kitchen, stepped onto it, removed most of the spider webs and opened the hatch. It was no problem opening it and he could see that there was sufficient space in the loft, just as George had explained. On the floor in the kitchen there were a few cartons of condensed milk and coffee so he could stack these on the chair which would allow him to reach up high enough to pull himself through the hatch. It looked feasible at that point. He would deal with how to get down on the other side later.

Considering Frank's planned venture in the evening he was uneasy and stressed all day, which went by at a snail's pace. He dealt with some minor tasks of a more administrative nature and finalised several small matters he had left pending for some days. He held a few meetings but all the time had the planned trip to the loft on his mind and found it particularly difficult to concentrate.

Mid-afternoon he called Ifeoma because he wanted to know how she was doing. She sounded distant when answering his call. "Well, how are you? Did you talk to the colonel?" he asked, and could tell that she was feeling bad.

"Where are you now, honey?"

"I'm at my sister's but I'll come to your place later. I hope you'll be home," she said with a weak voice.

"I have some things I need to take care of in the office tonight so I won't be home early but look forward to seeing you later," he said. "But are you OK? You sound a bit … a bit under pressure."

"Yeah, It's … I'm OK," she answered, without convincing him.

"Just come as soon as you're ready. I'll call the cook and tell him to let you in. Then we'll see each other later," he said.

She sounded relieved and said thanks.

When it was almost 5 p.m. he asked Mrs Adebayo to call Godwin and he sent him home. The explanation he gave the driver was that he had several urgent matters to finalise in the office so he expected that he would be late. There was no reason for Godwin to sit and wait when Frank just expected to go straight home later he explained. Godwin did not mind, although he did look sceptical as he was not used to being off duty so early.

Just after 7 p.m. it was again quiet on the first floor as all heads of department and secretaries with offices in this section had gone home. Frank made an effort to look very busy when the human resources manager, as the last person to leave, peeped in and said goodnight. Then he was ready for his climbing exercise.

He fetched the torch, the large screwdriver and the working gloves. Then he locked the door again and stacked the food cartons on the guest chair in the kitchen. It was a distinctly unstable arrangement and a ladder would have been much better. However, it allowed him, slowly and unsurely, to reach sufficiently high to open the hatch and get most of his upper body through the hole. It gave him goosebumps as it seemed gloomy and scary in the loft and the torch quickly revealed a massive spread of rat shit. The sun had been shining on the aluminium roof all afternoon so it was still hot in the stagnant humid air. Frank was already breathing heavily and estimated his heart rate to be around 120 before pulling himself up. This was the kind of situation where one would have wished to weigh 15-20 pounds less and Frank cursed himself that he was not in better shape but got up into the loft without too much trouble.

The working gloves came in handy in this situation because the loft was disgusting to touch – a good blend of old dust, rat shit and indeterminate goo about an inch thick. He was quite happy wearing jeans so the exercise did not cost him a pair of his better trousers. He began crawling forward very slowly but became unsure of the direction and had to look down into the kitchen to get a clear picture of the building's layout. Then he adjusted his course by about 30 degrees and crawled more determinedly ahead accompanied by a rat – fortunately scampering away from him, judging from the sound.

He stopped from time to time and lit up the loft around him with the torch to avoid close encounters with the confident rats which he could hear in the darkness. Otherwise he was pushing the torch ahead of him with the beam pointed forward. George had estimated the distance more or less correctly and Frank was happy that it was not 50 metres he had to crawl like this on a relatively weak knee on hard wood with plenty of splinters. By the wooden wall, where the warehouse had to be on the other side, he stopped to catch his breath. Then he lit along the wall and found the hatch, through which he needed to get down into the warehouse. It crossed his mind that he had not actually checked that the storekeeper had left but Frank assumed that he had because the gate to the warehouse was always closed when he left the office in the evening.

It now turned out that the locking device on the hatch to the warehouse was placed on the other side of the wall and he could not open the hatch from the loft-side. Frank pushed the hatch while lighting on it with the torch and he saw a microscopical opening opposite the hinges. He pushed a bit harder and saw the opening expanding slightly. The third time he put more weight behind the push and at the same time pressed the screwdriver into the opening. This type of task was most definitely not included in his job description but he did not really have anybody to complain to. So, he pushed again and maintained the pressure on the hatch while moving the screwdriver upwards until it hit metal. The hatch sprang open and Frank almost lost balance and nearly fell into the warehouse. He got hold of the wall with one hand while the screwdriver fell to the concrete floor inside the warehouse with, what Frank thought was, a deafening noise. Frank held his breath and expected to hear screaming and shouting from the area outside the warehouse but there was complete silence.

In most recent American action movies, it was always a little Chinese person or a dwarf handling these difficult climbing assignments where it was necessary to get through narrow passages. Here it was a big and slightly too heavy Dane who had the assignment but eventually he managed to push himself backwards through the hatch and found the steps on the wall with his feet. So far, so good.

Finally, Frank had firm ground under his feet again. It was not quite dark in the warehouse as light from the area outside shone through the open eaves. He easily found the storekeeper's desk and looked for the stock list which he found on a clipboard in an unlocked drawer.

Frank started going through the warehouse. He did not know exactly what he was looking for but he had a feeling that it would be useful to begin with the boxes from Nigerian Glass which had been driven past him on a forklift so quickly last time he visited the warehouse. He knew approximately where these boxes were placed in the large warehouse and soon found what he was looking for. He got started with the big screwdriver to open the first box. He succeeded in opening the lid and removing the first layer of wood shavings protecting the windows in the box. It did not take him long to ascertain that car windows were not the only contents in the box. Under five windscreens separated by corrugated carton there was a plywood plate, and underneath this plate Frank found a thin layer of rectangular packages running the entire length of the box. The packages were covered by a layer of wide brown tape so he could not see the contents but he pressed a small hole into one of the packages with the screwdriver. There was a little white powder stuck on the head of the screwdriver. Frank had never seen drugs in real life, only in American and British crime movies. He did not know what it smelled like, if it had a smell, or how it tasted for that matter. Nevertheless, he was convinced that what he had found in the box was cocaine. He closed the box quickly, since his primary purpose of visiting the warehouse had been fulfilled, that is to confirm that a shady business was running right under his nose. A narcotics wholesale business was being run parallel to the car assembly activities, he assumed. Frank had no clue where the cocaine came from or how it got into the country but it certainly looked like West African Motors was used as a transit point, a hub to and from other countries in the region. Frank quickly opened another box to be absolutely sure and found exactly the same contents under the car windows.

No wonder the colonel was so anxious about keeping Okonkwo as a supplier and the contents of the box almost certainly explained part of the price increases that had been implemented.

Frank had seen enough. He put the clipboard with the stock list back in the drawer before climbing back up the metal steps on the wall while trying not to think about how high he had to climb to get through the hatch into the loft again or how solidly the metal steps had been cemented into the wall. Sweat was running down his cheeks and the palm of his hands were wet inside the gloves. He clung desperately to each step and only let go with one hand when he was sure to have good grip with the other.

When he finally reached the open hatch, he held on firmly to the wall and pulled himself into the loft head first and crawled forward on his stomach. At that point he heard his jeans being torn and felt a sharp pain just above his right knee. There must have been a nail or another sharp object on the edge of the opening where his leg got stuck for a brief moment. He turned around and now sat inside the loft with his legs bent and examined the injury. His jeans were torn about two inches and he was bleeding – not a bloodbath but sufficient to leave a relatively large blood stain on his jeans.

'Shit,' Frank thought, and quickly turned around and crawled back towards the hatch in the kitchen which was easy to find as he had left the light on and placed the hatch cover next to the hole.

He managed to get down onto the chair on top of the cartons and push the hatch back in place, however, not without a lot of dust falling onto the floor in the kitchen. Then he quickly went to the toilet next to his office and fixed a handkerchief on the injury with some sticky tape around the leg to make sure it would stay in place. He worked fast and purposefully, swept up the dust in the kitchen and put the cartons back where they had been. After a quick inspection he thought that it looked as it had before his little expedition.

On the way to his car he carried his briefcase in such a way that it covered his leg where the trousers were torn and stained by blood. The watchmen at the main gate only noticed him when he started the car so he had made a smooth exit.

Chapter Thirty-Four

Ifeoma was relieved that Frank had called and looked forward to seeing him since she had not had a chance to discuss the horrible experience at the colonel's place with him. She was still shaken despite having slept on it and tried to distance herself from what she had seen. She was actually not completely sure that she had in fact experienced it and she needed to talk about it with somebody she trusted.

Ifeoma quickly packed a small bag with clothes and some toiletries, then she sent a text message to her sister informing her that she would spend the night at Frank's place. She jumped into the red Honda Civic which she had felt less and less comfortable with over the past couple of weeks. Especially when she thought about the way she had gotten it and the way things had developed recently. She had not driven it to Frank's place before as she did not want him to know that she had her own car. However, since he was now aware of her agreement with the colonel there was no reason to hide it any more.

When she arrived at Frank's house, she honked the horn a couple of times. One of the watchmen opened the gate slightly. He came outside to undertake a closer inspection as he did not recognise the car. He saw that it was her and made a sign that she should wait for a moment. A couple of minutes later, probably after having consulted the cook, he opened the gate completely and she drove up the driveway and parked in front of the garage. The cook came out from the kitchen section and wanted to carry her bag but she rejected his offer. "It's OK, Temitope". She was not used to having her things carried for her and did not really feel comfortable with it. Apart from that, the bag weighed no more than a couple of kilos so it was more a question of principle that the servants must carry the boss's things. But somehow she was only the boss's girlfriend and not Temitope's boss.

After having placed her bag in the bedroom, she fetched a coke in the fridge and switched on the TV. As usual, she found Africa Magic where they showed a Nollywood movie. Not because she particularly felt like following the movie but it helped her relax when these movies were on the TV. It was a movie starring Omotola Jalade Ekeinde. She liked Omotola and felt that she looked a bit like her. It was the traditional story with the uncontrollable, wild and slightly criminal boyfriend who treated Omotola badly and eventually dropped her for her best friend. However, in the end justice prevailed and God played a significant part in securing the right end to the drama. It reminded Ifeoma that she had not been to church or prayed very much recently. She had to catch up with what she had neglected on the spiritual front as soon as possible.

When the time was approaching 7 p.m., and she expected Frank to be home soon, she went and took a shower. She took her time in the shower. Then she rubbed her body in a nice-smelling lotion and found something slightly sexy to wear. A pair of tight shorts, a sleeveless shirt that she could wear without bra and leave open to show just about enough of her breasts to awaken Frank's instincts. Finally, a pair of high-heeled black suede shoes with straps up the calves. She had felt that he liked her slightly vulgar and she had no problem playing that role. Last time, when he had found out that she knew the colonel, he had refused to make love to her for the first time and she wanted to make absolutely sure that did not happen again. Hence, she was meticulous in preparing herself for his sake.

When she was done, she went back to Africa Magic to wait for Frank. She looked forward to seeing him. It felt strange to sit here in his sitting room waiting for him and she really wanted to be with him. He could be difficult to make out because he never talked much about things related to feelings but more about strictly practical issues. He could be so tender and thoughtful when they were together and she thought about his soft hands caressing her body. On the other hand, he could also be frighteningly tough, even ruthless, for instance in the way he had dealt with the robbers. It had been a shocking experience to see how cold and cynical he was in that situation even though she was, of course, happy that he had handled it. But it had been a huge risk, an almost desperate act, to attack the armed robbers who would not have hesitated in killing him. She did not dare imagine what would have happened to herself if they had found out that she was in the house.

Finally, Frank came home. She was not quite sure whether it was her shorts, the shoes or the shirt that did the trick but he looked hungrily at her from the moment he entered the sitting room.

She decided to play it cool to see how long it would take Frank to get started. She did not have to wait very long.

He went straight to the kitchen door to lock it, then came to her on the sofa and kneeled in front of her. "Wow, you're hot tonight, baby," he said, while taking the glass out of her hand and placing it on the small side table. She deliberately tried to follow the movie while he started unbuttoning her shirt, bent forward and kissed her breasts when they appeared and then frantically worked on opening her shorts. She helped him quickly so they could move on, lifted her butt slightly, pushed the shorts down over her thighs and threw them to one side with a little foot movement. Had he noticed that she had shaven her pussy very smooth? Judging from his breathing he had seen enough. Apart from the shoes she now lay completely naked with him on his knees between her legs, and she slid down in the sofa and licked her mouth while looking him in the eyes. He was almost ready now and lay down on her, started kissing her stomach and moved slowly towards her pussy. She loved it when he licked her and she could not hold back a little shriek when he found her most sensitive spot. Then she let him work with his tongue and felt the orgasm coming, slowly but surely.

Just as it was coming, she whispered. "Take me now, Frank, Quickly ... now." He responded to that with no further explanation needed. He sat up and she now saw that his stiff cock presented itself ready for action through the fly in his jeans. Then he grabbed her thighs, pulled her further out, so her butt was hanging out over the edge of the sofa, and he was inside her. She came with a little scream almost simultaneously with Frank falling down on top of her with a satisfied moan.

"Wow, Frank," she said, when she had caught her breath again. "That was a great fuck, you're amazing." She held his head between both hands and gave him a brief and wet kiss with her tongue. He looked surprised but did not say anything. 'Another sign that he does not find it easy to express his feeling,' she thought.

It was only when he got up, that she noticed the torn jeans and the blood stain. "Oh, Frank.

What happened to your leg?" she asked, and took a closer look.

"I was up climbing in the loft above the office but that's a long and boring story. There was a nail in the way and I got stuck on it but it's nothing too serious."

They left it at that.

She got up and went to the bedroom carrying her clothes and deliberately swinging her butt more than necessary. She was sure that he studied her behind thoroughly. Then she heard the cook try to open the kitchen door and Frank got up to open if.

When she came back to the sitting room the cook was serving their starter which today was avocado salad and Frank brought a bottle of sparkling wine from the kitchen. She had put on a pair of jeans and a T-shirt instead of the sexy clothes which had served their purpose. The high- heeled black shoes had also been replaced by a pair of flat sandals showing her dark-red varnished toenails. Ifeoma had not quite decided exactly how much she was going to tell Frank about her experience with the colonel but she knew that, somehow, they had to have a conversation about it. She wanted to tell him about it, had to get it out somehow, but how would he react?

He smiled at her but her thoughts were back to the harsh realities and the horrible sight in the colonel's guesthouse. Suddenly she felt sick. The room started spinning and her stomach somersaulted. "I'm scared, Frank," she whispered, her voice trembling.

"What's the matter? Did something unpleasant happen to you?"

She walked past him and sat down at the dining table where she poured a large glass and took a healthy gulp. "It's the colonel. He's completely mad and he has killed my friend."

She held her hands in front of her face and sobbed uncontrollably. She felt his hand on her shoulders when he sat down next to her. "Take it easy and tell me what has happened so we can find a solution to the problem," he said.

"But there is no solution, baby. He's capable of anything and nobody will believe us if we involve other people – least of all the police. He's got them in his pocket."

She told him the whole story about her last visit to the colonel's house but left out the details of the powder she had been given to poison Frank.

'There's no reason to worry him unnecessarily,' she thought and, anyway, she did not intend to use it. He listened carefully and they had completely forgotten to eat the starters but the cook had understood that they were having an important conversation, that he should not interrupt, so he was scrambling around with pots and pans in the kitchen.

She felt bad about having been mixed up in this entire matter and sincerely hoped that Frank would believe her. She wished that she had met him under different circumstances, a more positive and honest way, but it was too late for regrets now. She had needed the money and tried to justify to herself what she had done, even though she knew deep down inside that it had been wrong. She tried to imagine a life with Frank but there were so many obstacles and maybe it was just an unrealistic dream.

"But, well, listen, Ifeoma. What do you think is going on out there in his guesthouse or whatever we should call it? Is he just killing people at random, or what? Can't you see that's just too crazy?" Frank's expression showed that he did not quite understand or accept the seriousness of it.

"He's involved in human sacrifices, Frank. It's like a cult, a kind of pact with the devil. It is actually not as unusual here as you think," she explained, but it did not sound convincing to her own ears. "To become rich, you promise the dark side to carry out evil acts. It could be fucking your mother, killing your sister or sacrificing other people to the devil himself. You somehow sell your soul for personal benefit, sign a contract with the dark powers and pay the price for it later in life or on the other side. Some people are so greedy that they will do anything to become rich and powerful. The colonel is obviously one of them."

She shook her head and did not dare look at Frank because she knew that, considering his background, he could not possibly believe this story and right now he was surely trying to find logical explanations for himself.

"It can't be fucking true that we know all of this and yet we can't do anything about it. Even in this country there must be something called goddamn law enforcement and crime can be reported to the police even if many of them are corrupt." Frank shook his head and did not look like he could digest the thought of what was going on, even if he desperately tried.

"I can't explain to you how serious this is, Frank. We're in great trouble and the best we can do is to run away from here, although the danger is that he and his people will follow us and find us anywhere else in the world. They have a large network which could be almost impossible to escape." What more could she do to put things in perspective for Frank?

He poured the last of the sparkling wine into their glasses and looked at her with mistrust written all over his face. "It's too crazy," he whispered to himself, stood up and walked around. "But one way or the other we have to find out what his kryptonite is."

"His what?" Ifeoma wondered. "Kryptonite. You know, Superman."

"Superman?"

"Yes, the guy wearing blue tights and a red cape flying around to save the world." "Flying around?"

"Yeah, have you never heard of Superman, for Christ's sake?"

"No, and what's that got to do with kryptoplamite?"

"Kryptonite. It's a material from the planet Krypton, where Superman was born, which weakens him. Otherwise, he is invulnerable but when he's exposed to kryptonite he quickly becomes weak. It's a fantasy story but the expression is used to describe the one thing that weakens somebody otherwise considered an invincible opponent."

She pondered the story of Superman for a while but did not want to ask any more questions as she was, apparently, expected to know about that kind of thing. The story of the stuff weakening Superman had completely escaped her attention.

"Have you got a cigarette?" Frank asked.

"Yes, but I thought you had stopped smoking again." She knew there was a package of Marlboro Lights in her handbag with at least 8-10 cigarettes but she wanted to avoid Frank smoking too much.

"You just made me start smoking again with your story so bring those cigarettes now. I know you always carry some in your handbag." She quickly found the package and threw it to him. He caught it and shook one cigarette out with one hand just enough to pick the filter between his lips and pull it out of the package. He then went over behind her, bent down and placed one hand on her breast.

"Light me," he whispered in her ear and dropped the cigarette down between her legs.

"Oh well, too bad, Mr Clumsy. Maybe that's a sign you should not be smoking," she said, smiling but picked up the cigarette from between her thighs and gave it to him.

"Maybe you should just kill me, perhaps break my neck when I have my head between your thighs. Isn't that what he wants you to do, the colonel – to kill me, I mean?" Frank suggested, and smiled which made her so annoyed.

"Could you just be serious for two minutes, Frank – it's not a fucking joke, you know," she shouted and took the package of cigarettes from the table. He stood and looked like a school boy so she got up and put her arms around him. "You big fool – try to take it seriously, won't you?"

"Oh well. I'm just trying to lift the mood a bit," Frank mumbled.

"Don't," she snarled. They sat in silence and smoked for a while until Temitope carefully peeked through the door with a questioning expression on his face.

"You can serve the main course," she said, in a sort of "madame of the house" confident voice and the cook did not hesitate for one moment.

They finished eating without saying very much to each other and were both mentally overwhelmed by what was happening to them. When he had finished eating, Frank pushed his plate away and let a burp slip out, apparently without even noticing. She got up and opened the kitchen door.

"Temitope, come and clear the table and then make some coffee, please," she said politely and there were no protests. "Oh, and by the way, could you ask the watchman to run down to the corner shop and buy two packs of Marlboro Lights. Master is in the mood for smoking, I can see."

She sat down at the table again and noticed that Frank was deep in thought. He ran his fingers up to his slightly high temples as she had noticed he often did when he was mulling over something.

"So, let's try to brainstorm a bit over who could be expected to be on our side, OK? If there's anybody at all," he said with a little gesture as a sign of action, she assumed. "I mean simply prepare a list of "for" and "against" and then see where that leads us," he rounded up, leaned back in the chair and looked for the cigarettes. "Shit, there's hardly any cigarettes left," he said, surprised. So, he had not heard that she asked Temitope to send the watchman buy two more packs. Frank got up and went to the office to fetch a paper pad and a pen.

"If we start with those who are against us, assuming of course, that you and I are together, and we are, aren't we? Anyway, I'll give you the benefit of the doubt," he said, and sent her a wry smile. She was about to jump on him but he seemed so sweet and innocent that she gave it up and just nodded. "Well then. We can write the police on the negative side right away; do we agree on that?"

She nodded again.

"What about the chairman of the board in your company, the big Chief Adeyemi? He's a powerful person with strong connections," she asked, but he immediately shook his head.

"Maybe he is not involved in the colonel's conspiracy but he's supporting him in one way or the other. Also, he thinks that I should manage the situation myself. We won't get very far along that road." They sat without speaking for a few minutes before Frank added: "And the other board members are much too impressed by the chairman. None of them dare go against him and are afraid of getting involved in anything before having the green light from the almighty chairman."

"Are there any of the heads of department who are on your side?" she asked, and was quite happy with the way they made progress now. It felt wise to map the situation in this way. She would not have thought about that herself.

"George, clearly, but he's been shot and is missing half a leg so he can't do much," Frank said, and his fingers were up at his temples again. "Maybe Funmi, the national sales manager. She's reasonable enough and certainly not a criminal but she's not exactly a commando soldier, is she? She almost went into a coma when the Frenchman was kidnapped."

"This guy, Okonkwo from the window company – we can write him on the against-side, I believe. I saw him over at the colonel's place the other day." Frank opened his eyes wide and stared at her for a moment, then gazed at infinity.

"Hell yes. He's a real crook, that guy. He wanted to bribe me the very first day and I threw him out. We can consider him as enemy in category A+."

"Do you have any partners or suppliers who you know a little and could talk to," she suggested, and immediately saw that she had hit on something.

Frank rose from the table while nodding and mumbling to himself: "Yes, yes, maybe." After a little tour of the sitting room he sat down again and immediately his hand was at his temples again.

"Did I say something sensible for a change?" she asked.

"You're a genius," he answered. "We have an agent who assists us with contact to various decision makers in the public sector. When we need to "see" them, I mean. You know what I'm talking about, don't you?" She did. Everybody in Nigeria was familiar with the expression to "see" somebody which often involved handing over a brown envelope as appreciation of business- oriented services.

They were interrupted for a brief moment when Temitope brought the cigarettes and put them on the table with the change. "Take," Ifeoma said, gave him the change and he lit up in a big smile. Frank seemed to be completely absorbed in his own thoughts and lit another cigarette with a distant look on his face.

"His name is Segun Ajibola and I'll call him tomorrow so we can try to meet. I don't know him that well but we were in Abuja together to visit the minister and he seemed like a decent guy. Of course, he knows the colonel but I'm not sure how close they are. At least it's worth a try," Frank said, and turned to her with a smile. "Bring your sexy ass over here and get a kiss. You're amazing."

"Will I get a good fuck tonight then?" She said in her best schoolgirl voice.

"No, I don't want to bother," he answered laughing, and she grabbed his hair with one hand so he winced.

"Then I'll just rape you. You're an easy prey." She sat across his lap and kissed him. When she felt that he was getting hard in his pants she rose and said, "Are we not having a cognac today, baby?", but there was no more cognac because Frank messed around over in the bar with clinking bottles and cursed. "Just give me something else, if you don't have any cognac," she said, and he came back with a bottle of Bailey's; her favourite drink.

Later they were sitting together on the sofa flicking through the satellite channels without finding anything interesting enough to watch. They only spoke a little and mainly about trivialities but they were sitting closely together enjoying each other's company. It was a good feeling which she hoped there would be much more of in the future. Then reality returned and she tried to concentrate on the television instead. Around midnight Frank yawned uncontrollably and suggested that they go to bed. He did not look like having intimate activities in mind when he rose, scratched his stomach and yawned again. They lay in each other's arms and she stayed there until he began snoring. Then she moved away and gave him a push on the back.

"Frank, you're snoring, man." He grunted a couple of times and rolled over on his side where his snoring stopped and became ordinary heavy breathing.

She sat up on the edge of the bed, folded her hands, closed her eyes and prayed to God that she and Frank would get through this situation safely. Then she lay down again but could not sleep immediately. It took at least an hour of fretful thought before she felt sleep slowly embrace her.

Chapter Thirty-Five

Ifeoma was not there when Frank woke up in the morning and he could not see her bag anywhere either, but on the bedside table there was a small note.

"Frank, my darling. I have gone to Lagos to my church. I need some spiritual guidance to show me the way forward. I love you more than anything. Trust me. Big kiss and behave yourself," the little handwritten note said. A couple of months ago he would have found it strange but now he was not so surprised that she had chosen to consult her church in such a tense situation. Frank folded the note and put it in his wallet.

He remembered that he had to call Segun Ajibola but did not want to call too early as he did not know the man's programme and daily routines, so he planned to call around nine o'clock.

From the shower he could see through the window and into the front yard where there was a large flamboyant tree, popularly also called an African flame tree. He thought that it was about this time of the year, when the dry season had settled in, that it would blossom. It was a beautiful sight when it presented its red-orange flowers. A short uneven trunk, some gnarled branches which formed a flat and wide top with these spectacular flowers on top, thus creating an impression of flames. Until now there were no flowers visible, however, and Frank thought that he might be mistaken about the timing or perhaps it was just an unusual year.

Godwin was washing the car in front of the garage. Incredible how conscientious that man was, always on time and never sick. Yes, and perhaps most importantly, he could find his way from A to B without needing an explanation several times. He could not read a map, so Lagos Street Finder would be a useless book in Godwin's hands, but he had a well-developed sense of locality and only had to drive somewhere once to know the route forever. It was remarkable and Frank made a mental note that he should remember to give Godwin a proper raise at the end of the year. Then he pushed that little detail out to the periphery of his mind where he had several other, and more demanding, matters to struggle with.

When he arrived at the office he somehow thought that Mrs Adebayo had polished herself up compared to how she normally looked. She was a nice and attractive lady and always well-dressed. Not exactly a sex bomb but this morning she actually looked really good. He came to think about the charming hippopotamus, Gloria, in the animation movie, Madagascar and wondered if her husband looked like a giraffe. She also smiled more than usual this morning, Mrs Adebayo.

"Good morning, Frank," she shined, went to the archive room and came back with a bouquet of flowers and a basket with mixed food and drinks, mostly coffee, wine and spirits.

"What on earth is going on? It's not Christmas yet, is it?" he said, and her smile became even bigger.

"No, but me and some of the other secretaries thought that it has been so difficult for you since you arrived. So, we wanted to give you this and wish you good luck in the future." He was touched. "You're such a lovely boss, Frank", she said, and now he just stood there staring with open mouth and she came over to him and put her arms around him. He clearly felt her voluminous upper body including where her back was folding when he put his arm around her. He almost called her Gloria.

"I'm completely speechless," he said. "You shouldn't have – I don't know what to say."

"Don't say anything, just continue being our boss the way you are now." She was suddenly shy and went to sit down at her desk but had forgotten that she always made coffee for him in the morning and got up again to go to the kitchen.

"Yeah, hello Segun, it's Frank Grabowski from West African Motors. We were in Abuja together not too long ago." It took just slightly longer than usual when you call people and Segun clearly needed a few extra seconds to realise who he was talking to.

"Yes, of course, Frank, yes. How are you? Is business going well these days?" Frank thought that Segun had not expected it to be him calling. Frank had never called him before so he had probably seen an unknown number on the display on his phone.

"I'm OK ... yeah ... I'm fine," Frank said, and thought about how to continue. "However, we have had various problems of which some were quite unusual." He gave Segun a few seconds to let this remark sink in. "Yeah, we've had a number of incidents which I would like to discuss with you. I was thinking whether we could meet somewhere in the not too distant future ... or rather as soon as possible."

"Yes, of course, Frank. We can meet, no problem. When should it be? I'm in Lagos now and will be here until tomorrow afternoon. So, if we could meet in Lagos it could be either tonight or tomorrow for lunch." Frank was relieved that Segun was happy to meet just like that and that made it somewhat easier for him to present his problems to him. He still had to be very careful though and find the right way to bring up the problems to Segun. After all, he did not know him that well.

"I can drive down to Lagos this afternoon and then we can meet at any time after 6 p.m. Where would it be convenient for you to meet?" Frank said, and tried to lead Segun to accept meeting the same evening as he would like to have it done as soon as possible.

"Do you know Isaac John Street in Ikeja? Where the Protea Hotel is." "Yes, I have an idea where that is," Frank confirmed.

"Opposite the Protea there is a small, sort of a boutique hotel called Savoy Suites. That's where I'm staying and I can make a reservation for you too. It's a quiet and discreet place where we can sit and talk undisturbed." Segun had guessed correctly in his assumption that Frank wanted to talk privately and preferred discretion. "Just send me a text message when you've arrived, Frank. I'll be in town for a meeting late afternoon but should be back in the hotel at the latest around 7 p.m., maybe quarter past.

"I really appreciate it, Segun. See you tonight."

As Frank wanted to avoid being out on the Ibadan-Lagos Expressway too late, he left the office at 3:00p.m. and drove home to pack a small travel bag with the necessities for one night. Wise from the experience at the Airport Hotel, and taking into consideration that he did not know Savoy Suites, he packed a set of bed linen in the bag.

Now that he was alone, he felt a little pinch in his heart thinking about Ifeoma who had left without waking him up to say goodbye. He also worried about her and could not get her out of his mind. It had started with her seducing him, almost like an escort girl, which technically she had been when they met. Now he felt so good with her around him every day. He pushed the thought aside, lifted his bag and went to the car.

They only saw one accident on the way to Lagos which had probably happened the night before, so he avoided feeling sick over seeing human bodies mutilated or burned beyond recognition in macabre traffic accidents caused by irresponsible, reckless and often drunk or drugged drivers. They were lucky with the traffic and only hit the first traffic jam at Ojota where the expressway merges with Ikorodu Road in a huge interchange. A veritable chaos played out before their eyes with impatient drivers using their horns in an infernal cacophony and bus stops where the shouters tried to call customers to various destinations and thereby contributed to the extreme noise level. There were children and youngsters, of whom some were wearing school uniforms, others only partly dressed; adults and elderly people walking in something that looked like a mixture of dried mud and faeces. Frank was in the process of thanking the higher powers that he had been born in a time and place where he avoided living under these conditions. In the middle of this thought process a 4-5-year-old boy passed the car at a distance of only a few metres, suddenly needed to relieve himself, pulled down his worn-out shorts, squatted and quickly pressed out a long brown "sausage" on the ground. Then the boy pulled up his pants again and walked on like nothing had happened. Immediately thereafter traffic eased up and they now moved forward at around 25-30 kilometres per hour which was a big improvement. Soon they were away from the swamp of mud and faeces. Nigeria in general, but particularly Lagos, was truly a special place, even for Frank who had travelled and worked in different African countries for years.

Godwin was at home in Lagos as well as in Ibadan and obviously knew Isaac John Street. So they went straight to Savoy Suites where a young lady in a neat and tight-fitting uniform of African material on a slim and well-proportioned body was handling the reception

"I suppose that's Mr Grabowski?" she said smilingly, and he was already quite content with Segun's choice of hotel.

"Yes, it is. I didn't know that I was already famous here in Lagos."

She smiled and played along. "It's because Mr Ajibola said that we should expect a tall handsome man around this time so I guessed that it had to be you." That was damn professional work by a receptionist and customers are generally easy to please if you treat them well. Nobody refuses a compliment unless something is terribly wrong.

"If I may take a copy of your passport, then you can fill in this form with name, address and signature – all the other information is not needed when it's Mr Ajibola making the reservation for you." Frank became dizzy from all this well-functioning and polite efficiency. He just hoped that the bathroom, bed and linen would live up to the high standards set. He thanked the nice young lady and politely rejected assistance carrying his small travel bag to room 106 on the first floor. He also noticed from her tag that her name was Funke and thought that the start to his stay at Savoy Suites had been positive.

Frank left his bag in the room, confirmed that the bed was hard but the sheets clean and then went to the bar for a beer. The bar was furnished with some large heavy sofas with low tables in between. The walls were decorated with large pictures of Nigerian artists, dominated by Fela Kuti, the legendary musician and songwriter who died of aids towards the end of the 90s. There was also a picture of his son, Femi Kuti, standing on a suspicious-looking stage with naked upper body and smoking something that definitely did not look like an ordinary cigarette. Frank ordered a Star and some peanuts and they were able to deliver half of the order, namely the beer. The bar was very quiet as only two other guests were sitting at a table in the opposite corner speaking very softly. There was no Joy, Happy or other service-minded young ladies as he had experienced at the Sheraton the first night. It suited him just fine to be alone while waiting for Segun so he could prepare mentally for the conversation.

At 8:10 p.m., when Frank was halfway through the second beer, Segun turned up. He had, obviously, also had a couple of beers during his meeting and looked happy and relaxed.

'A good beginning,' Frank thought, and felt relieved. Segun tried ordering peanuts as well but had no more luck than Frank and complained a bit before accepting defeat.

"Should we sit at the terrace at the back?" Segun suggested. Frank did not even know there was an outdoor terrace but agreed. Segun ordered a Star and, to avoid sitting outside and waiting to be served when the next beer was needed, Frank did the same.

"Thank you for agreeing to meet with such short notice," Frank opened up, and Segun shook his head.

"No problem," he said. "I'm the company's agent and when the managing director wants to see me, I am, of course, available. Furthermore, I noticed that you mentioned having some problems. This is not the easiest country for a foreigner to work in so if there's something I can do, I'm here."

'Perfect start,' Frank thought, and prepared to tell Segun enough of what had happened to enable him estimate where he stood in relation to the colonel.

He gave a quick summary of the worst incidents, including the snake in the bedroom, the attack on George and partly mentioned the unfortunate situation at Kakanfo Inn which, however, he did not want Segun to know about in detail for the time being. He also mentioned Ifeoma but without saying how close they had become and explained it more like a practical arrangement.

Finally, he gave some indication of his doubts about the colonel's loyalty to himself and to the company. He was playing a risky game but he had no choice as he had to find an ally, if at all possible. It was the only way he would have any chance of survival, career-wise and perhaps even physically.

Segun took a long drink of his beer. Slowly but surely, he gulped down most of a large glass of beer and wiped the foam off his upper lip. "OK," he said. "That's a big deal. My God." He looked thoughtful for a little while. "First of all, Frank, you don't need to worry about talking openly to me. I have no special obligations to anybody else in the company but you. It's true that I have known Colonel Chuks for years, and he was the one who got me appointed as agent to handle certain, shall we call it, difficult tasks. It's been good business for me but it has also been a tough way to earn money. Not something anybody can do and there are huge risks involved." He was thirsty again and Frank imagined that they would soon need to place the next order for drinks.

Segun was ready again. "Chuks has given me a lot of assignments and we have been out together many times on these special and confidential missions to secure business for the company as well as support from authorities. So, we've had our drunken nights together and enjoyed the luxury that follows good business and a lot of money. Having said that, you should know that he's changed over the last couple of years." Another large gulp of beer and Frank realised that he would find it difficult following Segun on the beer-drinking front. "Chuks has become strange lately and it's difficult to explain exactly how or why but he's not the relaxed "bon vivant" I got to know. I'm just guessing now but I think he imagined that he could become the managing director when your predecessor died ... I heard some rumours and he seemed very confident but it wasn't to be. Maybe that's one of the reasons he started being suspicious, extremely temperamental and sometimes even mean, I think." Segun paused and looked with interest at Frank, as if he wanted to check his reaction.

"There's money disappearing from the system in the company and other strange occurrences, possibly in connivance with one of the company's suppliers, Nigeria Glass, where we buy the windows and ..." Frank said, but Segun interrupted him eagerly.

"That guy, Okonkwo, is it him? He's a hardened criminal and a nasty fellow. You have to be very careful with him. He's avoiding me because he knows that I don't like him but watch out for him, Frank."

"Oh, yeah. I understood that right from the beginning when he tried to bribe me and I threw him out of my office."

"Oh, no," Segun said. "That was a bad start but then the good news is that you won't risk getting too close to him. They probably tried to set you up in a trap to have something on you if you should prove difficult later on."

Frank wanted to go a little further with Segun and took a chance on giving him some more information. "At the colonel's place something fishy is going on. I don't know what to believe but he has some kind of guest house, or whatever we should call it, out in the back yard where cult- like activities take place. I can't prove it but I'm pretty sure it's not empty rumours."

Segun, who was otherwise unimpressed about most things, looked shocked. "I hope he's not into something extreme such as sacrificing disappeared or kidnapped people. It actually happens from time to time in this part of the world."

Segun got up and went inside to order a couple more beers, Frank assumed. He came back quickly with a waiter following him with two cold beers, condensation on the bottles. The waiter took his time opening the beers perhaps hoping to catch a few sentences of their conversation.

However, they drank in silence for a few minutes and waited until he had left and closed the door before speaking again.

"Listen, Frank. I haven't seen Chuks since we were in Abuja together but I'll try to call him and hear if we can meet. My contract expires soon and he's usually the one I negotiate the extension with so that's quite convenient."

It sounded like a good idea to Frank who was confident that Segun knew how to handle the colonel. Frank asked Segun about where the colonel lived and the geography around his house.

He knew approximately where the house was situated but had never been there and did not particularly feel like going there after what Ifeoma had told him. According to Segun, the house was in a cul-de-sac and at the end of the street there were some empty plots giving access to the back of the colonel's house and the houses next to it. The area was very quiet, as several of the neighbours did not stay there permanently but only used their houses as residence during shorter stays in Ibadan.

"Whatever I find out, Frank, I'll make sure to let you know so you're aware which precautions to take. Is that all right?"

It was. They shook hands and changed the subject to discuss where to have dinner as Segun was of the candid opinion that they should not sample the Savoy Suites' cuisine. That left a lot to be desired according to his experience. The choice fell on a Chinese restaurant, New China in Opic Plaza next to the Sheraton and thus right around the corner from Savoy Suites. Frank felt comfortable with that and they finished their drinks to get going before it was too late.

A couple of hours later they had, over a bottle of red wine and a good dinner with soup, spring rolls and three main courses between them, elaborated on the situation and had become much closer. They agreed that neither of them had the energy for further bar or nightclub visits so they went back to their respective rooms and Frank said goodnight to a now bleary-eyed Funke at the reception.

Chapter Thirty-Six

Godwin had apparently been sleeping in the car because there was a nasty smell of sweat and yesterday's dinner mixed with a foul morning breath, so Frank left the window open for the first 10-15 minutes on the way out of Lagos. He tried to call Ifeoma but her phone was still off. It worried him.

The biggest advantage with long car rides at high speed on bad roads and amongst incompetent drivers was that he could sit and philosophise over serious issues. And so he did this early morning on the way north from Lagos to Ibadan. Before they passed the road to Sagamu, about halfway to Ibadan, it was already clear to him that it all moved towards a direct confrontation between him and the colonel – most likely even of the violent kind. That now seemed inevitable. The colonel avoided him and now only showed up in the office at mysterious times, primarily when he knew that Frank would not be there. It was still not an openly declared war but they were heading in that direction. He wondered why he had not reached this conclusion much earlier, that he had overlooked so many warning signs along the way. He had wanted to arrange things without violent clashes and perhaps that was the reason he had postponed facing the facts for so long. He felt clearer in his head now and had a strong feeling that the time for action was approaching. He found it hard to find excuses for his own lack of initiative but also felt good that he was now ready.

He asked Godwin to stop the car at the first suitable opportunity as he needed to relieve himself. Godwin quickly found what, in local conditions, could be called a rest area and stopped the car with two wheels on the grass, the two wheels on Frank's side of the car. He looked very well on the ground before stepping out and heard a sound in the tall dry grass and saw the back of a snake which escaped hurriedly. Was that a good sign? Well, at least he had not been bitten and that could only be positive. He and Godwin finished peeing and Frank smiled to himself when he noticed that they were shaking it at the same time before zipping up their flies and then went back in the car. Without further comments they continued full speed towards Ibadan.

The plan was taking shape. In the evening he would send Godwin over to the area around the colonel's house in a taxi to scout. He would also promise him a nice bonus if he could give sufficiently detailed information about the area. Frank would rather not play the action hero and then be swallowed by a large quicksand pool to disappear without trace. But, on the other hand, he did not want to play this game any longer where he pretended that nothing serious was going on. Somewhere along the line something really ugly would happen and he no longer believed that diplomacy would take him to victory.

The Glock 17, that he got from Mama Sade, was still in the safe at home and he regretted that he had not done some more training with it. He was not sure how the gun would react in his hand when firing it with live ammunition or how precisely he was even able to shoot any more. It would have been useful to have a few more magazines, which he could prepare in advance but he only had the two she had given him. Two times 17 shots were, therefore, the maximum and it had to be enough. The chairman's management principles were, obviously, correct and under normal circumstance they would have been the way forward. However, at this point they were far beyond the point where such principles could make any difference.

Another big question was how his timing should be in relation to the fact that Segun wanted to visit the colonel. Could he wait for that or was it too risky? Should he try going there alone in the night or should it be when Segun was also there? One of his main concerns was when Ifeoma expected to be there and how it would develop if the colonel saw her and did not believe what she was telling him. What could he do to her? In any case, her phone was not usually switched off for this long. It was an alarming sign and he really worried now.

When they were on the way into Ibadan and struggling with the traffic in Challenge he called Mrs Adebayo to tell her that he was on the way back and wanted to work from home for a couple of hours and then come to the office. As usual, she had some papers to be signed so they agreed that he would send Godwin to the office. That would give him a few hours at home to mentally prepare for what lay ahead of him. There were still a lot of details missing from the plan.

Finally, they stopped in front of the gate, Godwin honked the horn and one of the watchmen jumped out like a jack-in-the-box happily saluting them as Godwin sped up the driveway past him.

Frank grabbed his bag himself and said to Godwin: "Go to the office. Mrs Adebayo has some documents to be signed urgently. I'll stay here until after lunchtime." No reaction from Godwin except a quick glance in the rear-view mirror and a little nod. Frank was happy that his driver was not a chatterbox and that he did not get involved in things unless he was specifically asked.

When he entered the house he once again felt this emptiness in his stomach. It would have been great if Ifeoma was sitting with a beer watching a silly Nollywood movie. However, the TV was not on and it was hot in the sitting room because the air conditioner had not been on since the day before.

He called Temitope. "Could you make some coffee for me? And then at 12.30 I would like some light lunch, just a couple of fried eggs and some sausages." Temitope bowed. "Of course, master."

When the coffee was served, Frank poured himself a cup and went to his office where he locked the door. Then he collected the gun from the safe and started dismantling it, assembled it again, emptied the magazine and filled it up again a sufficient number of times to feel comfortable handling it. He tested how long it took to press out one magazine and put in the other and went through this procedure several times. It was important to be able to load the filled magazine into the gun quickly when you had just fired the last shot and stood in front of a possibly heavily-armed enemy. He regretted not having had the opportunity to fire the Glock as it was important to feel how it would react in his hand especially if he had to fire several shots in succession. He had fired guns in the past, when he was in the military, but it had been a long time ago, and he felt a little rusty which made him nervous.

He decided to call Segun just to thank him for a nice evening although Frank had paid for dinner. It would also remind him about their conversation, but without specifically mentioning the agreement that Segun would contact the colonel. Frank got the impression that Segun was still at the hotel and that he had female company in his room. He smiled to himself. Segun would call him back a little later and Frank imagined that he probably needed to handle some things before checking out.

Frank saw that Caroline was online on Skype and he sent her a short message. "Hey, Caroline, how is it going at home?" She replied quickly with a small complaint about her mother having grounded her for coming home late last weekend when her boyfriend had invited her out.

'Teenage girls and their mothers, a complicated matter,' Frank thought, and sent her a few encouraging comments before disconnecting again. He deliberately avoided getting himself involved in that kind of issue between the ex-wife and the daughter as he had a bad experience. Actually, he had, a couple of times, succeeded in becoming unpopular with both parties and he was fed up with that. And it was not made easier by him being so far away and he felt a little sting of guilty conscience that he was not closer to his daughter at a time when she needed him.

Segun called him back around 12.15 and sounded a happy man who had had a pleasant morning. Apart from being happy he also sounded anxious. "Listen, Frank. I thought about whether we should go to see Chuks together. We've been together before and we can use the excuse about my contract as the reason." Frank was in doubt what he thought about this idea. Why would he and Segun have discussed the contract when it was usually done between the colonel and him? Segun read his mind. "We'll explain to him that we coincidentally ran into each other at Savoy in Lagos and had a few beers together. You asked questions about the conditions on which we cooperate and I took the opportunity to bring up the issue of a contract extension. Sounds plausible, right?"

'He's rather quick, this Segun,' Frank thought.

"Yes, that could be the way forward ... but," he said, while trying to give himself some time to consider the issue.

But Segun gave him no time to think. "OK, then I'll call and agree on a meeting with the colonel tomorrow night if he's available – and he has to be." Before Frank could express his scepticism, Segun had hung up.

'What mental strength,' Frank thought and smiled.

He got lost in his own thoughts and just sat there for a while staring into space. Then he cleared his desk. Godwin was back with the documents from the office including a cheque book filled with cheques to be signed. Frank sighed and began. Then a text message from Segun beeped in, confirming that he had agreed to meet with the colonel at his house the following day at 8 p.m. That was agreed then, and Frank stopped worrying whether it was a good idea or not and what they really hoped to achieve at the meeting. Under any circumstance, it had to be a good idea to have the meeting and get the opportunity to test the atmosphere. He packed the Glock and put it back in the safe.

Suddenly a text message came in from Ifeoma informing him that she was still at church and that he could not call her as she was busy with prayers. She still expected to finish in the evening. He did not quite understand what it was all about but gave up wondering about it. He did not grow up going to church on a regular basis and certainly not being involved in prayers for hours, let alone days, but he knew how important religion was in Africa and accepted it. He had also known from the beginning that with Ifeoma it was not something you questioned and especially not something you made fun of. He answered her text briefly and continued the signing. How nice it would have been to have Ifeoma there now and it was not to sign cheques that he needed her.

A moment later he received another text from her in which she said that she would pass by the colonel's place the following day on the way from church. Frank was disturbed. He almost panicked because he could not speak to her. Why did she actually want to see the colonel again? Were there unanswered questions? Had he found out that in reality she did not work for him and if so did that put Ifeoma in a very dangerous situation?

'Nothing must happen to her,' Frank thought. 'When all of this is over, when we just get this over with, if just …' He could not finish the sentence in his head but sincerely hoped Ifeoma would be part of his life in the future – that he was certain about now.

Temitope knocked on the door and confirmed that the long-awaited eggs and sausages were ready for consumption in the dining room and Frank left his office to eat lunch. As he now knew when to meet with Segun and the colonel and therefore had nothing scheduled that evening he decided to be efficient. So, he called Mrs Adebayo.

"I expect to be in the office around 2 p.m. and would appreciate if you could plan meetings with Funmi, the accountant and the factory manager in the board room at about 45-minute intervals." Perhaps Segun's energy was contagious.

In the office, Frank took his time in each of the meetings and was thorough in dealing with the latest developments with each of the heads of department he had asked to see. They expressed their satisfaction that he took the time to see them and all had several issues to be discussed. He sensed a certain relief, or perhaps rather appreciation, of the interest he showed them. At 6.30p.m. he was drained of energy and packed his things. Godwin sat on the guest chair in front of Frank's office and waited with an expressionless face as he always did when it was late and most of the other drivers had left. Otherwise he would sit in the drivers' room next to the security office at the main gate.

On the way home, Frank stopped at a small Indian-owned grocery store where he bought supplies of wine, liquor and other basic foodstuffs for the evening. He wanted to start by sweating for about half an hour on the exercise bike and then undo the good work with a couple of large whiskies and a bottle of wine with the food. He would have loved to talk to George or Mama Sade but remembered her instruction not to come to the bar again. He had great respect for that as he knew that he, and perhaps also Sade, could be under surveillance by a paranoid colonel and his henchmen.

Godwin followed him around in the shop and carried the basket. 'Another one of those practical things that were difficult to change in Africa,' Frank thought. All that he needed to do was actually place the items in the basket and pay the cashier, then everything was carried around in the shop, out to the car and into the house – even placed in the fridge or the bar.

Everything was organised down to the smallest detail which could be a big advantage in the daily routines. However, it could be very difficult if you wanted to change such established systems. That could be a major challenge he had learned during his relatively short stay.

Just as they left the grocery store, Segun called. "It's very strange but now Chuks has just called me and cancelled our meeting tomorrow. He was very brief and said that something important had come up so he can't meet us tomorrow."

"Did he say when it would be possible the meet then?" Frank asked.

"No. Not at all and he actually hung up in the middle of a sentence just as I was asking."

Segun was big and calm guy but now he sounded agitated and spoke faster than he usually did.

"OK," Frank said. "Thanks for calling me. It sounds very strange, indeed. I'll think about how to handle the situation. Maybe I should still go there and pretend to have misunderstood the message but I'll think about that and we'll talk tomorrow." Frank was aware that if any action needed to be taken, he would have to do it himself. He would spend the evening making his plans. The time for meetings, discussions and diplomacy had run out. He had to plan completely different and practical measures.

They went up the driveway and Frank said to Godwin. "Godwin, when you've parked the car, come to the sitting room. There's something I want you to do for me. A big favour actually and a kind of secret mission." Godwin looked at him in the rear-view mirror with open bewilderment but said nothing. Frank sat down at the dining table and when Godwin brought his briefcase from the car he stood at the other side of the table.

"Yes sir," which meant something like; "I'm ready to hear what you want me to do." Godwin did not use the word "master" about this boss but "sir" which was not less respectful but for the employee seemed less submissive.

"I would appreciate if you don't talk about this to anybody else but I have a little assignment for you. Do you know Colonel Chukwuemeka's house in Bodija?" Godwin did, and it would have surprised Frank if he did not. "Then I'll give you money for a taxi to go there but you don't go to the house itself and you must not be seen. You just need to pass by and see how many houses are on each side of the colonel's house and where it looks like people are at home. Is that clear enough?"

Godwin nodded seriously. "Is something wrong, sir?" he asked.

"I don't know yet but there's something I want to investigate and you're a loyal employee that I can trust – one of the few," Frank said, and Godwin stood straight-backed and looked serious, perhaps even determined. "I believe there are some empty plots at the end of the street where he lives. Find out if it is possible to go from there around the back of the house on the colonel's side of the street. Still clear enough?" Godwin confirmed that it was, now even more straight-backed than before. "Here's the money for the taxi and be careful not to be seen. Then come back as soon as you have scouted."

Apparently, that was not a word included in Godwin's otherwise excellent vocabulary. "When I have what?" he asked hesitantly.

"Yes, when you have checked, shall we say spied a bit in the area." Then Godwin understood and smiled, clicked his heels and left on his mission.

Frank looked into the kitchen and said to Temitope that he should serve the food as soon as it was ready which he confirmed with no hesitation. "And then fill the ice bucket with ice cubes. I feel like having whisky tonight." Temitope dropped all other kitchen utensils and quickly attacked the latest assignment and carried it out speedily.

At the bar, Frank filled a drink glass with ice cubes and twisted off the cap of the newly acquired Whyte & Mackay. 'A bit of a slave whisky,' he thought, and already looked forward to the first taste while swinging the ice cubes around in the glass and letting the whisky melt the surface slightly before taking the first taste. He stood behind the bar in the corner of the sitting room, put a Freddie Mercury CD on the music system at the end of the bar and started drawing small figures on a piece of paper. At times, when he did not want to sit alone in his home office, he used the bar as workspace sitting on a bar stool with his laptop on the bar.

'Not quite orthodox,' he thought, but rather practical and the height of the bar was also suitable for standing up and working if one felt like stretching the legs and the back. That was supposed to be good for the blood circulation he had read somewhere.

"The fact that time is running out, for us all. Time waits for nobody. Time waits for nobody,' sang Freddie Mercury.

Around 10 p.m. Godwin came back and reported to him. He had obtained a very clear picture of the area around the colonel's house and had focused especially on the slightly remote corner with 3-4 empty plots from where one could move behind the row of houses where the colonel's house was situated, with two houses on one side and three on the other. However, only one of houses looked inhabited and it was very quiet and dark in that area, Godwin remarked in a worried voice.

Frank thanked Godwin, said goodnight and gave him some more money for a taxi home plus a little extra pocket money. Then he went to the bar, poured a large whisky and started working on a sketch of the area around the colonel's house. He managed, on the basis of Godwin's information, to prepare a decent map. On the back of the drawing he scribbled a few notes, a kind of shopping list for the decisive battle to take place the following day. One of the most important points was wearing shoes with a rubber sole, probably tennis shoes, he wrote. At that time the whisky gave him one last bright moment before going blank. He quickly noted that he needed to pass by the local builders' store, if you could call Charlie's messy shop that – it did not resemble any builders' warehouse in Denmark. At Charlie's he needed to buy a solid rope and a metal hook, not for mountaineering, but to help him over a tall wall if that should prove necessary.

Freddie was replaced by opera – late Luciano Pavarotti from a concert in New York many years earlier – and the whisky replaced by a cold Star around midnight. At the same time the plans began to blur for Frank, who was now sitting on a bar stool with both elbows on the bar without being worried about the blood circulation in his legs – one of which had actually gone to sleep.

'It's about time to turn in,' he thought.

Chapter Thirty-Seven

Later in the day Frank could not remember how he got up in the morning, how he had gone to the office or most of what he had done during the day. He had been on autopilot most of the day also helped by the fact that it was Saturday and therefore very quiet in the office. This mental autopilot was switched on until he stepped inside his home just after nightfall. From that point on, everything became crystal clear to him and he noticed every little detail of what was going on around him. The world had, all at once, become high definition and his mind was clearer than it had been at any time since he landed in Lagos, when Nigeria started affecting him mentally and pushing his sanity out into the tiniest vessels in his brain and pulling his nerves to breaking point.

In order not to spoil his clarity he abstained from drinking alcohol but took a cup of coffee with him to the office where he took out the Glock and checked it thoroughly one last time. Thereafter, he tried how best to carry the gun so that it was not visible but could still be brought out without becoming entangled in clothing. He wanted, at all costs, to avoid a situation where he lost vital seconds if he ran out of luck. He ended up with a solution with the gun pushed down in his belt at the back and a shirt worn loose over the trousers. For the same reason he chose to wear a shirt that was slightly too large, looked himself in the mirror and was happy with the result.

"You talkin' to me? You talkin' to me? I'm the only one here. Who the fuck do you think you are talkin' to?" He chuckled a bit over his imitation of Robert De Niro in Taxi Driver, tried to pull out the gun a few times, thought it worked well and dropped the fooling around.

Godwin was waiting in the car in silence. He often sat and listened to the local news when Frank came out in the morning but not tonight. No radio. He probably sensed the seriousness of the situation and was perhaps a bit proud of being involved in a sort of secret mission and where he played an important part.

At around 9:00p.m. Frank went to the car and, acting on a sudden impulse, he asked Godwin to go to Kokodome from where he took a taxi to Sadelicious. He enjoyed Sade's surprised but pleased expression when he arrived.

"Frank, are you still alive?" She came to him and gave him a tight hug and a kiss on the cheek.

"I told you it was better not to come here. You remember that, or is it early dementia setting in?"

Yes, Frank remembered it but reassured her that he had used a decoy on the way there.

"Smart guy, Frank, but I can see that you have something on your mind tonight. What's going to happen and why do you have your Glock in the belt on the back? Are you going to war?"

'She had, of course, felt it immediately,' he thought. It was interesting that he had not noticed it when she touched the gun. She had probably distracted him with her huge breasts and then let her hand slide down his back. Perhaps she was really a commando soldier or a secret agent.

In any case, he felt good having her on his side.

"There was a reason you gave it to me and I thought it could be useful tonight. Do you have a few minutes in private?" Frank asked. She nodded and pulled him inside the backroom.

"How's George?" he asked.

"He's much better and will soon come home but then he begins a long recovery. He should also have a good prosthesis, a leg prosthesis that is – the other one works very well." She laughed when Frank did not immediately understand what she meant. "Sit down, Frank. I'll get you a drink, is it beer or G & T today?"

"Just a soda water today," he replied, and sat down.

"She was back quickly with his soda and served it to him. "This your colonel is onto something crazy," she said, and looked at him.

"Yes, I have the same feeling and I'm damn nervous about what's going on," Frank replied.

"I checked around a bit and there are some of his friends coming from different places in the country for the time being. Some people are talking about their brotherhood but I can't find out exactly what it stands for. It's probably some kind of lodge or order, perhaps even something more secret and mysterious like a cult," Mama Sade whispered, while looking around the small room as if there could be spies or microphones. "He is doing something, that's for sure. Have you seen him in the office lately?"

Frank's heart was beating fast and he started sweating.

'Ifeoma,' he thought. 'She's in danger … in serious danger now. If cult-like activities are going on at the colonel's place her life could be at great risk.' His throat closed up and he was breathing in short bursts. He became impatient to get going to the colonel's house but he knew that there would be a greater risk of being seen if he came too early.

"Frank, are you feeling sick?" Mama Sade asked.

"No, no. I'm OK. It's just … I was just thinking … but you asked if I had seen the colonel. No, actually I haven't seen him for a while. For some reason he's always out of town when I'm in and in the office when I'm away."

"Hmm. What are your plans for tonight?" she asked.

"I plan to spy a bit around his house. I think I can get around the back of the house where it's dark and quiet and perhaps get inside the perimeter," he said, and anxiously awaited her reaction.

"You must have had a stroke, man. He has heavily armed policemen as his guards – you risk being shot to pieces before you can think of your little toy pistol," she said agitatedly.

"As far as I have been informed, those policemen mostly sit at the parking lot, drink and have a good time. They don't think there is any real danger since the colonel shot a burglar from his window with a shotgun last year. Everybody knows it's a dangerous house to approach," Frank said.

"Yes, exactly and now you want to ride in and start a personal vendetta, armed with a little Glock and two magazines. You do have both magazines, don't you?"

she said, and pressed her index finger into his chest. "Have you trained with it? Maybe fired it and got used to handling it at least?"

"Yes, I have been sitting and fumbling with it. Now it only takes me eight minutes to release the safety so I can shoot and 14 minutes to change the magazine. As long as I don't need more than 17 shots that should be OK, yes?"

She shook her head and smiled. "You're a good kid, Frank but please don't get shot today. Please. Maybe I should go there with you myself."

They sat for a while and thought it over. "But, Frank. If you really go there, then point number one: be careful and run away if you see that it becomes too dangerous. And point number two: don't shoot anybody unless it is unavoidable. Certainly not a policeman.

"Could you write that down for me on a little note. My memory is not very good. No, jokes aside, I have understood. Maybe I should just knock on the door and ask what they hell is going on." He scratched his chin as if pondering over this option.

"Be serious, Frank. It is a question of life or death." She looked sincerely worried.

After a quick exchange about how they imagined things could develop and which risks he was up against it was almost 11 p.m. and it was about time to get going. He did not dare to wait any longer.

"OK, Frank. Like last time, the young lady can accompany you to your car so it looks like you've come to pick her up. Then she'll find her way back again."

"Thank you for everything you've done for me. What would I do without you?" Frank said.

She took his head between her hands and looked at him with wet eyes. "You be careful now, my son, and also this time he got a kiss on the mouth and a little pat on the cheek. "Off you go then," she said, and Frank knew that it was time to move on.

She gave instructions to the girl who smiled at Frank and nodded. Maybe she thought it was becoming a recurring job and did not look like she minded that assignment. They held hands, walked to the street and hired a taxi.

When they got to Kokodome she continued without any farewell formalities and he jumped into his own car which was parked in the shade next to the Christian book store. A lone drunkard came wobbling out from Kokodome arguing with himself but otherwise there was nobody in sight.

Frank concluded that it was not the place to go on a Saturday evening for the time being. There were also very few cars in the streets in the area which made Frank feel sure that he was not being followed.

They rolled out from the large parking lot in front of Kokodome and Cocoa House which stood like a threatening mastodon with its 24 storeys, dark and ghost-like.

Godwin knew where they were going and nothing was said in the car. Frank sat with his legs slightly to one side, as the gun was uncomfortable against his back.

"Godwin, when we get there, drive slowly so we can see if there are any policemen outside the gate. If there are, we'll take a detour. I don't want them to see us," Frank said, when they were approaching the colonel's house.

"OK, sir, but I didn't see any yesterday. I think they are sitting inside on the parking lot drinking, sir." Frank hoped they would be doing just that this evening as well.

They were getting closer to the area and turned down the colonel's street. There was a side street two houses before his, so they could turn off if they saw a policeman outside but everything was quiet and they drove past the house.

"Just continue up to the end and park the car so it's not visible, Godwin," Frank said. He got another, "OK, sir," in response.

Godwin manoeuvred the car in between a couple of trees in an expert way and switched off the engine and headlights so the only sound heard was the noise from the cicadas. Frank wondered whether they actually sang or if they made the loud noise by rubbing their feet or wings against each other. He dropped the thought and would have to Google it if he survived this evening. However, it had reminded him about the mobile phone which he now put on silent – phew, what a blunder that could have been.

He slowly got out of the car and said to Godwin, "You stay here in the car and keep an eye on what's going on further up the street. We may need to get out of here fast. Oh yeah, and if you see anything important send me a text."

"OK, sir. I will leave the windows open so I can hear what's going on," he whispered to Frank, who nodded, gave him the thumbs up and started walking towards the empty plots on the same side of the street as the colonel's house.

The grass was tall and dry as it had not rained in more than a month now and with every step he took, it crunched under his feet. He worried a bit about snakes and moved slowly forward so they had a chance to escape when they felt the shaking from his footsteps. The moon was now behind a cloud and it had become very dark except for the colonel's clearly lit house further up the street.

Frank passed a large pile of garbage. So, this was where people dumped their trash when living in this fashionable area. The smell from the pile was a nauseating mixture of rotten foodstuffs and burned rubber. He heard a rustle from the pile and assumed it was a rat. He walked around the pile and had almost reached the last house in the street where obviously nobody was home. At the back of the house he saw a small lake but fortunately there was just enough space between the wall around the house and the lake for him to pass without needing to swim. He was pleased that it was not the rainy season and checked that the gun was secure in his belt and that there was no sign that the extra magazine and the box of bullets would jump out of his pockets. He stood with his back against the wall of the first house. The air was warm and humid while the uneven surface of the wall felt cool through his shirt.

Slowly, but surely, he moved sideways with small steps and made it past the lake without incident. From there the vegetation became more dense and taller and hid him from any possible curious passer-by. Not that he could imagine who would be going for an evening stroll in such a place so late in the evening. He decided to relieve himself to avoid doing it later at a more critical time. There were plenty of mosquitoes in the thicket which he now moved through with difficulty. If he survived, he would most likely need an anti-malarial treatment within a couple of weeks, but that was the least of his worries right now.

Finally, he reached the colonel's house which he could not see from the ground but knew was the fourth house from the empty plot, and he could easily count that far even in pitch darkness and in a particularly tense situation.

He stood and caught his breath under a large mango tree. He had the rope with the hook around his waist and was lucky that the large tree had a branch which went over the wall, so he could climb the tree, push himself along the branch and then lower himself down inside the wall around the colonel's house. Lower down, another large branch had been cut off but that was obviously a long time ago. Lucky, because there were, as he had expected, electrical wires on top of the wall and he would rather avoid colliding with these.

Frank was not very comfortable with heights but here he was looking at about four metres and that should not give him serious problems, especially as he was helped by the darkness.

He was already out of breath from the excitement when he threw the rope with the hook up in the air and it gave a loud plonk when it hit the branch. He feared that the loud noise had been heard about 12-14 kilometres away but he noticed no reaction. The hook landed a few inches from his foot so until now luck had been on his side. Two more attempts and the hook got hold of a smaller branch higher up than the large branch Frank wanted to climb up to. He pulled the rope hard to confirm that the hook was fixed firmly to the smaller branch.

He began pulling himself up while walking his feet up the tree trunk which was fortunately very rough giving him a solid grip. The biggest part of this circus act was getting from standing out vertically into the air with both hands around the rope to sitting on the branch. He wished that he had had some training in this exercise. It was something they had omitted teaching them at Copenhagen Business School and it would be a very inconvenient place and time to fall down and break an ankle, never mind the neck. At one point he hung by his forearms from the branch with his legs freely kicking in the air but then he got his legs wrapped around the rope. That gave him enough support to pull himself onto the branch. He was wildly out of breath and his hands were shaking from exhaustion but he was sure that there were many other challenges in store for him and he took a deep breath. Sitting on the large branch, Frank could just reach the smaller branch over his head to loosen the hook from it. As he needed the rope to lower himself down inside the wall he wrapped it around his waist again and fixed the hook so it would not hang loose. He then started pulling himself across the branch in tiny movements and was surprised how complicated this, in principle simple, exercise actually was. He had, some time in his adolescence, ridden a horse without a saddle together with a girlfriend but then he had, in the absence of stirrups, had the fat stomach of the pony as stabilising point. Here his legs hung freely in the air and it felt very insecure and awkward. At one point he almost lost his balance and had to throw his upper body along the branch and hold on to it with both hands to avoid falling down.

'Phew, that was close,' he thought with relief.

When he reached the wall, he had to keep his legs bent as he did not want to touch the electrical wire on the wall and perhaps be electrocuted. You never knew how much power a madman like the colonel had run through the wire. It was probably just plugged into a normal electrical socket. It made it even harder to move forward along the branch with his legs bent and he must have looked ridiculous up there on the branch with bent legs, moving forward with tiny skips of about five inches at the time.

Frank could now see the guest house inside the garden, from where a soft red light filtered out through the windows. He saw movement from shadows in the windows but had no idea what was going on in there and he also had to concentrate on the branch balancing act up in the tree.

Just as he had passed the wall and prepared to descend into the garden, he heard footsteps in the dry grass and saw the glowing end of a cigarette over by the guest house. It came closer.

Frank lay down over the branch and hoped that he would not fall down onto the head of a person in the garden. He assumed it was an armed guard who would probably not waste much time on investigative conversation.

In-depth investigations did not seem to be the police's main strength in this region. Frank heard his own breathing which sounded deafening in his own ears but he kept his balance on the branch. How he would have loved to be somewhere else right now. How likely was it that the guard in the garden would look up?

He assumed that the people who had accepted armed guard duties would rarely walk around admiring the beautiful moon, which was now hidden by clouds to Frank's great relief.

He could just about make out the silhouette of the guard who made a swinging movement with his upper body, probably to put his AK-47 on this back. Then Frank heard urination in the dry vegetation and the man let a loud fart slip out with a little moan and spat on the ground. He zipped up his pants and started walking back towards the guest house then around it. Frank hoped that this was a routine patrol and that the next round would be much later in the night. He sat up and straightened his back while reassuring himself that he was far enough from the wall to straighten his legs. The next difficult trick was to fix the rope to the branch and lower himself into the garden. He had reached a crucial time where, in a moment, he would have reached the point beyond which retreat would be problematic and inconvenient, if not downright impossible.

He found a suitable place to fix the hook where it would stay in place, hanging there as a possible escape route. Then he swung out his legs over the branch, got hold of the rope with both hand and feet and then lowered himself slowly to the ground. The rope was a good solid but local quality and it left him with a few small splinters in the palm of his hands, but that was the least of his problems.

He still had the gun in his belt and Frank now decided to bring it out so he was prepared for whatever might happen while he moved as quietly as possible through the dry grass towards the guest house. His heart was galloping from nervousness over what he might find.

Before he dared to look in through the windows he first walked to one side of the house to ensure that there was nobody there. Then he checked the other side but the guard, who had previously made a round, had apparently returned to his guard headquarters at the parking in front of the main building. Then Frank went to one of the windows. The blinds were closed on the inside but they did not cover completely, and he peeped through a small opening between two slats into the room which was bathed in a dark-red light.

The room was only lit by a large number of candles and wall lamps with dark-red shades. It was quite gloomy in the room and it took some time before Frank could make out the detail in there because of the small aperture in the blinds. Slowly, he understood the horrible scenario and the act that was underway in the so-called guest house. It really looked like a place where you would never invite guests to stay. On the walls were some symbols formed in black metal and, as far as Frank could see, it was not Christian symbols. He rather guessed that it was of the occult.

He touched his small golden cross that he carried around his neck, not particularly as a Christian symbol but rather as simple decoration. He made the sign of the cross and wondered where that came from. A longer prayer to the higher powers would have been appropriate but there was no time for that.

Inside the guest house, which only consisted of one large room, stood six people in long robes, black hats and gloves around a very large table on which was spread out a red cloth.

Frank's heart leapt when he saw a person lying with arms and legs tied to each corner of the table. The person was wearing a long dress and head gear in the same red colour as the cloth covering the large table. He felt dizzy when he recognised the woman on the table.

Chapter Thirty-Eight

It was Ifeoma who lay tied up on the table. Franks stomach turned itself upside down and he had to turn around for a moment and kneeled down on one knee, spat and waited for his stomach to find its right position again. He got up, looked in through the blinds again and confirmed to his horror that it really was Ifeoma. She seemed to be only partially conscious. She hardly moved at all and stared with open eyes at the ceiling. On each side of her stretched out body there was a row of lit candles which created long shadows and gave the entire scenario a chilling look.

He faintly heard music and a slow rhythm and deep tones from inside the room but he did not recognise it. The six men, because it was undoubtedly all men, approached the table and started walking around it with small steps and their gazes directed towards Ifeoma.

'This is gonna go wrong,' Frank thought, and was panicking with his heart racing away and sweat dripping from his face. If only he had an AK-47, he would have attacked immediately but with a weak little Glock 17 in his hand the six men inside the guest house would be the stronger force. He looked at his shaking hand with the gun and checked that the second magazine was where it should be in the trouser pocket, took a few deep breaths and licked the sweat off his upper lip.

'Okija shrine,' Frank thought, and shuddered at the thought of the atrocities left behind from human sacrifices which the police had found in Okija in Anambra State a few years ago. These sacrifices had taken place over a longer period of time and many body parts in various states of decomposition had been found. It shook the country to its core. So-called priests had killed a large number of people but insisted stubbornly that they had been killed by a divinity, despite evidence that the sick congregation had taken over the valuables of the deceased. Frank had the impression that his dear Ifeoma was about to be the sacrifice to something similar before his very eyes and his stomach took another full speed rollercoaster ride.

The procession of men in black robes inside the house continued slowly around the table. How much time did he have to save Ifeoma? Surely very little time, that was if she had not already been poisoned. It was extremely difficult to find hope in this situation but he certainly did not intend to give up in advance. Frank just managed to see the participants pull their long robes aside and each of them pull out a long, old-fashioned sword. Then the sound of metal hitting stone tore him out of his thoughts. He turned towards the main building from where the sound had come. It was the armed guard again, or perhaps one of his colleagues, who came stumbling towards the guest house. Frank quickly jumped around the corner to the back of the house and waited for a moment. The guard was out of breath and swayed heavily which was in line with the rumours that they were sitting in a group drinking in the parking lot at night. This guard had, like the first one, a need to relieve himself. After having placed his AK-47 against the wall he emptied his bladder with a copious amount of urine spraying against the guest house wall. Then he became curious and wanted to look through the blinds at the secret scene but he had difficulty finding an opening in the blinds. Exactly at that point, Frank jumped around the corner and, before the guard in his drunkenness could react, Frank hammered the barrel of the pistol into his temple. The effect was dramatic as Frank had hit a vein resulting in blood pumping about an inch out of the wound in the forehead. The bad news was that the guard had fallen over forwards with a loud scream before he fell to the ground and the first spray of blood had hit the guest house window.

'Somebody inside the house must have heard the noise,' Frank thought. He did not investigate the matter further but placed his pistol in the belt, this time in front, and grabbed the guard's AK-47. Once again Okafor's brief instruction at the Sheraton proved useful. Frank quickly clicked out the magazine and checked the contents – it was full. He put it back in and set the lever on the right-hand side of the weapon to automatic.

The blinds were pulled open and a face appeared in the window. Frank turned around and fired a brief burst into the head of the person sending splintering glass flying around his head.

He was pretty sure to have hit even with his eyes closed. Then he jumped around to the back of the guest house and walked to the other side which had similar windows. He saw nobody in the windows, threw himself on the ground and crawled forward towards the entrance of the guest house from where a person came running out in total panic. Frank fired a burst into his back and the man fell to the ground on his face, kicked with one leg in cramps a couple of times then lay completely still. That was two and he had seen six people inside the house, but then there were also the guards who must have heard the shooting and would come sprinting in a moment.

Frank ran to the front door with the machine gun ready to fire. One of the other participants, still wearing his long black robe but now without his hat, came storming out of the door with his sword lifted up high. He recognised Okonkwo and it made him hesitate so long that he only just evaded it enough to make the sword hit his loose shirt, fortunately without doing him any harm. The weight of the sword coming from up high made Okonkwo lose his balance when the sword hit the ground next to Frank's foot and he rolled over the grass for a couple of metres until Frank's next burst sent three bullets into his left thigh. Okonkwo sat up and screamed with both hands around his thigh, when Frank fired another short burst and hit him with one shot in the forehead. Frank did not know how many shots were normally in an AK-47 magazine and tried to keep the bursts short but it was difficult in the heat of moment. He had a feeling that he would soon run out of ammunition. There was no time to waste. Frank no longer deliberated about his actions. He was running on autopilot although he had no clue how it had been coded into him – perhaps in an earlier life.

He ran through the door into the guest house well aware that they were probably waiting for him inside the door. He jumped into the room and rolled the first couple of metres over the floor before getting back on his feet to turn around. There was a dark silhouette on each side of the door and Frank hit one in the chest with a short burst that made the machine gun run out of ammunition. The other person came running towards him with his sword held high and Frank had to throw himself aside to avoid having his head split into two. When the man passed him, Frank just had enough time to swing the machine gun around and hit him in the face with the butt. From the sound Frank estimated that bones had been crushed. Frank immediately threw the machine gun on the floor, pulled his Glock out of the belt, cocked the gun and fired three shots into the back of the man lying next to him. All of a sudden, everything was quiet apart from the slow and gloomy music playing on a music system somewhere in the room. No shots, no noise from running guards, no heavy breathing and worst of all not a sound from Ifeoma lying less than two metres from where he stood. He could see that she was still alive but he knew that there was still one of the men of darkness left in the room. He knew that both he and Ifeoma, if she was still alive, were in extreme danger. Who was the last one? Frank was not sure but he had a strong feeling that it was the worst of them all, the man who had proved to be his worst enemy, Colonel Chuks.

Frank stood with his back against one wall, right hand with the gun stretched out in front of him and with the left hand as support while he moved the arm from side to side to cover the room as well as possible. He should have sufficient bullets left in the magazine to do what was necessary. Suddenly two things happened simultaneously; a guard came in through the door and looked around the room in confusion – it was the colonel's special bodyguard, Okafor, and the colonel rose behind the large table with a loud growl and lifted his long heavy sword above his head and down along his back. There he stopped the movement but he was ready to swing the sword forward at any time. The colonel stared at Frank with wild eyes and a macabre stiff smile on his mouth. He looked like a person in a trance.

Okafor held his machine gun and looked from side to side from Frank to the colonel. He seemed puzzled but then pulled himself together and pointed it directly at Frank. "Drop the gun, Mr Frank," he shouted and made a slight movement with the machine gun to indicate to Frank that he should drop the gun on the floor.

The colonel was still standing with this mad expression frozen on his face, staring at Frank without speaking. Frank pointed at the colonel with the gun in his right hand supported with the left. Okafor, pointing his AK-47 at Frank, would probably not hesitate to shoot him. The colonel held the heavy sword in both hands down behind his back ready to swing it at Ifeoma who was apparently not sufficiently conscious to understand what was going on. They stood like that for some seconds, perhaps five, maybe ten, probably not more than that … it felt like an eternity.

Frank heard the two shots but did not fathom where they came from. He turned his head towards the entrance just in time to see Okafor, with a gaping hole in his forehead and a baffled expression on his face, fall over forward and land on the floor with a bizarre thump. Segun was standing at the door with a gun in his hands. They looked at each other for a split second and then shifted focus to the colonel who had now set the sword in motion in a big arch over his head.

Frank and Segun fired their guns almost at the same time, several shots in succession. One shot tore a hole in the colonel's black robe at his right shoulder but did not hit him. A second went through his throat and a third cleared his upper mouth of teeth. The last shot Frank fired removed the colonel's left eye and left a dark hole while a cloud of brain mass sprayed out of the back of his head. The shots were lethal but they did not stop the colonel in his movement. The sword had been set in motion, forward and downwards and continued down towards Ifeoma tied to the large table. Frank saw it all in slow motion but without any option of pressing the pause button. He was too far from the table to stop the sword. He fired a couple of shots hoping to divert the sword but missed and it continued its path down towards Ifeoma until it, in the now lifeless hands of the colonel, hacked into Ifeoma's throat.

The sound was horrible and Frank screamed desperately as loudly as he could; "Noooooo," while he saw the blood cascade into the air. He knew instantly that it was all over. He had lost Ifeoma to this sickening human sacrifice ritual and a completely mad colonel, whom he and Segun had just shot to pieces. Frank fell forward, hit the edge of the table and was down on his knees. He was dizzy and felt nausea and stayed down with one knee on the floor while trying to pull himself together. He felt Segun grab him under his arms and pull him to his legs. He stood swaying for a moment.

"Where the hell did you come from?" he asked Segun.

"I heard you say something about coming here alone and it worried me. My driver had gotten your driver's number when we were in Lagos so he found out about your plans. And the rest is history as one says."

"What about the other guards?" Frank asked.

I lit a fire down the street and shouted for help. Then they came storming out the gate in their drunkenness and I could wander in without problems."

"If I had just shot the colonel immediately and not waited for him to swing the sword ..." Frank found it difficult to speak and became dizzy again.

"You did everything humanly possible to save her and don't forget that the policeman was standing there pointing his gun at you. You can't blame yourself."

Frank went to the table where he loosened the ropes around Ifeoma's hands and legs. He could hardly bear looking at her face but forced himself to do so one last time. He closed her eyes, bowed down and kissed her hand. Then he threw the gun on the floor and stumbled out of the guest house supported by Segun. Away from this horrible place. Away from the worst experience he had ever had.

Chapter Thirty-Nine

Frank had gone down to Lagos in the afternoon to take the night flight to Amsterdam. On arrival in Lagos, there was still some time left before KLM would begin check-in and he considered for a moment driving over to Savoy Suites to have a beer and wondered if Funke's service was still as impeccable and her smile as sweet as he remembered it. However, he dropped the idea and instead asked Godwin to go to the Protea Hotel in the same street, where he went to the bar and ordered a small bottle of Nederburg while observing the British Airways crew which had just arrived and de-stressed with some large draught beers and gin & tonics. He tried to guess who was the captain, the first officer, the purser and who were the new stewards and stewardesses and he thought, from their behaviour and interaction, that he more or less got it right.

Then he finished his drink, paid the bill and went to the airport. He would rather make sure he got through the security circus in good time and have some waiting time in the airport than get there at the last minute and be stressed.

In the departure terminal there was the usual noise and general commotion around check-in. Here there was no sign that the peace of Christmas would sink in any time soon. The airport's computer system had broken down and the entire check-in procedure had to be done manually. Frank was happy to have arrived early and was sweating like a pig in the crowded and warm terminal while he slowly moved forward in the queue at the check-in counter. An African gentleman with a load of hand luggage, heavy winter coat and bowler hat tried to jump him in the queue and Frank was ready to go on the warpath but then dropped the idea. He looked at the man and just shook his head.

This time Frank had succeeded in getting a seat in business class and he enjoyed the service and the food which was several levels above what he had had to consume on so many other flights over the years. When Frank was served his coffee and cognac, he switched off his reading lamp and sat philosophising over what he had been through over the past few months.

After the scary experience in the colonel's garden, Frank had been on a strict diet of Valium, healthy balanced food and zero alcohol for a week. He had needed the Valium for a few days but had then scaled down and was beginning to feel normal again. Emotionally, a part of him had been amputated but he was functioning on a strictly practical level.

He had managed to be sufficiently alert, with Mrs Adebayo's assistance, to arrange for Ifeoma's body to be collected by a professional undertaker who had prepared it for the funeral. This, however, had been planned to take place in Owerri and her family had collected the body. As Frank was not able to participate in the funeral, they had held a simple and private ceremony in a small chapel at the undertaker's place where Frank said his goodbyes to her. It had just been her closest family and a few friends, apart from Frank, and it had been quiet but influenced by her deep religious philosophy. A strong spiritual experience which had touched Frank deeply and which he felt would influence him for the rest of his life.

Thereafter, the company had arranged an impressive farewell reception for him where even the chairman was present. The short man with the big ego had been almost humble which was very different from his usual exaggerated confidence. He had praised Frank for his drive, offered him to return if he was interested and even rounded off with a "well done" and a slap on the shoulder.

It had been a very generous farewell reception and it had even crossed Frank's mind who would have to approve the bill but, fortunately, that was no longer his headache. It had been good, but also sad, to say goodbye to Segun, Mrs Adebayo, Funmi and several of the other people.

However, the highlight had been to see George arrive together with Mama Sade and the separation had been moving despite the short time they had known each other.

Frank was feeling sleepy and moved the seat back as far as possible, which was not quite horizontal but sufficiently low for his head to fall comfortably back. He succeeded in getting about two and half hours of proper sleep before the cabin crew started scrambling with the breakfast trolley.

In Schiphol airport the luxury ended as there was a passport control, which took forever, just outside the plane and Frank had to run like a madman to catch his connecting flight.

Consequently, he was the last passenger, out of breath and sweating, to get onboard the KLM Boeing 737 to Copenhagen. He had just fastened his seat belt when the crew announced, with a Dutch accent, "Boarding completed" and a moment later; "Yellow door selectors to automatic and cross check".

It being an old habit of his, he kept an eye on the cabin crew checking that the handle had in fact been put at automatic on the other side of the plane. 'Routines in an aircraft are well-oiled and the personnel well-trained,' he thought, and wished that the same could always be the case in other companies where he had worked over the years.

About an hour later they flew out over the Bay of Køge and continued to the Swedish coast line before the pilot made a soft left turn, passed over Saltholm and prepared for landing in a grey and windy Copenhagen.

The screen stated 19 minutes to delivery of baggage from KL1125 when Frank reached the baggage delivery area and he switched his brain to standby but suddenly he remembered his mobile phone. He quickly changed his Nigerian SIM card to the Danish card which he used during stays in Denmark, short or long. The baggage began rolling out onto the conveyor belt and his two large Samsonite suitcases were among the first. Onto the baggage trolley and off through the green exit at customs.

After a short stop at 7-Eleven to buy a bottle of water and some liquorice he took the airport shuttle to the car rental centre near the domestic terminal. A young Swedish blonde at the Hertz office gave him a professional and service-minded smile while making sure he got his Volvo XC-60 which he had booked online. He thanked Swedish Anika for her good service.

He accidentally pushed over a small child when turning his baggage trolley quickly and excused himself to an angry American mother after which he soon found the dark-blue XC-60 and threw the luggage in the back, adjusted the seat, started the engine and put on the butt heating at full strength. The radio was on Danish Radio programme 3 which happily played Mariah Carey's "All I want for Christmas is you".

Before driving out of the parking at the airport, he sent a similar text message to both children. "Hi, Nikolaj and Caroline. I have landed and am on my way. Are you ready? Then we'll go to the summer house. I'll send a text when I'm outside." He was sure that they understood that he could not handle being confronted with their mother on such a morning after having travelled all night. Into "drive" with the automatic gear and off to the highway, then towards Gentofte to collect the children.

They drove across the bridge in Frederikssund around noon and continued toward Kulhuse after passing Jaegerspris Castle. A couple of kilometres before Kulhuse, they passed the relatively new and charming church in Skoven, where Frank thought he might become a regular customer. He had never been there but it looked appealing from outside – humbler than what he had seen in Nigeria but probably more in line with his own temperament.

They stopped to buy some provisions at the supermarket, before going to open the summer house further up Krakasvej. It was cold inside the house, and the first thing Frank did, after having carried the luggage inside, was to light up the fireplace. A retired neighbour, who helped him with practical things in the house, had cut down a couple of large pines the previous year and there was plenty of firewood stacked against the house outside. They switched on the TV and the children installed themselves in their rooms where they had often stayed when visiting him. He made some popcorn in the microwave and opened a bottle of Amarone from 2009 which he had kept for a special occasion. Then he found the cigar that he had just bought in the supermarket, put on his jacket again and went outside as he was very anxious about the non- smoking principle inside the house.

Outside on the terrace he stood in his slippers and heavy leather jacket with a glass of red wine in his hand while smoking his cigar; the first one in a very long time. The air was fresh and crisp, in contrast to the warm and humid air in West Africa, and there was an ice-cold wind biting his nose and prickling his cheeks. He stood observing his overgrown garden which needed some looking after. It was good to be home. He felt a tear run down his cheek in the cold air, wiped it away with the back of his hand before it froze to ice and almost choked. Nikolaj opened the door and shouted, "Dad, isn't it fucking cold out there? Why don't you come in and watch a movie? I have the latest Planet of the Apes." Frank turned around and nodded. Then Caroline came outside and stood next to him as if they observed the scenario together. She took his hand.

"Dad, we know it was difficult in Nigeria but let's have a good time please. You can tell us about it when you're ready, OK?" She paused a moment. "And we have to decorate for Christmas as well, right?"

Frank swallowed a lump in his throat. "Thank you, Caroline," he said, and gave her a hug. "I'll just smoke a bit more of this cigar, then I'll come in and watch a movie."

She nodded and went inside.

Printed in the United States
by Baker & Taylor Publisher Services